"From what you told me, I would say you drank a drop of demon's blood," said the magician with a cheerful smile.

"I'm glad you didn't mention all this before breakfast," said Daniel.

"Look on the bright side." Rogan filled his cup, offering to pour for Daniel, who declined. "You're perfectly safe, for the moment."

"For the moment?"

"Well, there's no telling what will happen when I call the demon tonight." Rogan took a languid sip of wine. "I imagine he will be happy to see you. You know, you may be the first dinner to have escaped him in the last five or ten thousand years."

Daniel decided perhaps he'd have some wine after all. . . .

THE DOOR TO AMBERMERE

J. CALVIN PIERCE

ACE BOOKS, NEW YORK

This book is an Ace original edition, and has never
been previously published.

THE DOOR TO AMBERMERE

An Ace Book/published by arrangement with
the author

PRINTING HISTORY
Ace edition/June 1992

ISBN: 0-441-15944-3

Ace Books are published by The Berkley Publishing Group,
200 Madison Avenue, New York, New York 10016.
The name "ACE" and the "A" logo are trademarks
belonging to Charter Communications, Inc.

PRINTED IN THE UNITED STATES OF AMERICA

10 9 8 7 6 5 4 3 2 1

To my mother and father

THE DOOR TO AMBERMERE

CHAPTER
· 1 ·

To an observer viewing the avenue from behind a low garden wall, the object, passing as though in languorous flight, would have been something of a mystery, though one perhaps more likely to prompt speculation than active investigation. Could certain little-known plants walk the tops of garden walls? Had slinking cats taken to wearing disguises of leaves, berries, and dried flowers and grasses, cunningly woven together with bits of ribbon?

The object was, in fact, a hat. It sat, squared and true, on the head of a gray-haired woman who was rather short (a little over five feet in the kingdom of Ambermere, a little under five feet in the neighboring kingdoms) and who walked with such an unvarying perpendicularity, such a rigid straightness of spine, that her hat neither dipped nor swayed with her step, but drove forward as though traveling through the air by magic.

As it happened, there were no observers, or low garden walls either, on this particular avenue in the city of Ambermere. The only person observing anything was the lady beneath the hat, who had her eyes fixed on a point far down the street, where a different sort of mystery presented itself.

At first, Mistress Hannah did not recognize the light as an aura. In the distance it seemed only a spot of unexplained bril-

1

liance, as though a small hot fire blazed on the street three crossings away.

She kept her eye on the light as she walked. Surely no smith worked a forge on a city thoroughfare, blowing showers of bright sparks to dance and die on the paving stones. This would accord neither with the usual practice of smiths, nor with the customs of the city, and Ambermere was not a place where innovation was common.

Hannah wondered briefly if a magician might be busy with some mischief there, but the streets were nearly empty. With dark summer rain clouds rushing nightfall, all sensible folk were behind their doors, enjoying the aromas of supper bubbling in the pot. Hannah thought all magicians fools, but none was such a fool as to perform his tricks for no audience.

She crossed the next street. No farmers' wains, no tradesmen's carts crowded the way at this hour. The only sign that this city had a population was in the wavering glow from lamps and candles to be seen against the curtains at every window.

When she realized the distant light was an aura, Hannah stopped. Her first impulse, which she would not allow herself to obey, was to turn and leave, to avoid a meeting that was certain to be awkward, perhaps dangerous. Had her posture not long ago forgotten that it was possible to depart from the erect, that there were other angles than right, her shoulders would have slumped.

"Complications," she said. She turned to look back down the cobbled street. In a moment a small shadowy cat trotted into view from behind a hedge. It stopped and sat licking a paw.

"You may as well go back and wait for me," Hannah called, as though fully expecting the cat to understand her words. She turned and continued in the direction of the light. The cat lowered its paw gently to the ground, gazed after the receding hat for a moment, then turned and disappeared behind the hedge.

Hannah walked neither faster nor slower than she had before. She was accustomed to controlling more compelling forces than her own curiosity or anxiety. She would allow herself neither to hasten nor delay the moment when she must confront the source of the disquieting radiance.

Just ahead, a door opened and released a child, who darted

past her on some urgent household errand. A woman wearing an apron and holding a long wooden spoon came and stood beneath the lintel. As Hannah passed she gave the matron a word and a nod, grateful for the chance to let her eye linger for a moment on an aura of no unusual properties, one that did not blaze like a beacon on a hilltop.

Waiting at the corner that had been Hannah's destination, a young woman sat on a bench under a flowering tree. Her hair was dark, her build slight, and her clothing plain. Seen as most would see her, without the light and colors of the nimbus, she would be just another maiden, youthfully pretty, but not a girl to arrest the eye. For Hannah, the aura was so dazzling, it was hard to remember that to all but the rare adept among women, and to every man without exception—beggars, barristers, even wizards and necromancers—it was completely invisible.

A good thing at that, she thought. If everyone could see auras, much of a social intercourse, dependent as it was upon deception, charitable and otherwise, would be soured. The ordinary woman, blind to the auras of her friends and family, suffered quite enough, in Hannah's view, from the workings of her natural sensitivity to the nuances of word and glance.

At Hannah's approach the girl did not rise, but gestured for the older woman to take a seat at her side. Mistress Hannah settled herself on the bench, her back and neck still immovably upright, and folded her hands on the dark cloth of her long plain skirt.

They spoke together briefly, the girl saying little, Hannah less, then rose and walked together down the lane that left the avenue. Though the way was narrow, it was paved with heavy stones, for it ran by many warehouse doors where goods came and went daily by groaning wagons. In the middle of the block there was a tavern, marked by a faded wooden sign that hung above the door.

Inside, the aromas of cheese, smoked fish, wine, and ale mingled in the shadowy lamplight. A few old men sat around a table by the window; a serving girl, tall and slender, like an elegantly elongated figure in a painting, was propped against the bar as though she never meant to move again. Hannah left her companion among the empty tables and exchanged a few words with the barman before leading the way to a dark corner at the rear of the room. There the two women passed through a heavy door. They crossed a storeroom filled with barrels and crates and left by a door at the other side.

They found themselves again in a tavern, similar in some ways to the one on the other side of the storeroom, but with no warm light of flickering lamps, and no heavy aromas of kitchen and cellar. As in the tavern they had just left, a few men sat by a window. Behind the bar was a stout, white-bearded man in an apron.

"Greetings, Master Hugo," said Hannah. "How is it we find you at work in this place and not with your Brothers at the table?"

"Well," the man said with a nod to both of them, "Errin has gone to look at something with Jackson, and Gavas and Mervin are off somewhere, so I am left to tend the shop."

Hannah introduced the young woman. "This is Miss Elise. I have brought her from Ambermere to assist Master Errin for a time, if your Order will permit it."

Hugo bowed politely. "You are most welcome, miss." To Hannah he said, "Any adept you present is acceptable, and I am sure young Errin will be delighted. He will hope it means his apprenticeship is coming to an end. In any event, Miss Elise will find much instruction from those who gather here and those who pass this way."

After being introduced to the others, Elise left, promising to return with Mistress Hannah the next day.

Hugo watched the heavy door close behind her, then stared at it as though lost in thought. He turned to Hannah. "She didn't stay long," he said. "She didn't even bother to look out onto the street." He gestured toward a door at the other end of the room. "Most who are sent here manage at least a peek on their first visit. Of course, I don't know her Order or her rank; perhaps she's no novice despite her youth and her quiet way." He folded his hands across his ample midriff. "In any event, we must not interrogate our guests. We are here to watch, and sometimes to teach, not to ask idle questions." He looked at Hannah with an innocent expression. "I suppose one with your talents can see things in her aura that are hidden from me."

Hannah nodded with a quiet smile. "Trust one of your Brotherhood to be curious, Master. You must remember that we all have our talents. And yours are many; you have no need to envy mine." She made a completely unnecessary adjustment to her hat, which sat with blameless symmetry atop her gray hair.

"And now to my other errand." She waved in passing to the men at the table and left by the street door.

On the sidewalk, she did not immediately set out, but gave herself a moment, as she always did on her visits, to get used to the noise and the smells. She stood by the door, her hands clasped in front of her, and looked slowly up and down the street. Beside her the neon sign, long dead, inertly spelled the word BAR in the window.

The evening snarl of cars and trucks sat motionless, filling the air with noise and noxious gasses. The trapped vehicles were making no more progress than the parking meters that stood like sentinels along the curb. Exhaust fumes hung so thick in the damp atmosphere that Hannah almost feared for the health of the herbs and berries in her hat. Hoping for fresher air on a wider street, she started in the direction of the nearest corner, where a malfunctioning traffic light stuck on yellow dangled above the intersection.

She turned the corner onto a boulevard where instead of two lanes of traffic, six were locked in perplexity. Like Master Hugo, she thought. It was said of his Brotherhood that its members pursued perfect awareness. Yet he talked of Elise's aura, certain to be forever an abstraction to him, and said no word of her strange deep green eyes.

Daniel was thinking about Hell. He pushed through the revolving door from the hotel lobby to the street outside. Hell would probably be a bridge tournament, he had decided—one in which his particular punishment would be to have his sister-in-law Margaret as a partner for all eternity. And as the eons slipped by and the infinite future added inexhaustibly to an endlessly lengthening afternoon at the card table, she would never, ever progress beyond the level of smug incompetence.

On the street the situation was about normal for early evening, except instead of moving at an agonizing crawl, the rush-hour traffic had overflowed the intersection from all directions and come to a halt that looked permanent. Daniel watched in awe, wondering if he was witnessing the historical moment at which utter and irreversible gridlock finally took hold. But it wouldn't do, he realized, to underestimate the resilience of the motoring public. For instance, though they appeared to be hopelessly trapped, many of the commuters had the presence of mind to blow their horns and swear.

The sun had disappeared behind the horizon of tall office buildings without noticeably lowering the temperature outside, but after a long afternoon of air-conditioned duplicate bridge, Daniel felt his body soaking up the heat like a stiff dry sponge softening in a hot bath. He enjoyed the sensation, knowing that his pleasure would be brief. Like rush hour, hot weather in the city had not been designed for pleasure.

He glanced back at the hotel entrance just in time to see a little wisp of a man make a narrow escape from the revolving door and stumble onto the sidewalk. He saw Daniel and came toward him grinning maliciously. Daniel felt ten degrees hotter just looking at the wrinkled wool suit, and the tie cinched tightly around the skinny neck like a noose. He tried to remember if he had ever seen old Milton wear another outfit.

"Hi, Milton. Congratulations on the win," he said. "You played great."

"Sure. I do okay. I been a bridge bum for fifty years, so how else should I play?" He looked around suspiciously and patted his suit jacket in the region of the inner pocket. "Plus, I get paid to play good," he whispered. Milton was short. He leaned back to look up at the younger man and raised his upper lip to expose his front teeth in something between a grin and a sneer. "I hope you got a good price, too; you deserve it just for the suffering."

Daniel sighed. "I wasn't playing for money."

"What, you was playing for the fun of it? With that woman? Don't make me laugh."

"She's my sister-in-law."

"Oh." Milton seemed to be pondering the fresh information. "She's old enough to be your mother," he said.

"Almost," said Daniel. "My brother's a lot older than I am." Milton looked irritably at the sea of noisy automobiles.

"Why don't these people go home?" he said. He lifted his hat by the brim and brushed his white hair back. "So, big shot, you wanna play poker on Friday?" Before Daniel could answer, the old man waved the hat in his face.

"Don't tell me the stakes ain't high enough, either," he growled. "This is a totally different game. Not like that other one."

Daniel took a step back to get out of range of the fedora. "I have a Friday game," he said. "Charlie's. Every week."

Milton clamped his hat back on his head. "Okay, you *are* a big shot." He leaned toward Daniel and looked up at him from under his hat. "But you're a kid, so I'm gonna give you some free advice, which is: be careful. You gotta watch yourself with those people."

"Thanks, Milton, but I'm not a kid, I'm just irresponsible. Ask my sister-in-law. Or my brother." He smiled. "Actually, I'm thirty-one years old."

Milton chuckled and shook his head. "That's what I said. You're a kid. I'm telling you, you gotta watch your step. Those things you hear about Charlie, you know? They're true."

For a second Daniel looked troubled, then he smiled again. "It's just poker, Milton. Most of the players are businessmen."

"It's your funeral," said the old man in a cheerful voice. He waved and started down the street. After he had gone about ten steps he turned around and trudged back.

"Hey. You wanna shoot some pool?"

Daniel grinned and shook his head.

"One-pocket," said Milton. "Just for fun. My eyes are gone—I can't play no more." He examined his fingernails as though he had just noticed them for the first time. "Maybe fifty a game," he said casually. He looked up with eyebrows raised. Daniel said nothing.

"C'mon, we can make a game," he said. "I'll give you a ball." He paused. "And the break."

Daniel shook his head again. "You know I'm not going—"

"Two balls," said Milton.

"Have you ever seen me in a poolroom, Milton?"

"We'll play nine-ball, then. That's a young man's game. You'll kill me."

"No, thanks."

"The seven. I'll give you the seven and the break. Twenty dollars a game."

Daniel waited for him to subside. "Why don't I just give you the money right now and save myself the agony?"

"Nah," said Milton with an impatient wave of his hand. He started down the street again.

In a moment he was back. Daniel braced himself for another onslaught.

"I forgot," said Milton, planting himself in front of Daniel. "I wanted to say about that one hand you played—if this had been a chess tournament, you'd have copped the brilliancy prize for making that ridiculous heart contract your partner stuck you with. I felt like standing up to cheer when you pulled that swindle with the clubs, but I don't think Dr. Lennox"—Milton raised his chin and pursed his lips in imitation of his paying partner's air of prissy hauteur—"would have liked it."

This time when Milton left he didn't come back. He stalked off and was soon out of sight among the after-work crowds.

Daniel didn't bother to daydream about getting a cab; the traffic was still glued to the street. As he strolled to the corner he noticed that the signal above the intersection was stuck on yellow.

He left the curb and began to pick his way among the cars. His apartment house was three or four miles uptown. If he wasn't overcome by carbon monoxide or run down by a frenzied suburbanite, he could expect to be home within an hour.

And in the mountains by tomorrow, he reminded himself. He had been neglecting his hobby, besides which, a nice lengthy rock-climbing trip might go a long way toward solving his current problems. Given Roxy's presumed attention span, she probably wouldn't even remember who he was by the time he got back, let alone think she was in love with him. And Charlie, having no way of knowing where he was, would not be tempted to do anything rash.

Daniel was trying to imagine Charlie as a father-in-law. It proved as difficult as imagining Charlie's daughter as a wife.

"Take the girl out for a pizza. Give her a thrill. She thinks you look like a movie star."

For someone who had been frequently referred to as a "reputed crime figure" in the newspapers, Charlie had been almost diffident, even shy, as though he brought the matter up with reluctance. Just a doting father indulging the whim of a silly girl. Daniel had been certain, erroneously as it turned out, that Charlie thought of this as a trivial matter—a twenty-two-year-old's version of a schoolgirl crush.

Now, just a few weeks later, Daniel found himself facing the crime family equivalent of a breach-of-promise suit, the imagined penalties of which did little to encourage an optimistic outlook.

"I'm a reasonable man," Charlie had said. His charming smile was reassuring. For a foolish moment Daniel had dared to imagine he was off the hook. "But if somebody breaks my little girl's heart, I'm naturally not going to be happy." The smile had vanished. "And if I'm not happy, I'm gonna make sure he's not happy, either. You understand what I'm tryin' to say?"

Daniel walked several blocks before he saw any vehicle move more than five yards. He turned to look back down the street. For as far as he could see behind him, the signals at every corner were yellow. He wondered if Margaret had managed to get out of the hotel parking lot yet.

"I just don't see how you manage without a car," she had said today, borrowing from his brother's stock of inevitable remarks. "Of course, when a person doesn't have a steady job . . ."

Daniel had waited, knowing the script.

"Have you checked with the high schools for the fall?" she asked. "They say there's a shortage of teachers."

"I'm not surprised."

Margaret had not fulfilled her obligation to remind him that he was not in his twenties anymore, because she had been anxious to say some extremely silly things about the Bath coup, a fine point of bridge that she misunderstood thoroughly and, Daniel was sure, permanently.

The traffic rumbled and muttered like a mob in a bad mood. The assembled horsepower was having its usual effect on the city air but achieving little else. Daniel wondered how many buses it would take to hold every cursing commuter trapped in the acres of idling cars.

A half a block behind him a man who looked like a professional wrestler all dressed up for Sunday school was peering intently into a shop window. Daniel continued up the street. After two blocks of walking at a good clip, he looked over his shoulder. Half a block back, the man was rolling along in his wake.

Twenty minutes later Daniel was already thoroughly bored with playing silly games. He had walked around a block and cut through the same department store three times, and he still could not tell whether he was being followed. All he had accomplished was to attract the attention of a stunning clerk at the makeup counter who looked as though she was made of porcelain.

Still, if Charlie was having him followed, it would be by someone who was good at it. The big man he had thought might be shadowing him had turned off a few blocks back, but that didn't mean someone hadn't taken his place. Daniel didn't really know how subtle Charlie's employees might be. He decided to stop thinking about it. If he was being followed, so be it. He was only on his way home anyway, and Charlie already knew where he lived. Besides, if he walked by the makeup counter a few more times, the porcelain figurine was either going to call a store detective or offer him a key to her apartment, and he already had one girlfriend too many.

On the street, the traffic had finally begun to move. When an empty cab appeared at the curb, he grabbed it. On the way to his place he occupied himself with an attempt to think neither of hired thugs or bridge tournaments. He thought about his livelihood instead. He probably should have accepted Milton's invitation to the poker game. Despite what he had said to the old hustler, he would not be showing up at Charlie's until this soap opera with Roxy had been resolved.

In his apartment, he mixed a scotch and water and sat down to ponder his options. His experience as a gambler had taught him that in life, as in poker, you could usually keep out of trouble if you stayed alert. You did, however, need some cards to play, or at least fold, and in this game, Charlie seemed to hold all fifty-two.

Life with Roxy. That was one of the options. But Daniel

could not imagine spending a lot of time with someone who thought television talk shows were "stimulating," and whose most animated conversation was on the subject of the private lives of singers, actors, and anyone else who was grossly overpaid and notorious. Daniel did not think of himself as a particularly well educated man. He knew for an indisputable fact that his master's degree represented only very slight learning. Nonetheless, his interests strayed beyond the boundaries of commercial television and popular music. As far as he could tell, Roxy's did not.

"So much for Darwin," he said to his drink.

It occurred to him that his older brother had finally been right about something concerning "the kid." If he had pursued his high school teaching career, he doubtless would not even be acquainted with any crime lords, or at least none old enough to have marriageable daughters.

And, as his brother ("Remember, I'm old enough to be your father.") never tired of pointing out, with the extra money he could earn teaching a rock-climbing course at the community college, he would be "really set," as well as having a good time with his hobby. "Not to mention the prestige," his sister-in-law would be sure to add. Margaret seemed to be convinced that teaching rock climbing at a community college made her brother-in-law a college professor. As far as Daniel could tell, she considered it the equivalent of holding an endowed chair at Harvard or Yale.

The phone rang. He did not consider answering it. No great loss anyway. If it wasn't Roxy, it was probably his dentist, who occasionally called with a last-minute invitation to his Thursday-night poker party. But the play was of such low quality that Daniel felt like even more of an impostor than he usually did when playing with amateurs. And anyway, the stakes were too low. "Pretzel contest" was the term Charlie favored to describe suburban card games where the tables were always littered with snacks. "Hey, kid—you make any money at the pretzel contest last night?"

But Daniel didn't expect to hear any more avuncular ribbing from Charlie. Nor did he know when if ever he would be welcome again at Charlie's weekly poker game, which amounted to losing the income from a full-time job. Even counting the occasional losing night that was an unavoidable part of his trade, it had covered basic living expenses. In a way, he supposed, marrying Roxy would be like marrying the boss's daughter. Daniel sighed. All the more reason for Charlie to be offended at his obvious lack of enthusiasm.

The whole proposition was very simple from Charlie's point of view—Roxy wanted something; what else was there to say? It reminded Daniel of a novel—one by Faulkner, he thought—in which a father tells a grown son that a southern gentleman "never disappoints a lady."

He put off thinking about how he would get out of town if he was being followed. For one thing, it was difficult for him to imagine he could be in any real danger from his poker pal Charlie. Surely it wouldn't hurt to give things one more day. He could spend some time tomorrow wandering around the city and find out once and for all if anyone was watching him.

The phone rang again. He wondered if Margaret might be calling to talk over the day's triumphs. Sometimes after she had shanghaied him into a tournament she tried to interest him in playing with her regularly. She thought it scandalous that her young brother-in-law played poker often enough, and well enough, to live on his winnings; but somehow she thought it would do him a world of good to spend a few nights a week at the bridge table—after working all day, of course.

Over the past year her favorite comment had become, "When a person is past thirty, they're not a kid anymore." Daniel could tell that Margaret thought she was being subtle and oblique. His brother was usually more direct. "Grow up," was his standard advice, to which Daniel invariably replied, "No, thanks."

From time to time it occurred to Rand that his position as principal adviser to the king of Ambermere must be envied by many of his fellow subjects, especially at court, where the scarcity of common sense made foolish errors in reasoning routine. This notion usually sought him out when he found himself in one of the thoroughly unenviable situations that were so frequently his lot.

"No, no," said the king from his immense chair, waving away

his valet, "I'm sure I wore that last time. Or maybe it was the time before. I don't want to arouse suspicions by appearing in the same disguise too often."

It was a sign of the well-known lack of justice in the universe, thought Rand, that a man of his years should find himself spending irreplaceable moments watching the king, who aside from his other attainments, was far the fattest man in the land, make meticulous choices from a collection of vast garments meant to counterfeit the dress of a prosperous commoner. This wardrobe existed for the purpose of allowing Asbrak the Fat, whose unmistakable silhouette appeared on signs over the doorways of tradesmen throughout the city, to pass unrecognized among his subjects.

The valet minced forth carrying a long jacket and a pair of pantaloons that together might have furnished the material for a capacious, if unusually colorful, tent. Rand turned his head fastidiously from the rude clash of patterns and hues as the little man spread the clothing before the king with a flourish.

"Perhaps," purred the valet with an affected lisp that he evidently thought made him sound like an aristocrat, "one might be permitted to offer this *ensemble* to His Majesty. If he will ignore its undoubted vulgarity, His Majesty will perhaps agree that it is otherwise quite nice."

"That might do. That might do." The king looked at the ceiling. "I wonder what Rand thinks," he said in the manner of one who is alone and talking to himself. He turned to his adviser. "What do you think, my Lord Rand?"

"As Your Majesty very well knows, I think it most imprudent for Your Majesty to go abroad unaccompanied, wandering the streets and alleys of the city in the middle of the night, inviting who knows what disaster."

"But I shall be disguised." The king turned laboriously on the thick cushions that lined his chair. "Men, and women, too, walk our streets unmolested." He fixed his adviser with the regal stare. "Surely you don't think I will be recognized?"

Though it was unthinkable, Rand thought of pointing out to the monarch that the very cats on the windowsills could not fail to recognize the king, however attired, by his unmatched girth and ponderous swaying gait alone.

"I concede that Your Majesty is a master of disguise," he said. The king never failed to beam at this particularly cherished compliment. "Nevertheless, I find it difficult to understand how your deception can hope to succeed."

Rand knew that to leap to his feet the king would need the help of some sort of mechanical contrivance; nonetheless, the glint in the monarch's eye suggested that he had leapt to his feet in spirit.

"Please explain yourself, my Lord Rand."

"Why, it should be obvious to anyone," said the older man, covertly enjoying the growing incredulity of the kingly glare. He paused to relish the moment before continuing. Such sport was small recompense for hours wasted, but better than none at all.

"When Your Majesty appears among the populace, however cunningly disguised, it must be a wonder that you are not at once discovered." He paused again for as long as he dared. "Your Majesty's noble bearing must be obvious to all. Your kingly eye. Your . . ."—he brought his hands together and stared at them, as though searching for exactly the right word— "presence. These things could not escape the attention of the least alert of our citizens."

The king was beaming again. He struggled from the chair and moved himself with stately step to the center of the room.

"But this, you see, Rand"—he turned as though better to display his kingly lineaments. Rand thought he looked rather like a large trained animal attempting a pirouette—"this is the essence of my disguise. What you say is undoubtedly true, my bearing, my carriage, and so on, but I can suppress it. I don't change only my clothing when I go among the people; I change my glance, my step . . . everything. I think that had I been born poor, I would have made a success on the stage."

To Rand, this was at once the most sympathetic and the most frustrating quality of his ruler. The man, a widower and a father, and old enough to be a grandfather, was in many ways like an immense boy. For all his bulk, and the gray in his beard, he spoke of his adventures with the enthusiasm of an urchin brandishing a wooden sword.

"As I said, Your Majesty is a master of disguise. But still I wish you would allow me to persuade Your Highness to stay at home tonight." He walked to a window set deep in the stone wall. "You see, Your Majesty, that now it begins to rain, so you must abandon your plan."

The king joined him at the window. Lights were already showing at the windows of the houses and shops beyond the castle walls. In the fading glow of day the colors of the tile roofs deepened as they were glazed by the soft rain.

"Rand, you came here during my father's reign, and I myself have been on the throne for more than twenty-five years, so you are not a newcomer in this land." The king gestured toward the sky. "It is dusk. At this time of year it rains every day at dusk. I point this out to you in case you have failed to notice it. It is no more unexpected than the midday bells."

"But there is no need for Your Majesty to go abroad in this way."

The king turned to his valet. "Leave us. I will ring when I am ready."

The valet bowed and left quietly by an inner door. The king raised his hand to forestall conversation and listened in the silent room. He peered along the walls and into the shadowy corners as though there might be forgotten or hitherto unnoticed visitors with them in his dressing room. Or perhaps, Rand thought disconsolately, he was just counting the chairs. Asbrak stepped away from the window.

"I hope to learn something that may help us," he said in a soft voice pregnant with significance.

Rand suppressed a sigh. "Your Highness, the only things that will help us are an army large enough to defeat King Razenor's, which we do not have, or patience, which we must have."

The king paced to the window and looked out at the rain.

"An army. How I wish I could ride to the walls of Ascroval at the head of my great-grandsire's host. How sweetly our neighbor the viper-king would smile as he invented excuses for his vile treachery. And when he handed over the princess unharmed, perhaps, but only perhaps, I would not put his head on a spike, though my military ancestor would not have been so forgiving."

"Your Majesty must remember that in those days a captured

enemy could get his head on a spike for smiling too much—or not enough—or wearing colors that clashed."

"But to have such an army!"

"Those armies and warriors, and their wars, are all long dead, Your Majesty. Your great-grandsire led troops who knew all the tricks of the battlefield and thirsted for the blood of their foes. Our soldiers know all the tricks of the parade ground and are acquainted with no thirst that cannot be quenched at a tavern. We live now in a world of bargains and diplomacy."

"And vile treachery."

"To be sure, Majesty. Always treachery."

"But on the streets or in the taverns I may hear something that will be of use."

"Your Majesty, we know everything we need to know. Our neighbor, King Razenor—"

"Son of my father's cousin, and a lying snake his whole life!"

"Indeed, Your Highness. King Razenor, perhaps with the help of the wizard he is reputed to have in his service—"

"Rogan says that cannot be, that he may be a magician of high rank, but that wizards do not attach themselves to courts."

"Your Majesty knows how earnest is my respect for our palace magician, Rogan the Obscure, as he wishes he could persuade everyone to call him."

"He is very learned in his Art, and very long in its practice."

"He is certainly old, I will grant. And that may be magical, considering the quantities of wine that disappear into his apartments. But speaking as a survivor of his recent fireworks demonstration, I am not inclined to overvalue his abilities." The adviser's lips turned to a near smile. "I will concede that, considering the livestock and stored grain that with a slight shift in the wind might well have been reduced to ash, it was the most terrifying celebration I ever attended."

The king sighed and gazed from the window at the darkening sky. "Yes," he said in a quiet voice, "the celebration of the engagement of the Princess Iris to the son of our richest neighbor. The marriage that will seal an alliance of endless prosperity and security."

He turned back to his adviser. "And where," he asked in a voice loud with anger and bitterness, "is our princess, my daughter, the Lovely Iris, Fairest Flower of the Kingdom? Held by Razenor the Snake, who does not wish to see this alliance become a reality." The king clenched his hands as though they grasped his enemy by the throat. "He holds her there in his castle, and yet will not acknowledge it."

"Not officially, Your Majesty. But his emissary has made it clear to me, nonetheless, in the customary way, without admitting anything."

"I wish you had told me before allowing the 'emissary' to leave. I would have sent him back without his ears."

Rand disregarded this, knowing it to be bluster. Aside from everything else, the oversize monarch was far too kindly and softhearted to mistreat even a diplomat.

"In any event, Your Majesty, I am confident we shall soon be in receipt of King Razenor's terms."

"Terms?" thundered the king. "I will give him 'terms' to consider when my magician finds a way to deal with this viper!" The king pointed to the ceiling. "Up there in his tower, Rogan the Obscure is working without rest to find a way to bring Razenor the Snake to his knees."

Rand had frequently suspected the palace magician of drinking without rest, but he doubted he could be expected to persevere in any other project. Still, bringing a snake to its knees seemed one worthy of his talents.

"I hope Your Majesty will not be disappointed. His trade is ceremonial magic. And while I don't think anyone is truly safe with Rogan at work, I cannot imagine what he could possibly accomplish that would be of any use."

The king returned to his overstuffed chair, positioning himself carefully above it before dropping into it with a force that would have reduced most furniture to scraps of wood and cloth. Rand, who had witnessed this operation countless times, had always thought of it as the mirror image of leaping from a seat.

Once again the king sighed a royal sigh. "We must accomplish something soon. Secrets have short lives, and anyway, my subjects cannot be told endlessly that the Magnificent Iris has gone into seclusion to prepare herself for the great event of her life. The people expect to see her. The court, for that matter, expects to see her. And every lady of the court has a question on her lips, often about the choice of companion in this isolation, the commoner, what's-her-name."

"Modesty, Your Highness."

"What? Are you being impertinent, Rand?"

"It's the girl's name, Your Highness. Modesty."

"What? Oh. Ah, so it is. Yes . . . pretty thing. Not like the princess, of course, but . . . Yes, I know her. Speaks right up. Put that lord, what's-his-name, in his place. Very good. Yes . . ."

Both men were silent for a moment. A fragment of a distant song entered through the open window, then was lost in the soft noises of the rain.

"You see," said the king, "it's that she's not an aristocrat. But what are we to do? There are no unmarried girls now at the court, except for two or three whose company my daughter cannot abide for more than a few hours at a time. So this common girl . . . you say her name is Mystery? How unusual. I don't believe I care for it." The king's voice had become indignant. "Who are her parents?"

"The maiden's name is Modesty, my Liege."

"I'm sure you told me Mystery."

"I was mistaken, Majesty."

"Anyway, it's a good thing she is a commoner. What excuse could we make to her parents if they were at court?"

Rand said nothing. He wondered if the king might forget his plan to venture forth in disguise. He tried to think of some further distraction.

"Have I seen her parents?"

Rand looked blank. "I beg Your Majesty's pardon?" He leaned forward as though he had not heard the question.

The king sat up in his chair, straightening his back. He lifted his chin and fixed his adviser with a look of stern dignity.

"You must listen to me when I speak, Rand. I am the king."

"Always, Your Highness." The adviser bowed slightly. "What was the question?"

"What question?"

"I am sorry, Highness. I misunderstood."

"Try to be more attentive, Rand."

The adviser bowed again.

"Anyway," the king said in a more cheerful tone, "I will be

doing what I can in the taverns, and Rogan says, but in confidence, you understand—magicians must have their secrecy—that he has a plan that will cure all our problems." The king looked reproachfully at Rand. "He has given me great hope. Great hope."

The rain had stopped. In the highest window of the tower, looking down through the mist that still hung in the air, stood a tall, bony, gray-haired man. In one pale hand he held a piece of chalk; in the other, a goblet.

"Stars," he muttered in a cracked voice. "I want some stars. What I am to do can't be done on a cloudy night." He sipped from the goblet. "That's right, talk to yourself," he said, talking to himself. "That will fix everything."

He looked up and squinted, as though to penetrate the clouds and mist with his gaze. "I know you're there," he continued. "Show yourselves. I have a job to do."

He drained the goblet in one long swallow, his head tilted back, eyes closed.

"Fireworks," he said, returned his gaze to the dark landscape below. "I'll give them fireworks. Fireworks they'll still be talking about a hundred years from now." He turned his glance to the cloudy sky above. "If the clouds will go away and let me see the stars." He tried to sip from the empty goblet, then looked into it with an expression of mild surprise before placing it on the stone sill of the window.

"A wizard. Hah! Let us say Razenor does have a wizard, though I know very well he does not. Cannot." He spoke as though addressing an invisible audience suspended in midair outside his window, making flourishing gestures with his piece of chalk. "Let us say he has two wizards. Or twelve. Let us say twelve." He stabbed the air with his chalk as though counting a large number of wizards. "We give him twelve wizards to protect himself against the magic of one palace magician."

He turned from his imaginary audience, leaving the window empty. In a moment he returned carrying a dusty flask, from which he filled his goblet.

"Just one magician," he resumed, before raising the drink to his lips. "Rogan, master of fireworks and other carnival tricks.

A mere functionary. A humble servant of the monarch, like a cook. Or a hairdresser. No one mistakes Rogan for a wizard. No one fears the deep spells of power that might be wrought by Rogan. No, indeed. Rogan is to content himself working minute magic suitable for royal ceremony." He paused to sip, daintily, from the contents of the goblet before returning it to the sill. He stared into the mist outside the window.

"Twelve wizards, deep in artifice, fearsome in secret knowledge, awful in their collective power. Arrayed against the fabricator of fireworks, Rogan, palace prestidigitator. Let them combine in confabulation and set their workings in motion against mine. Against the skills of Rogan the Obscure!"

He laughed grimly, picturing a group of self-satisfied wizards sitting around smirking and speaking of him in a belittling and patronizing way. Suddenly their foolish complacency is shattered as they are confronted with and utterly confounded by his, Rogan's, little surprise. In confusion and dismay they are routed. Some attempt to flee, choosing doorways or windows, as they are close at hand. Some cower where they sit, too stunned to move. All have been undone. The opponent they derided and despised has prevailed. Rogan's triumph is complete.

The magician smiled, savoring the imaginary scene of sweet justice. It was too bad, he thought, that Razenor didn't actually have a wizard for him to overcome. He reached for the goblet, but brushed it with his hand, and saw it disappear over the edge of the windowsill and into the night. From far below, while he still stared at the spot it had occupied, came the faint clatter of metal striking stone.

A moment later he heard another noise. He peered through the gloom. It was just possible for him to make out the unmistakable figure of the king passing quietly through a private garden gate to the dark street beyond the palace walls.

CHAPTER

· **2** ·

Daniel had planned to stay home for the night, but didn't. After spending half the evening brooding about his unintentional entanglement with Roxy, the tedium of gambling as an occupation, Margaret's inability to bid a bridge hand rationally, and, finally, the futility of life, he realized that he was ravenously hungry. His only meal of the day had been a late lunch before the tournament.

On the way downtown, he looked out the back window of the taxi a number of times before conceding that one set of headlights looks much like another, and that any one of fifteen or twenty cars could be following him. In the restaurant he found a table that would have suited a frontier gunslinger in an unfriendly town—facing the door with a wall at his back. From time to time he glanced out the nearest window to see if there were any suspicious characters lurking under the street lamps.

His meal passed without drama. No burly goons arrived to harass him with ungrammatical comments about his personal life, no threatening notes fell from his napkin when he unfolded it. The steak was cooked the way he ordered it, and the french fries were not cold. Considering that he had never before tried the restaurant, and had picked it solely because it was not the sort of place where he would be likely to run into Roxy or Charlie, he felt lucky. His luck didn't run out until he ordered coffee, which was weak and tasted vaguely like flannel.

He ignored the coffee and listened to the Muzak instead, which had been monotonous and mildly annoying throughout his meal, but had suddenly become almost surrealistic. The tune leaking out of the cheap speaker above his table was from the seventies, and had originally been played at a volume meant to do permanent harm to the ear. This version was being whispered by violins in a saccharine arrangement and executed by studio musicians who played it with fatal precision. As he listened to the housebroken protest song, Daniel pushed his coffee away to get it out from under his nose.

As if he had been summoned by a bell, the maître d' came knifing across the carpet with quick, short steps. He was short and slight with swept-back hair and the posture of a man leaning into a stiff wind. His face in profile was triangular and culminated in an eager, outthrust nose. Daniel could not recall ever having seen such a streamlined human being. He appeared to have been designed entirely on aerodynamic principles.

He spoke in a bubbly Calcutta brogue. "Is your coffee cold, sir? I will sending you a fresh cup instantaneously."

Daniel declined, telling a polite lie about the quality of the coffee and asking for his bill.

He left the restaurant and sauntered casually through the streets, checking occasionally to see if anyone was following him. At night on busy sidewalks, though, this turned out to be of no more use than watching headlights from the cab had been. Anyone could have been following him, and he was about ninety-nine-percent sure that no one was.

From somewhere ahead he heard a voice rise above the ambient racket of the city streets. His first thought was that he was approaching a disturbance of some kind. He looked for flashing lights.

"Eeeeeeee." The wailing voice seemed to be coming from the next cross street. As Daniel turned the corner, the sound became momentarily louder, then trailed off into silence. Ahead was a small knot of people surrounding a man with a microphone in his hand. Daniel had nearly reached them when the man began broadcasting again.

"Jooooooze," he cried, waving a finger in the air as his amplified voice was overtaken by feedback. He dropped to one knee and twisted a knob on an amplifier at his feet. As he got back up he blew noisily into the microphone. He fixed his audience with a manic stare.

"Presbyteeeeeerians," he cried. Daniel stopped and joined the tiny congregation.

"Mooooormons." The man's burning eyes swept the people in front of him as though he suspected the presence of Mormons. He paused for a moment.

"Methodists!" he said in a conversational shout. He chuckled and shook his head sadly.

"You know where they're going?" he called, then repeated the question at a greater volume. *"Do you know where they're going?"* His amplified voice was loud enough for a much larger audience. "They're all going to Hell. The Devil's there waiting for them. Jews, Catholics, Mormons, Presbyterians, Mohammedans, all of them. They all have confirmed reservations in *Hotel Hell.*" He stared at his audience for a moment, then took a drink from the glass sitting on top of his single speaker.

'You can go, too!" he shouted suddenly. "They got plenty of room, my friends; they never turn a guest away."

A tall, thin man wearing an apron appeared in the doorway of the bar next door and stood watching with a frown. After a few seconds he turned and went back inside.

"And it's *cheap!*" The speaker crackled. "In fact, friends, it's *free*. Won't cost you a penny." The preacher tugged his tie loose. His shirt was wet with perspiration. "All they want is your *immortal soul.*" He took another drink and bent down to adjust the amplifier.

"But don't expect to see me there!" the preacher shouted as he rose from his crouch. "Because my plans are already made. I'm going to be in with God in glory!" he said, pronouncing the key words "gawd" and "glow-reh." He leaned back and smiled broadly up at the rooftops. "Hallelujah! Boshamu beemah! Oppilee Boshilee bah!" Once again he raised the volume on the amp.

"And you can come to!" he thundered. He jumped up and clicked his heels, then whirled, leaping over the microphone

cord like a jump rope. "Or you can go down to Hell, and fry
there with the *Jooooze* and the *Moooormons* and the
Caaaatholics and the *Presbyteeeeerians*, and all the other sin-
ners that are stuck there forever in the eternal pit of fire." He
looked eagerly across his audience. "Let me tell you again,
friends. Let me tell you who's down there in the fire, 'cause
there's lots of them."

As the preacher started back into his wailing chant, a large
barrel-shaped man burst out of the bar as though he had kicked
the door down. He pushed his way past the edge of the small audience, and without breaking stride, went to the loudspeaker
and yanked it off the ground. The water glass fell to the sidewalk and shattered in a splash of droplets and shards. The metal
amplifier bounced and skidded at the end of the speaker wire
until the man tramped on it and broke the connection with a
jerk. He took three or four rapid steps to the corner of the building and smashed the speaker against the angle of the brick wall.
The particle-board case crumbled, spilling speaker cones and
wires. The man let the pieces drop and, without a word or a
backward glance, went back into the bar.

The preacher was still holding his microphone and staring
down at the wreckage of his speaker. A tall gray-haired woman
wearing a winter coat sidled over to Daniel.

"See? They won't let you talk." She spoke in a near whisper
out of the side of her mouth. She leaned toward Daniel. "People
don't believe me," she murmured.

Daniel smiled politely at her as if she had mentioned the hu-
midity, then turned his attention to the preacher, who was quietly gathering up what remained of his equipment. He had a
placid expression on his face, as though what had happened had
not disturbed him in the slightest. A deeply wrinkled old man
with jet black hair that looked like it had been dyed with shoe
polish detached himself from the crowd. As he drifted past Daniel he remarked, "Guess that guy must have been a Presbyterian."

Daniel laughed, then stopped abruptly when he felt an elbow
in his ribs. The woman was looking at him with earnest concern
in her eyes.

"Presbyterian, nothing," she said. "Did you see that nose?"

Daniel found he didn't have a ready answer.

"He's a spy. They all are."

"Who?" said Daniel, knowing he shouldn't ask.

The woman looked around cautiously. "Jews." She spoke without moving her lips. "They're all foreign agents." She leaned closer to him. "The coloreds are in with them, too."

Daniel pretended to be engrossed in watching the preacher load his equipment into the trunk of a ten-year-old Buick. Then, like everyone else there, he stared after the man as he crossed the sidewalk with a jaunty step and went into the bar.

The woman nudged him again.

Daniel waited to hear her next revelation.

"Can you give me a dollar?" she said.

Daniel had nothing smaller than a ten.

"Sorry," he said with an apologetic smile. The woman turned and walked away slowly without saying anything. Daniel watched her wander off into the summer night in her heavy coat.

The barroom door was open.

Though it wasn't amplified, he recognized the preacher's voice from inside the bar. He started for the door, meaning to have a look. Then he stopped. "Nuts," he said, shaking his head wearily. He wheeled and set out at a quick stride. From the bar, he heard a faint "Joooooze . . . Mooormons . . ." trailing off in a mournful diminuendo.

When he caught up with the woman, he slowed down just long enough to hand her the bills he had taken from his wallet. As soon as she took them, he hurried on as though he had a plane to catch. It had made him feel good to give her money he would never miss—even demented bigots have to eat—but he didn't want to spend any more time with her. That would have been more charity than he was willing to extend.

He slowed down as soon as he dared. It was still too hot for any activity much more intense than a quiet stroll. He thought about looking up Milton in the poolroom. Milton had invited him to play poker, and not in a cheap game. It was probably worth looking into. It was certainly true that for the time being, his Fridays were open.

* * *

He tried to remember the location of the poolroom. It was somewhere nearby, he knew, and Milton would surely be there. He had told Daniel in the past that he only played cards to make money, but he played pool because he loved the game. The thought of Milton brought the crazy lady's warnings about Jews to mind. Daniel laughed aloud at the picture of the old hustler making clandestine reports to a sinister foreign agent in a trench coat.

Somehow, the thought of spies and intrigues brought to mind the Internal Revenue Service. As usual, he had been putting off the quarterly ordeal with his taxes, which was part of the reason it was always such an ordeal. If he went home right now, his conscience informed him, he could get everything in order tonight and be ready to actually complete the whole stupid affair and get the forms and the check in the mail by tomorrow afternoon.

As he was trying frantically to think of plausible reasons for putting the chore off until Saturday or Sunday, an empty cab came drifting by at about the speed of a brisk walk.

Daniel's shoulders slumped. "Providence," he said, and waved it down. The invigorated taxi leapt into the stream of traffic. Half a block back, a big black car with windows of reflecting glass left an illegal parking space. At the corner it went through a red light and drifted up the street behind Daniel's cab.

Dibrick the Roaster of Meats was engaged in a battle, or at any rate a skirmish, with his conscience. He was winning.

"As it is so early," he said gravely to the maid at the barrel, "I believe I will have . . . another blagon . . . flagon of beer. Before I go home. To my wife."

The girl took his pitcher and began to fill it.

"Do you know my . . . wife?" Dibrick said to her back.

She answered without turning from the barrel. "She is my mother's sister, Uncle Dibrick."

Dibrick screwed his face into a parody of incredulity. He leaned around the girl and squinted at her face from the side.

"Whose uncle are you?" he shouted in her ear.

She pushed him away, sloshing beer on his vest.

"I am got noing . . . Not going to pay for that," he said, brushing his front with careful inaccuracy. He looked up at his niece with an expression that was both befuddled and befuddling. He seemed to be trying to prove that he could smirk while blinking.

The maid took him by the elbow and began to steer him toward the door. "Go home to your supper, Uncle."

Dibrick grinned affably at the company on either side as the girl propelled his slender frame through the crowded common room.

"I roast meats," he announced a number of times before they reached the door.

Outside, he happened to glance down the street. In the distance he could see a figure approaching. He bent forward at the waist, nearly falling, and watched as the silhouetted man passed beneath a street lamp.

"By the gods and goddesses, it is the king," he said aloud, then clapped his forefinger to his lips.

"Shhh." Though there was no one there to wink at, he produced a laborious wink that seemed to involve every muscle in his face.

He addressed himself in a sibilant whisper. "In disguise. Again. Walking the streets like any man of the city." Dibrick set out with a stiff-legged and unintentionally meandering gait toward the advancing monarch.

"Like any doctor, or . . . or Roaster of Meats. Like a man that may be addressed by any other man." At the thought of the magnanimous condescension of the king, Dibrick's eyes began to fill with tears. He stopped and dabbed at them with his sleeve. He was startled, in fact amazed, if his feelings could be judged by the expression on his face, when a voice interrupted him.

"My man?"

Dibrick wondered how it could be that the king had reached him so quickly. He looked at him closely, congratulating himself on resisting the impulse to bow. When the king was in disguise, it was important not to do or say the wrong thing. He consciously arranged his features into an expression that would indicate to the monarch that the citizen who stood before him was a man of good humor, yet one of dignity and intelligence.

Before he opened his mouth, he reminded himself not to allow the bit of drink he had indulged in to slur his speech.

"I do not know you," he said, being very careful to pronounce each word distinctly. He lingered on the vowels, and turned them on his tongue, giving his speech, he thought, a distinctive lilt. Quite pleased both with himself, and with the sound of his new accent in private conversation with the sovereign, he decided to add a few words. It was probable, he suddenly realized, that he was impressing the king with his bearing and his discourse.

"Not," he said with a flourishing gesture that pulled him just a bit off balance, "having been seeing you before under . . . Previous circumstances."

Asbrak leaned forward, squinting, and put his hand to his ear. "What?" he said querulously. "I can't understand you. Who are you?"

Dibrick swayed before his sovereign. Before answering, he thought it wise to blink a few times in a judicious manner.

"Roaster of Meats," he said finally, and then winked at the king to demonstrate his complete lack of suspicion.

The king snorted and moved on without another word.

Dibrick watched the departing figure, then wiped his eyes again before striking out for home with a step resolute in intention if not execution.

"We shall see," he said with an air of triumph, "what my wife has to say to this!"

The king paused at the entrance of the tavern. From inside he could hear the sound of lively talk and laughter. But it was, he thought, an establishment too close to the palace, and too much attached to its own neighborhood, to be frequented by intriguers and spies. What he heard were the sounds of strictly local conviviality. He continued on his way, walking in the general direction of the waterfront. It was there that foreigners, from boats and pack trains both, drank, gambled, and talked far into the night.

In accord with local custom, he greeted everyone he passed with a word and a nod. He noted with pleasure the great civility of those he encountered, who never failed to yield the pavement to him in the many narrow walkways where there seemed somehow to be room for only one to pass. As was always the case on his anonymous visits to the city, the behavior of his subjects moved him to reflect that courtesy had the power to elevate all to the condition of royalty.

In fact, the king was satisfied that a city more gracious than his own was not to be found. Even the capital of King Finster the Munificent, though twice the size of his Ambermere, did not exceed it in grace and charm. In Asbrak's view, Felshalfen was too big to be comfortable. The fact that his daughter, once married to Finster's heir, Hilbert the Silent, would be residing in the metropolis was the only circumstance of the impending marriage that bothered anyone, and the only one it bothered was Iris herself.

It was not at all uncommon for a royal daughter to marry before the age of seventeen or eighteen. The Matchless Iris had celebrated her twenty-second birthday. She had been so long at her father's court at Ambermere and, as Asbrak himself had been aware to the point of despair if not panic, so long unmarried, that any change, even one so happy for her kingdom, was alarming to her. How lucky, as Asbrak the Fat reminded himself a hundred times a day, that the rather retiring and backward heir of the richest kingdom on the sea had conceived this passion, or what passed for one in his case, for the Stunning Iris.

Whether his daughter returned Hilbert's feelings was not a question Asbrak had inquired into. Certainly the princess would as a matter of royal duty accede to any union so advantageous to her kingdom and her people, but the king had heard no hint that his daughter was unhappy.

He walked for a while on a wide avenue where at every corner were to be found musicians, dancers, jugglers, or some other lively enterprise. The king stood among his subjects, joining them in the pleasures of the summer night. The clink of the coins they tossed at the feet of the entertainers was itself a music to lift the spirits. After lingering at a number of crossings, enchanted at one by the clever fingers of a lutanist, lost at the next in the melodies of a pretty singer, he remembered himself, recalled his duty, and pushed on.

On a quiet commercial lane dominated by warehouses and

the back doors of trading houses he found a small tavern. He
was yet some distance from the quays, but felt the need for
some refreshment and a chair. He squeezed himself through a
narrow entrance that opened not onto a hallway, as was usually
the case, but directly into a small one-room tavern. The king
looked for a spot from which he could listen and observe. As he
stood blinking in the lamplight, a tall slender girl arrived to con-
duct him to a table by the wall. He lowered himself with great
care onto a sturdy-looking stool and ordered wine.

A few minutes later, the king, who considered himself keenly
observant, noticed a woman enter the room from a door in a far
corner. She appeared to be a little older than he, perhaps Rand's
age, and was rather on the short side. Deducting for the outlandish hat she wore, he guessed her height at a little over five feet,
or under it in the many neighboring kingdoms that insisted on
using perverse and erroneous systems of measurement.

The woman looked around the room. Her posture, he noted,
was exemplary. The king tried to recall when he had last seen a
duchess who stood as straight as this commoner. Her eyes
scanned the company, and when they turned in his direction,
she waved. Asbrak shifted his gaze and pretended not to see her.
He was, after all, acting as a spy. Out of the corner of his eye he
saw her walk toward his table. As she drew nearer, he wondered
if he had been mistaken for someone else. To his immense relief, she passed him without a glance, and joined a number of
gray-bearded men nearby. They all rose in greeting, bowing as
the matron took a seat. Here was courtesy, thought the king with
a feeling of pride, that would have done credit to the court, if
only dressed in finer clothes.

He sat for quite a long time, sipping wine and half listening to
the seemingly aimless talk of the other patrons, who were
mostly gray-bearded elders. By the time he had poured the last
drops from his flagon, he had stopped listening entirely. After
all, he thought, the quiet talk of old men was unlikely to tell him
anything of the princess. He felt suddenly tired and discouraged. Rand was doubtless right. The king's intrigues, Rogan's
magic—these things would prove to be futile.

Although she presented a picture of perfect indolence when
she leaned inertly against the bar, the tall slender waitress

proved most attentive. Asbrak allowed her to renew his supply of wine and, at her suggestion, indulged in a small snack of bread, cheese, olives, and some rather fine smoked fish. The nourishment served to revive his flagging spirits. The barman very thoughtfully provided him with a warm and fragrant moistened napkin for his hands. It pleased the monarch greatly that in his capital, even the taverns in the alleys were not without their luxuries.

Paying for things not being part of the common experience of royalty, the king forgot, as he frequently did, to ask for a reckoning, yet remembered to leave a few coins for the girl.

Outside, the sky had cleared, and told him the hour was later than he would have guessed. He had stayed too long, plowing sterile soil. Under the uncountable stars, Asbrak set out in the direction of the docks.

With the advancing night, there were fewer and fewer citizens to be seen out of doors, but in the area of the harbor the streets were never entirely still or lonely. Even when it was so late that all the other songs in the city had stopped, there was always someone at the waterfront, if only an overly merry sailor or staggering drover, with a tune on his lips.

The king strolled for a while under the bows of the moored ships where the deep water came to the very doorways of the city. How many more ships, sailors, and all the other signs and engines of prosperity would soon be crowding the wharves and streets in this neighborhood! When the royal marriage had taken place, this port would become the favored partner of the biggest and richest trader on the sea.

King Finster, of course, was well aware of the imbalance of material advantages the impending connection would provide—many for Ambermere, few for Felshalfen. It seemed to him, and he had made no secret of it in his talks with Asbrak, that a passable bride could surely have been found in one of the forest kingdoms, which would have made for a more economically diversified alliance. But Hilbert the Silent had turned out to be Hilbert the Stubborn on this subject, and Finster, who with only one son was understandably nervous about the royal line, had decided to accept the good without regretting the best.

If it were revealed, though, that the Lord of Ascroval had

been able to detain the princess with so little difficulty, and defy his neighbor with so little to fear, this would be a strong hint that finances and other matters in Ambermere were on perhaps a less sound footing than Asbrak the Fat had been able to make the world believe they were. And this might (would, in Asbrak's opinion) be the thing that would make Finster more stubborn than his son. Finster the Munificent had not maintained and increased the wealth of his ancestors by living up to his name. Finster the Stingy, if too harsh, would have been at least closer to the truth.

The king entered one of the principal taverns devoted to the entertainment of travelers and foreigners. With the thought ever foremost in his mind of remaining inconspicuous, he stood completely filling the large archway between the passage and the common room as he surveyed the scene in an attempt to locate potential nests of intrigue where he might hope to eavesdrop.

The common room was a riot of conflicting chanteys, shouted talk, and the high-pitched laughter of women whose virtue had long since ceased to be questionable. Asbrak managed to secure a chair in a dark corner. There he slaked his thirst for ale but for nothing else. He heard no secrets; only seamen's gossip and the noisy wit of caravanners. In these surroundings the king was likely to witness no courtly courtesies.

He visited a number of other waterfront taverns. In one more staid than the others, he heard much talk of the benefits of the coming alliance with Felshalfen, but he gained no useful intelligence in any of the rooms he listened in.

It was at an hour past his normal bedtime that he made his way to the quiet place where he found his waiting groom with a footstool and a stout horse that would have looked more at home hauling a heavy wagon than bearing a cavalier. Once mounted, the monarch allowed the mighty beast to make its own way to the castle, and at its own pace. He was borne away from the harbor, through streets silent but for the fall of the hooves on the cobbles, brooding in his high saddle and mindless of the brilliant moon that shone above.

The night had cleared. The stars were thick in the sky above Rogan's tower. Inside, the magician brushed back a wisp of

long gray hair and peered at the results of his labor. He dropped
the last crumbling fragment of chalk on the powdery heap beside him and rose slowly to his feet. Now the circle, the runes,
the signs—all necessary elements—had been inscribed carefully and precisely on the ancient stone floor. The flask stood on
the shelf among clean goblets, ignored entirely while the critical
work with the chalk had been done. He retrieved a sheet of
parchment from the floor and walked around the circle slowly,
checking for one last time the accuracy of his copy.

When he had satisfied himself that the chalk marks on the
floor matched precisely and without variance the drawing in his
hand, he went to a high wooden table in the far corner of the
room. On it was a glowing lamp and a very large book that
looked as though it would suffer damage if touched by any but
the most gentle hand. Now, and with as much care as he had
checked the floor against the parchment, he compared the
parchment with a drawing in the book, not failing to trace each
feature of the design with a careful finger and a close and
squinting eye.

At length he lay the sheet aside. The circle on the floor was
correct. If he could but read the words and names of the spell
with equal precision—utter them without a mistake—he would
have a weapon against which his opponents would have no de-
fense. On the other hand, one mispronounced name, one formula incorrectly recited, and the very best he could hope for
would be a quick death.

He carefully turned the pages of the book to a place marked
with another sheet of parchment, larger than the first, on which
he had laboriously copied the spell. He resisted the temptation
to check it against the faded text in the book, a task he had performed repeatedly in recent days. It was accurate on the page;
his concern now was that it be as accurate on the lips.

Although he knew the words well, he had never spoken them.
Spells of this power were as far outside the province of a palace
magician as of the royal hairdresser. He had not been certain
that such a spell could be safely rehearsed aloud; he had been
certain that the answer to that question was not one that he cared
to pursue by experiment. He had always imagined that apprentice necromancers muttered spells of this sort by the hour and

repeated them before their masters in the course of perfecting their art. He felt that was probably true, and that he could have been practicing it in his tower from the day he had bought the book. It was easy to suppose that without the chalk circle, the words were only words, without the power to summon so much as a chambermaid. It was, however, not impossible that the spell alone would summon much more, and do so with no circle to hold in check that which had been so summoned.

Rogan lay the copied spell carefully on the table and went to the only unshuttered window in the room. He glanced at the stars. The middle hour of the night was only coming now. He nodded and turned his lips into a small, unhappy smile. As he reached for the shutter, his gaze wandered to the courtyards and lawns quiet in the night below. The king had long since made his furtive return. At this late hour, even the most restless courtiers were no longer abroad. By now, all but he had found the comforts of the bed—if none better, then their own.

He pulled the shutter to. From the shelf he retrieved the flask and a goblet, carrying them with him to a wooden chair near the circle.

"Just time for one measure," he said aloud.

The sound of his voice in the silent room startled him. Though he had spoken softly, the words seemed to echo from the stone walls and the shadows of the ceiling. It almost seemed that instead of his familiar chamber, this was a place he had never been before.

When he had emptied the goblet, he poured a little more, just to keep his throat from getting dry, as he put it to himself. He was quite sure that a spell of the sort he was going to cast had to be spoken without interruption, and this was a very long spell— very long and very complicated. Still, he reminded himself as he sipped, he had mastered this spell to the last syllable. He smiled comfortably in the direction of the chalk-marked floor. That work of this nature demanded close attention was undeniable, but he felt sure that he had executed it as well as any necromancer could. He replenished the depleted goblet.

Perhaps he had not, in the past, dealt with magic of this complexity, but he had wielded magic, nonetheless, all his life, save the first twelve years or so, and felt, really, quite comfortable, now that he happened to think of it, about what he was going to do. He emptied the goblet in small but frequent sips.

He began to pour again from the flask, then abruptly put it down. He hurried across the room and disappeared through a doorway in a corner. When he reappeared a few moments later, he was dressed in a deep blue robe that reached nearly to the floor and a high, pointed hat heavily decorated with a variety of magical insignia.

He filled the goblet past the halfway point, but not to a level that could have been considered full, then returned the flask to its place on the shelf. As he drank, he gazed calmly at the chalk circle on the floor. Far too much was made of this necromancer's sort of magic. Magic was magic, after all—simply a matter of technique. The very fact that he had been forced to acquire the Dark Book, undoubtedly stolen, from a carnival magician of no apparent talent or skill, was scandalous. Such knowledge should be available to those with the wisdom and experience to put it to use.

He rose. The time had come. Following the instructions he had memorized, he retrieved from a small wooden cask a candle that he himself had made, infusing the wax with certain fragrant oils and herbs. From the candle, after it had burned to an inscribed mark, he would light the lamp that sat alone on a stand that had been precisely positioned to define, along with the center of the chalk circle and the place where Rogan was to stand, the Three Points of the spell—the Mortal, the Immortal, and the Eternal.

"The caller, the called, and the law that binds them," said Rogan in a whisper.

The candle, once lit, burned more quickly than he had expected. It filled the room with a fragrance that was somehow disturbing. It suddenly occurred to Rogan to wonder if he was meddling with power too great for him.

He moved to the lamp, keeping his eye on the flame as it approached the mark. If he did not light the lamp, or lit it too early or too late, the spell would be afflicted in some unpredictable, and possibly hazardous, way. He wished the candle would not burn so fast, would give him time to think. He wished he could have one more cup of wine before beginning.

The candle had melted almost to the mark. Now was the moment to act. By force of will he stiffened his resolve. He straightened his back—lifted his chin. Now would he be more than the mere royal worker of petty spells. Now would his old hands know the deeper power. He touched the candle to the lamp. Now would he be one who dared to hold in his grasp the tether of a demon.

He moved to his point, the Mortal. He drew the parchment from his sleeve and held it so that it caught the glow from the lamp. It was only then that he noticed, greatly to his consternation, that every candle in the room had died.

"Baldersnarp," he said in a shaky voice. The parchment trembled lightly in his hand, as though being troubled by a breeze. "Rassaddersnatt," he continued. The names seemed longer when they were read aloud. Rogan wondered what would happen if a spell were simply abandoned, but this was another question that could not be prudently pursued by experiment. He read on, the syllables echoing in his dark, lonely chamber.

And elsewhere.

There was no sky in the Lower Regions. No day, no night. No sunny blue, no jeweled blackness. Instead, there was a reeking haze. Pools of sluggish waters reflected weak light that seemed a property of the atmosphere itself, as though the air were glowing. Low clouds of foul dark smoke drifted in the absence of any wind, walking the suffocating landscape, kicking at the reluctant haze. But no sky was overhead to be gazed on. No one there turned an eye to open heavens above.

Castles stood there under no sky, as did shanties, huts, and secret holes in the hot, rocky ground. Ways were marked by worn paths, ancient ruts, threading across the bare jagged hills and hollow valleys. And every fork and turning was lit by the eerie ambient glow.

And some there walked the ways, or crawled, or slithered, or lay in wait, lurking at places where the path was steep. And some hid in their holes, gnawing old flesh, cracking old bones. And some quarreled in their huts and shanties, brooding on their hates.

And some took their ease on cool stone slabs within their castle walls.

The names bit at him like rats worrying a corpse.

He stirred, disturbing the viscous yellow haze that lay around him. A season of repose, lying unthinking, beyond place, like a toad on a rock—this was to be interrupted. He raised himself. And by whom? He listened to the voice, as much inside his pointed ear as in the air around him.

Who dared to disturb the Lower Regions? What meddling fool with a Book called his names? Awakened, he felt empty. Hungry. Perhaps this incantation would go awry, as others had in the past. How astonished they always were, these mages, when they got something a little wrong and their chalk circles were only useless marks on a floor.

And if that is to be, then let him be a plump little witch-man, thought the demon, not gross and fat, but tender and appetizing. A feast to settle into. Or else, he thought, considering further as his appetite grew, he might be lean and muscular, meaty instead of fatty. But not scrawny; not all skin and gristle, all feet and elbows.

After a time, when all his names had been pronounced correctly, he rose to listen to the words that followed. The spell was an old one. Complicated beyond necessity, but of great potency. Hidden among the pointless formulations was a vocabulary of power that could not be ignored. He could feel it seize him as one by one the words of meaning emerged.

And yet he did not recognize the one who called. Numbered among those mortals of the Middle Regions who would dare to summon him were none who would use this wordy, bookish spell—this extravagant necromantic peroration. As the grasp of the magic closed around him, he listened for a mistake. The voice, almost faint at first, was louder now. Let it stumble on the wrong word, falter at the wrong time, and a circle of chalk, however carefully rendered, would not contain him.

Still in his own form, but no longer in his keep, he moved by the power of the spell through the sulfurous haze that veiled every feature of the landscape. In his eyes, as in those of all the inhabitants of this place, was reflected the dull yellow of the atmosphere. Ahead he could begin to see the image of the hated circle, growing ever closer. As he was forced toward it, the yellow mist gave way to a thick white fog, the veil of the Middle Regions.

The circle filled his path. He stopped before it. It remained only to be ordered through to stand in the presence of his captor. How he would seethe, bound and impotent in a circle before a cringing magician.

But if not on the magician, then on the magician's enemies would he have the chance to be revenged. Someone in the Middle Regions was certainly meant to be the victim of this spell. Rarely did anyone call a demon but to do violence.

The voice droned on, becoming louder with each phrase, and then stopped. Now beyond the circle a figure could be seen, dimly—an old man in a pointed hat, bending to pick up a parchment from the floor. He retrieved it, dropped it, and picked it up again, turning it rapidly from front to back and top to bottom in his trembling hands.

". . . the, ah, the summons so delivered, come or go ye then to some Middle Regions such as commanded, and by thy names so uttered, leaving the Lower Regions, and thy blood and substance, ah, rather, with . . . with thy blood and substance, and by forms, ah, my, that is, thy form so ordered as by my form, that is, my order . . . command . . . to, ah . . . such region be ye bound to my call. . . . Drat!"

The page dropped again, this time sailing across the circle before coming to rest on the floor. The demon watched the magician hesitate, squinting uncertainly in his direction, and then make a dash after the sheet of parchment.

The view of the circle faded, and with it the mist. The demon felt himself drifting. The fool of a magician had turned the spell inside out with his blundering. The mist cleared completely. The Lower Regions were gone. The magician was gone. Only the power of the spell remained.

He stood between high walls in a narrow space. Above, between the rooftops, he could see the full moon shining in a cloudless sky. Ten paces from him, an old man dressed in ragged clothing slept in a doorway. No one else was near. He could smell the man's flesh. He wrinkled his nose in disgust. He was no trifling devil of one or two names, or even one or two dozen, and would not sit down to such a supper. This was a meal for slaves that dwelt in stinking holes, or shacks built against his castle walls.

The man awoke. He opened his eyes and looked directly at the demon across the alley, hideous with horns, fangs, and glowing yellow eyes. He started and gasped, stared for a moment from frightened eyes, then shrugged, turning his glance to the empty bottle under his hand.

Using the old man as a model, the demon transformed himself, squeezed himself, into the image of the tattered wino. He first contracted and distorted his shape, then molded his form until the demon was gone and the wino's twin stood in his place.

The tramp in the doorway stumbled to his feet. His mouth hung open as he steadied himself against a garbage can.

"Hey, buddy. You got anything to drink?" He spoke in an almost incomprehensible whine.

By timeless custom, those whose forms were copied were always left a little better off than they were found.

"What is your wish?" said the wino's double. His voice did not resemble the old man's.

The man staggered closer. He began to laugh, but his weak chuckle turned into a coughing fit.

"You look jus' like my old man," he said, laughing and coughing as he stumbled back against the wall.

He slid to the ground. He began to weep.

"But my old man's dead. Been dead." He began to cough again, holding his chest.

"They're all dead now. All dead." He looked at his empty bottle, at the garbage can next to him.

"Wish't I was dead," he said.

And in a moment, he was. The demon lifted him to his feet with one hand, broke his neck with a single heavy blow, and left his still corpse among the trash in the gutter.

He of the hundred names shuffled from the alley like an old drunk. The power of the spell, if not renewed, would dimin-

ish in time. The night air was heavy with smells, the street
noisy with talk and music. The demon smiled. The color of
his teeth matched the dull yellow of his eyes. This was
not where he would choose to be, but it was where he
was.

CHAPTER

· 3 ·

The Friday lunch-hour crowds had thinned. Marcia left the park, hoping that if she took a brief walk, Hannah would be sitting on their bench when she got back. She checked the time. Surely it would be safe to be away fifteen or twenty minutes. In the way she had perfected by long habit, she began immediately to worry about her decision. Maybe ten minutes would be better, she thought. With a final glance over her shoulder, she crossed the street and set out at a brisk pace. At the first corner, she turned, not because she had any particular destination in mind, but just to avoid the neighborhood where she worked.

Up ahead, a group of well-dressed men emerged from an office building and turned in her direction. They walked three abreast, filling the sidewalk. As they approached, they looked toward her and through her but not at her, as if they had all been trained as waiters. At the last minute she sidled out of their way, squeezing between a parking meter and a pickup truck as the men breezed past in a flurry of small talk and cologne. She wondered, as she always did when this happened to her, what they would have done if she had simply stood in the middle of the sidewalk. Trampled her underfoot and gone on, she supposed. It was as though she were invisible. At times like this, Marcia wished that instead of 120, she weighed, say, 350 pounds. She imagined a great rotund version of herself plowing into a group of these movers and shakers and scattering them like a cluster of tenpins dressed in three-piece suits.

Marcia was beginning to regret taking the afternoon off. Hannah was late—probably not coming—and Mr. Figge had reacted as though he thought Marcia's absence would threaten the survival of the firm.

"What about the Owens file?" he had demanded.

"Well, it's already—"

"Just one moment, if you please, Marcia," he snapped in the tone of a man who has been driven to the end of his patience. He frowned and shook his head. "I'll have to check this with Colette."

Colette, who was almost twenty years younger than Marcia and, nominally at least, lower in the company hierarchy, was disposed to be generous. "Don't you worry, Mr. Figge. The team can cope. I was going to work through lunch anyway."

Mr. Figge beamed.

Marcia started to speak in a timid voice. "All of my work is up—"

Mr. Figge interrupted. "Just one moment, if you please, Marcia." Mr. Figge was not a man to vary a locution lightly. "After all, it is your problem that Colette and I are discussing." He smiled at Colette. "You have everything under control, then?"

"Yes, sir. We're talking all systems totally go."

Nervous as she was, Marcia could not suppress a slight smile. She wondered how long it would take Colette to learn that their fastidious boss hated all fads, particularly in speech, that had arisen since his childhood. Prominent among the many things Mr. Figge did not approve of were the expressions "we're talking," "I was, like," and all their kin. Yet Colette went to the trouble to arrange the things she said so that frequent occasions for their use would arise. When they did, she would roll her eyes, lower her voice portentously, and utter the appropriate formula.

Three blocks of daydreaming and inattention brought Marcia to the seediest downtown section the city had to offer. Strip joints and stores dedicated to the distribution of pornography— written, photographed, and filmed—were the principal enter-

prises. Marcia hurried past the shills and loiterers outside the
bars, keeping her eyes in front of her. She was making for the
nearest corner when she saw something that stopped her.

The man loomed on the sidewalk. He was a sneer surrounded
by stringy long hair, numerous tattoos, and an ample belly that
was not entirely covered by the dirty T-shirt he wore under his
black leather vest. Marcia hesitated for a moment, then crossed
the street, both to keep her purse out of his reach, and to avoid a
painfully close look at his especially nasty aura. Not that her
ability to see auras yielded any extra information in his case. A
glance was enough to convince anyone with common sense to
stay out of his way.

That was often the case with auras. Marcia had been seeing
them for as long as she could remember, and had found that frequently they only confirmed the conclusions she would have
drawn without them. But not always. She had never really figured out if her natural pessimism was strengthened by her unusual talent. Certainly the ability to see auras and compare them
with outward appearances did nothing to encourage a rosy view
of the world.

From across the street, her eyes were drawn to the man. She
did not often see an aura that dark, not even in the city with its
hordes of people. She wondered what Hannah would say about
it. She glanced at her watch. There was really little hope of seeing Hannah today, she supposed. She sighed.

She had dreaded asking for the afternoon off, and Mr. Figge,
who never troubled to hide the slightest displeasure from an
employee and was never without an obsequious smile in the
presence of his superiors, had behaved as expected. Now it appeared that she could have saved herself the agony. She fully
expected the park bench to be empty when she got back; it was
well past the customary time for Hannah to arrive.

Marcia was positively dejected. She had looked forward to
Friday all week, and was full of questions about the things Hannah had told her last time. She recalled their first meeting, only
a few weeks ago. She had brought her lunch to the park and was
alone on her favorite bench when she noticed the small woman
with the irreproachable posture and the very strange hat. Not
wishing to stare or, more accurately, not wishing to be caught

staring, she kept her eyes on her sandwich and waited for the lady to pass.

That Marcia did not actually jump when she sat down beside her was to her credit. The woman arranged her long dark skirt and sat quietly with her hands folded in her lap. Marcia finished her lunch, keeping her eyes away from her companion.

As she sat politely pretending that the woman next to her did not exist, she thought about urban etiquette and the lengths people went to in observing it. Anyone who spent much time in the city developed impressive skills of strategic avoidance. Marcia was pretty sure the ability of each passenger on a crowded elevator to find a different empty space to stare at proved the existence of a fourth dimension.

She finished her lunch and brushed a few imaginary crumbs from her lap. She folded her lunch bag with self-conscious neatness, then consulted her wristwatch. It was still early, but she decided to leave rather than sit there feeling uncomfortable. As she was getting up from the bench, she glanced at the woman with an impersonal smile meant to communicate a nice anonymous urban farewell.

She bent forward to rise, then stopped, her smile replaced by an undisguised look of astonishment. She settled slowly back to her seat without taking her eyes from the woman and the aura that surrounded her. How, she wondered, had she failed to notice it? True, it was subtle and muted, but it was totally unlike any in her experience. Auras simply didn't look like that. She stared as frankly as a three-year-old.

"Ahhh," said the woman, smiling broadly and raising her hands from her lap. "I was sure you were not blind, my young witch."

The combined effect of being referred to as "young" and "witch" left Marcia without a reply.

"My name is Hannah. May I call you Marcia?"

Marcia closed her mouth and nodded.

"You do talk?"

Marcia swallowed. "How do you know my name?"

"A trick. One that a person of your abilities can easily learn. I will teach it to you next time, if you like."

Marcia found herself picturing a cheap storefront with a sign that said MADAME HANNAH, READER AND ADVISER.

"Next time?"

Hannah appeared not to notice the question. She looked around her with an expression of disapproval.

"In these surroundings, it's a wonder you have been able to develop at all." She was silent for a moment. "Is it always so noisy?"

Marcia, who came to the park because it was comparatively quiet, could only nod.

"Well, it will have to do, at least for now. After you've made some progress, I'll see about finding us a more peaceful place. At least the tavern."

Since Marcia didn't have the slightest idea what the woman was talking about, she did not offer a comment.

"No one has ever been in touch with you, have they?"

"I beg your pardon?"

"I am the first," said Hannah. She smoothed her skirt over her legs.

"First what?"

"Witch, of course. Really, my dear, you must try to remain alert."

Marcia had returned quite late from lunch that day, and then ruined Mr. Figge's afternoon by being too distracted to cringe at his displeasure.

And now today Hannah had not arrived for their meeting. It was the first time she had not shown up when she had said she would. Marcia checked her watch again. She looked once more at the aura of the man across the street, then left to sit in the park for a while, just in case.

At the edge of the city of Ambermere, on a quiet unpaved street by the river, was a modest shrine dedicated to one of the obscure but potent goddesses of the Elder Truths. It was set well back from the road, among a grove of fruit trees.

The rays of the afternoon sun were just beginning to reach the small building, warming the stones of the ancient walls. Inside, the cooler air of the morning lingered. In front of the altar, a middle-aged woman with her hair wrapped in a bandanna applied a small broom to the floor.

Renzel never rushed at her work in the shrine. She felt whatever was done there was done in the presence of the goddess, and should be done with care and reverence, in the manner of a prayer. She thought, in fact, that anything done in the shrine was a sort of prayer, even if it was only the caretaker sweeping and polishing. Each bend and taper of the worn wooden rail before the altar she had rubbed to a glow, so that the humble material itself appeared to have received the blessing of the goddess.

She was surprised to hear the sound of voices through the open door. Midday visitors were not common except at times of public worship or festivals, nor had guests begun arriving for the long-awaited wedding of the Peerless Iris, Royal Daughter of the Beloved Monarch.

Nonetheless, of the two who entered, one was a stranger, a dark-haired girl. Or perhaps a woman just beyond youth; Renzel couldn't tell. For one thing, the dim candlelight at the altar was reflected in the girl's eyes in an unusual and distracting way.

She might be suspected of being an early-arriving royal visitor to the wedding, but for her clothing, which was plain, and her companion, not one to be found in the company of royalty.

Renzel put her broom aside.

"Good day, Mistress Hannah," she said to the older woman, nodding politely to the other.

The witch returned her greeting distractedly and looked, Renzel thought, very much as though she wished she were elsewhere. Perhaps the dark one was royal, and liked to disguise herself, as the king did. Or might she be a witch of rank? Renzel didn't think so.

The two visitors fulfilled the minimum obligations of respect to the altar of the goddess, then strolled around the small shrine examining the ornaments and decorations. When they had finished, the girl came to Renzel.

"You are the priestess?" she asked. Renzel was still holding her polishing rag. She found the girl's eyes disturbing—something about the way they caught the light. Though not given to flights of fancy, Renzel found herself imagining what it would be like to look into the eyes of a wolf.

"No, miss. I tend the shrine." Out of courtesy, Renzel tried to hide her disapproval. It pleased her when the shrine was admired, but when a visitor came only to admire it, that showed, in Renzel's view, a lack of respect for the goddess.

The woman—girl?—looked again at the altar and the other appointments. She smiled at Renzel.

"You tend it well. It is exactly as it should be. I will visit it again soon."

They had left before Renzel could decide if the stranger was an impertinent child or a visiting duchess. The witch, who had been known to linger for a comfortable chat, barely muttered a word of farewell on her way out.

Now Renzel, done with her chores, had leisure to worry about her niece, also a dark-haired beauty. How long was she to be absent, sending no word apart from the relayed messages from a palace functionary? Companion to the princess, she was, and off with her without a word of warning, but "expected back imminently," she and the princess both. Renzel wished as she had many times in recent days that highborn girls were more plentiful in the city. Then her niece could admire the palace from without like the rest of the commoners rather than being a permanent resident there.

It had been put out by the palace that the Inimitable Iris Who Shamed Perfection had decided to spend the last weeks before her nuptials in seclusion and might not reappear until the eve of the event itself. The populace, apart from a number of merchants inconvenienced by her unavailability, and the royal dressmaker, who seemed to have achieved a permanent state of hysteria, were content that the Dazzling Iris should absent herself during her last days of virginity if that was her whim. But the populace had not had its niece vanish without a word, and did not have to endure explanations that always seemed to sound as though they were being improvised.

The door opened to admit the priestess. Her silk frock appeared to glow in the dim light.

"Are you still here?" she asked in a sharp tone.

"Yes, madam. Making the shrine tidy."

"The shrine is tidy enough. You are to be working in the house today. I have guests coming for the wedding, as you know very well." She looked around the shrine. "I don't know what you find to do in here every day. You should devote more time to the domicile of your priestess. I need attention over there. You do not have to swipe at every mote of dust with your cloth, while I am without anyone to do anything for me." She walked up to the altar without ceremony, which never failed to shock Renzel, no matter how many times she witnessed it, and picked up the coins from the wooden bowl.

"Not much here," she said with a hard look in Renzel's direction.

Renzel said nothing. It was a religious obligation to respect the priestess, and Renzel took religious obligations seriously.

The priestess strode to the door. "I expect the house to be finished by tonight," she said. "When I permitted you to stay after the old priestess died, I explained that whoever cares for the shrine must care for the priestess as well. When you neglect me, it is like neglecting the shrine, or the goddess."

Shocked again, Renzel could only nod. The priestess had absolute power over the shrine. Renzel could care for it only by her leave. In any event, whatever the priestess said was right by definition. She continued as priestess, the faithful had to presume, on sufferance of the goddess. And had she not been invested more than four months ago?

And of course with a new priestess some changes were to be expected. She had wasted no time in removing Renzel from the cottage behind the residence to a small room within it.

"I want you in my house, so you will be near when I have need of you," she had explained. "It was not proper in my predecessor that she allowed you the use of the cottage. The cottage is too big for you. A small room in the residence is enough. You must remember that it is a great honor to serve the goddess, even in the meanest capacity."

Renzel smiled. The fact that she spent more time in the shrine than anyone, and that she was allowed to care for it, was all that was really important to her. She had never been asked to act as a servant to the old priestess, who had in fact tended the shrine herself before her great age made it necessary to have help. But

Renzel would do what she had to. She allowed herself the space of a few deep breaths before following her mistress through the door.

The bartender was seated, with his knees drawn up to his chest, on the bar itself. He was a small, sandy-haired young man, and looked, in the dim light, like an elf in a picture book.

The word BAR could be read on the floor, drawn there by the sun as it slanted past the neon tubing in the dirty window. The bartender, appreciating the marvel of the city sun penetrating to street level, however briefly, concentrated on the phenomenon. His Brotherhood taught that nothing was without its meaning, and it was through concentration that meaning could be sought.

At a large table in a corner seven men talked quietly, their murmurings punctuated occasionally by soft laughter. None were young, a few were old. One, a rather fat man who was dozing in his chair, appeared to be of great age. He was bald but for a fringe of wispy white hair and wore a thinning unkempt beard. Like all the men at the table, he was dressed in nondescript casual clothing that looked well used and comfortable.

The street door opened, admitting a surprising quantity of noise from outside, and a young man dressed in a business suit. When the door closed behind him, all the sounds of traffic and machinery were gone again, as though the bar were located in a deep woods somewhere far from civilization.

The bartender withdrew his attention from the shadow on the floor.

"Greetings, Jackson," he called. "You look just like a local." He slid himself to the edge of the bar and dropped lightly to the floor.

The newcomer took a seat.

"If you remember, Errin, I am a local. And speaking of locals, I have been meaning to ask why we don't have a rebuff at the door."

"No one seems to think it necessary. Gavas says an unnecessary spell is a bad spell."

"Yes, Gavas always seems to have an axiom, when he's awake. Has anyone come through since I was here last?"

"No. Nothing has happened. Mistress Hannah makes her regular trips."

"That can hardly be considered news."

Errin shrugged. "Oh, I forgot. There is one thing. I am to have help. In fact, she is late."

"She?"

"A barmaid."

"Not a local?"

"No, connected with some Order or another. An apprentice of some sort, I suppose. Who knows? Imagine, someone junior to me." He struck a pose of exaggerated dignity.

"Mitzi," he said sternly, "a glass here for Master Jackson, and be quick about it."

"And," Jackson added in a low voice, "a pillow for Master Gavas." They both burst into laughter.

They were still recovering when a heavy door at the back of the room opened with a low-pitched moan from the hinges.

Errin leaned toward Jackson. "Perfect for a witch," he whispered, at which they both began to laugh again.

"As you see, my dear, not all wizards are old, or dignified."

Hannah stood with a dark-haired girl at her side. The young men bowed.

"This is Miss Elise," she said. "This is Master Errin and Master Jackson. It is Master Errin you will work with, I believe. Master Jackson is a traveler and only stops from time to time."

They presented Elise to the others. Even old Gavas got to his feet to greet her properly, at which Jackson caught Errin's eye.

"It's because she's so pretty, and I'm so old, young sir," he said in his cracked voice, astonishing Jackson, who had imagined he was being subtle. "Pray you find out someday what I mean." Like many of the utterances of Gavas, this one was ambiguous.

"Come," said a gray-haired man of middle years, "you must sit and join us." He addressed Hannah, already on her way to the street door. "Mistress, won't you linger and tell us what you've been up to lately? I had dealings with one of your Sisterhood when I was last away."

"Thank you, Brother Mervin, but I am late for a meeting with the adept I am trying to cultivate. I hope she is still waiting. I must fly. Figuratively speaking, of course."

After they had joined in a glass with the table, Elise and the two young men returned to the bar.

"You see," said Jackson, glancing toward Gavas, "he is asleep again. I confess he is sometimes sharp, but I do not see what use he is asleep. Even in the small things I do, I would be grateful for some help sometimes."

"Well," said Errin, "I will speak to Gavas for you. Perhaps he will go with you."

"That is not what I meant. But what about you? Now that Elise is here, maybe they mean to release you. You are long since ready."

"No. Thank you, but I think they mean for me to be an apprentice forever. You heard what Mervin said about beginning Elise's instruction. Not," he said, turning to the girl, "that it will not be my very great pleasure to do so. You must not take our chatter too seriously." He jumped up onto the bar and dropped to the other side.

"I will prepare us some tea, and you can take advantage of the presence of Master Jackson for some instruction at the hands of an expert." He busied himself at the end of the bar.

Elise smiled at Jackson. "Please do not trouble yourself," she said.

"Oh, it's no trouble. We all like to talk," he said, making a gesture that took in everyone in the room. "Are you familiar with the Orders and Sisterhoods and so on? It really doesn't do to be confused on that subject. There is no telling who might pass through a place like this. And not just the travelers of the Middle Regions. An arch-wizard was here once, openly, and stayed for half a day. I actually saw him, and spoke to him. I had wondered before that if there really was such a thing as an arch-wizard."

Elise looked at him questioningly.

"Well, not doubted, exactly. Arch-wizard is really just another name for necromancer. But it is one thing to tread the paths that I do, or even that you just did in order to get to this place from Ambermere, but to pass through other Regions . . . It is as though Errin were to tell us he had spent last night at the bottom of the river."

Errin appeared with three cups of tea.

"As promised," he said. "And I didn't."

"Didn't what?" asked Jackson.

"Didn't spend last night at the bottom of the river. But since Master Hugo was minding the store, so to speak, I did spend the evening in Ambermere. And," he said with a flourishing gesture, "I saw the king. In fact, I stood right next to him."

Jackson looked puzzled for a moment. "Oh, that's right," he said. "He's the one with the disguises."

"Asbrak," said Errin. "The Fat. I didn't even notice him at first. Everyone recognizes him, of course, but they just ignore him. Anyway, there were some musicians and a pair of jugglers performing at a crossing on the avenue. The jugglers did some amazing things. And not magic, either, not a trace. Just skill and concentration."

Jackson nodded in the direction of the street. "I'd like to see the mayor try walking around this city alone at night."

The front door opened and the room was flooded with noise.

Jackson watched as three men approached the bar. He turned to Errin.

"Locals," he said. "I think Gavas should have to wait on them."

They had only been out for forty-five minutes, according to Judy's watch, and already they had startled three or four men, and completely terrified one jerk who had been walking a dog of his own.

"You're a real good dog, Monster, real good." Monster, a veteran of attack training and many months of Judy's walks, held his position. The two of them took up the entire sidewalk on this quiet side street. Judy was not petite, and Monster, who unlike his mistress was all muscle, outweighed her by a couple of pounds.

Judy looked admiringly at Monster's new collar.

"Spikes!" her uncle had said, touching them as though to verify the evidence of his eyes. "Now I know you're nuts. What the hell does that dog need spikes around his neck for?"

"In case some other dog attacks him."

"What dog's going to attack him, the Hound of the Baskervilles?"

Judy looked interested. "The hound of what?" she asked.

"Never mind. It's from a book."

"Oh," she said with no enthusiasm at all.

Judy was pleased to see that even on a cloudy evening, the spikes were noticeable, especially when they walked under a streetlight. She decided to take Monster downtown tomorrow. Saturday was a good day for a downtown walk. People would be sure to notice his collar as they jumped out of the way. She wrapped the leash around her wrist one more turn, still leaving plenty of slack. The leash was a stout cord of braided leather, purchased when Monster graduated from the choke chain.

"That's a hell of a leash," the clerk at the store had commented.

"I got a hell of a dog," had been Judy's reply.

A block ahead, she saw someone cross to the other side of the street. She crossed immediately, leading the big dog between the cars and vans parked at the curbs.

There was not enough light for her to tell at that distance if the man had noticed Monster. Sometimes people crossed the street to avoid passing him. Those that didn't, usually slowed down, and then gave Judy and her dog wide berth.

The man was getting closer. When he was nearly to them, Judy flicked the leash with her wrist. Monster bared his teeth and snarled at the approaching man, who jumped back in a very satisfactory way.

"That's enough, boy," she said as they passed the astonished pedestrian. "Just a warning to let them know you're here, that's all."

"What the hell's the matter with you, lady?" shouted the man from behind her. Judy's heart began to pound. She turned, pulling on the leash. Monster growled and moved toward the man.

"You looking for trouble, mister?" she said in a loud voice. "You keep bothering me, and I'll turn him loose." Monster pulled on the leash, straining toward the man, who was backing up. Judy took a triumphant step forward.

The man retreated.

"I'm not bothering anyone," he said angrily.

Judy advanced another step.

"You better get away from me," she said with conviction. "I mean it."

As the man turned with a curse and walked away, quickly, Judy had a mental image of Monster unleashed, chasing him down.

"One of these days," she muttered, "some bastard's going to push me too far." She turned.

"Heel!" she said with an angry and unnecessary tug on the leash.

For the next twenty minutes, the walk was boring. Judy was getting ready to call it a night when she saw the wino at a lighted intersection two blocks ahead. Though not fond of moving fast, she quickened her pace. She was able to slow down a moment later when the man began to walk in her direction.

"Here he comes, Monster," she whispered. Her pulse quickened again. One of these days she was going to have to turn the dog loose on someone. Who knew when?

The man, dressed in rags, crossed the next street. He didn't turn off. Judy took a deep breath. He was half a block away. Her pulse quickened. If he had noticed them, he didn't show it. He was walking right toward them. Probably half-drunk. Judy almost grinned. She knew a way to sober him up.

"He better not act up," she said fiercely to her pet. It was almost time. She made sure she was taking up all of the sidewalk, moving Monster a little to the right.

Without warning, the dog halted, staring at the approaching figure and sniffing the air. Judy was almost pulled off her feet.

"What's the matter with you?"

Monster whined and looked up at his mistress.

"Shut up," she said. She took another turn of the leash around her wrist. The wino was only thirty feet or so away. She pulled on the leash, putting her weight and her temper into it, but without success.

"What do you want with a pet that's stronger than you are?" her uncle had asked.

She thought of those words now as her pet began pulling her up the street. Judy pulled back as though in a tug-of-war. She stared at the heavy spiked collar where the leash was attached with a metal ring. Step by step she was pulled along. She glanced over her shoulder. The bum was almost to them.

With a yelp echoed by a scream from Judy, the huge dog took off at a gallop. For a few steps Judy kept her feet under her, running madly and clawing at the leash on her wrist, and screaming in rage at Monster to stop. She tripped, stumbled forward, recovered, and then fell and was dragged, screaming, over curbs and pavements for almost a half a block before the leash parted from the collar, leaving her writhing and bloody in the middle of the street.

The houses in the neighborhood emptied, and Judy was surrounded by a crowd of people who couldn't imagine what had befallen her. No one noticed the dirty little man with the yellow eyes who passed the scene with no sign of curiosity.

Ferris was getting tired of waiting for Jaybee. Jaybee had money that belonged to him, and he wanted it. Jaybee was a tough man, but he wasn't so tough that he wanted to mess around with Ferris. Ferris had advice for people that were in danger of annoying him. He advised them not to make him mad. Jaybee was beginning to annoy him.

He looked up and down the street. It was Friday night, and every strip joint and barroom was full. Harsh, icy light spilled onto the pavement from the windows of the twenty-four-hour bookstores. Among the crowds of college boys, punks, and winos, the hookers in their working clothes and makeup glowed like neon signs.

But no sign of Jaybee. Ferris's practiced eye noted a young man in expensive clothes half stumble from a bar opposite and walk unsteadily up the street. He considered following him. He could always find a use for some easy money. A punch and a kick and that powder puff would be offering to put him in his will.

Before he had made up his mind, his potential victim had stopped to talk to a miserable little wino he had practically tripped over. The young man was making extravagant gestures and laughing as though he had run into a bosom friend. As Ferris watched, he took out his wallet and handed the tattered old man some money. After a parting oration, he continued down the street.

The bum shoved the money carelessly into a pocket and shuffled ahead until he was just opposite Ferris. There he stopped and peered across the street, grinning at the big man as though overcome with delight at the mere sight of him.

Ferris directed his sneer toward the wino. He couldn't believe the puny little bum was standing there grinning at him. Maybe he thought Ferris couldn't see him. Maybe his brain was so fogged with booze and old age he thought he was a long way away. But he was just across the street, and Ferris could see him just fine.

"So what about it, Ferris?"

"What about what, Marsh?" he asked. He knew what Marsh wanted. He was surprised that he had the guts to mention it.

"The twenty dollars."

"Yeah?" He sneered down at him. Marsh was only about six feet tall. Someone Marsh's size was a midget to Ferris.

Marsh seemed to have run out of ideas.

"Come on, Ferris," he said with a cautious whine, "you said you'd pay me last week."

Before answering him, Ferris stared at him for a long moment.

"You don't want to make me mad, man."

"But . . ."

"You don't want to make me mad, man." Ferris liked to say things twice when he was bullying people. He didn't know why; it was just something he enjoyed. That, and kicking someone who was trying to get up and run away, were both really fun, in his view. Maybe Marsh would get mad, or brave, and try to mess with him. He hoped so. He pulled on the lapels of his leather vest.

When he looked across the street, the little bum was still there, still staring. Ferris didn't like people to stare at him. Not openly. He liked it when they pretended not to see him but were careful not to get too close. He liked it when they glanced and whispered and looked scared. But this old guy was staring right at him, and grinning, and looked like he wasn't planning to quit.

Ferris wondered how much money the kid had handed the

wino. No telling, plastered as he was. He pushed himself away from the building he was leaning against.

"I'll be back in a minute. If Jaybee comes by, you tell him." He walked across the street slowly, doing his best to disrupt traffic, and hoping someone wanted to make something of it.

By the time he had crossed the street, the little bum had gone. He just caught a glimpse of him turning into an alley in the middle of the block. Ferris smiled as he followed. Two days ago, a construction crew had blocked the alley at the other end. He had been down there this afternoon, looking. He wondered if the man would try to fight. When old guys tried to fight, it was really funny. They sputtered and swore, and got red in the face, and swung their fists like babies. Or sometimes they tried to box, stumbling over their own footwork as they tried to land their puny jabs.

The bum was all the way at the end of the alley, sitting on a large barrel swinging his legs. Ferris wondered how he had gotten up on it without breaking his neck. The man looked calm. He was even smiling as Ferris walked up.

"That smile's not going to look like much when I knock your teeth out." Ferris spoke in a conversational tone. "Of course, it don't look like much now."

The old man continued to smile. "This is not your lucky day," he said in a soft voice that didn't go with his appearance.

"Talk's not gonna help you, pop. Want you want to do is give me that money in your pocket."

"Except for being unappetizing," the man continued. "That's luck of a sort, I suppose."

Ferris was conscious of the muscles in his arms. Conscious of just how hard he could punch. He felt good, and strong, and in control. This would be a nice little warm-up. He looked forward to an entertaining night.

"You talk an awful lot for someone in bad trouble," he said.

He was surprised when the old man began to laugh. He was also mad. Ferris didn't like to be surprised, and he didn't like people to make him mad.

He stood still for a moment longer, feeling his anger turn to something hotter. When he was finished with this joker, the wino was going to hurt all over, and real bad. He leapt forward suddenly, reaching out to snatch the wino off his barrel. It would be a long time, he thought, before this old bastard laughed again.

Ferris felt like he had walked into a tree. As his head cleared, he could see the old man standing over him. He realized he was sitting on the sidewalk. Grunting and swearing, he began to struggle to his feet, only to be slapped down again with what felt like a shovel. He put his hands up to his face and groaned. He looked around. There was no one there but him and the bum. And the bum was empty-handed. Ferris groaned again. Someone was hitting him with something heavy. The bum was old and skinny, more than a foot shorter than Ferris, and less than half his weight. It had to be someone else. He looked around again. There was no one else there.

"You are completely repulsive," said the old man. He made it sound like a compliment. He reached down with one hand and, without noticeable effort, pulled Ferris to his feet by the arm, as though he were a teddy bear stuffed with cotton.

Ferris stared into his dull yellow eyes.

"Perfect," the man said softly. He didn't sound old. "And more my size."

It was just getting through to Ferris that this skinny old man had picked him up with one hand. He had reached down like a mother grabbing a two-year-old. Ferris was puzzled. It couldn't be that he was some kind of former athlete. Ferris had been around plenty of those. Last year he had beaten a dilapidated old ex-heavyweight boxer nearly to death without ever getting hit.

"You don't get a wish," the man said, addressing Ferris, "but then, you don't get ripped open, and that's something."

He let Ferris's arm drop and slapped him, almost lightly, with his open hand.

Ferris saw the slap coming, but couldn't make his arms move. When the hand hit his cheek, it felt like a brick. He was unconscious before he hit the ground.

When Ferris stumbled from the alley ten minutes later, he was in a state of total confusion. He felt weak and sick. It seemed a great effort to make it to the curb and steady himself on a parking meter. His vision was blurred. He blinked repeatedly, expecting it to clear up. Across the street he saw, dimly, a big man in dark clothing. He moved closer, staggering through the traffic. He was almost too tired to cross the street. When he finally made it, he leaned against, almost lay across, a parked car and peered at the man standing thirty feet away. One by one, he looked at the tattoos, remembering each one, then at the T-shirt and leather vest, and finally at the stringy hair and at the sneer . . . on his face . . . with the yellow eyes staring at him. He shifted his eyes to the window of the car, focusing on his reflection there. Ferris tried to scream, but it came out a coughing fit. As they passed, people stared at the little old man dressed in rags leaning against the car, coughing and staring into its window.

CHAPTER

✦ 4 ✦

Rogan awoke in his chair well after dark. He went hurriedly to the window and was relieved to see that the time for beginning the spell had not passed. He closed the shutters and poured himself some wine.

A full day had passed since his first attempt with the spell. He couldn't imagine what had gone wrong. One or two times, it was true, he had not been quite perfect in his recitation, but still, he had almost seen the demon, almost had him trapped in the circle of chalk.

The lamp still burned. At the proper hour he would take his position and begin again to call the names. Tonight he would surely be successful.

By late Friday afternoon, Daniel had had enough of his apartment and of tax forms and poorly kept records. He had finally unplugged his phone the night before. It had been somewhat discouraging for him to realize what a small sacrifice it was to do without that particular contraption. What it amounted to was that there was no one he cared to hear from anyway. Of course, there was the danger of missing a telephonic lecture from his brother on the virtues of steady employment, but he had decided to take the risk.

He had given up on the idea of Milton's game. At the mo-

ment, an evening of cards and bets sounded positively purgato-
rial. He went downtown and caught the early showing of a
movie that had sounded interesting but wasn't. Afterward he
treated himself to what he secretly regarded as a perfectly bal-
anced meal—a pizza and a half bottle of Chianti Riserva. He
was persuaded to indulge in dessert because of a new Italian
item on the menu that was translated alluringly as "a simple
country tart."

By the time he finished dinner it was dark outside. He walked
the main streets for a while, enjoying the summer evening and
the Friday-night crowds. He found himself thinking that maybe
things would straighten themselves out with Charlie. Maybe a
week from tonight he would be back at the game.

He strolled along the waterfront and ended up going farther
than he had intended. Daniel liked long walks, but not after dark
in the wrong part of town. He struck out for home by the short-
est route, which took him through a downtown fringe the mayor
and Chamber of Commerce would have gladly seen burned to
the sidewalks. The main enterprises, other than empty store-
fronts, were adult bookstores, and bars that advertised exotic
dancers. It was remarkable, Daniel thought, that this was the
only part of the city that could in any way be represented as being devoted to literature and the performing arts.

A pretty girl in boots and denim skipped out of a bar ahead of
him and took off up the street with a businesslike stride calcu-
lated to cover ground in a hurry. You could always pick out the
dancers on the strip. They were the only people that looked
wholesome and healthy. The prostitutes dressed, used makeup,
and fixed their hair in ways that made them look like recent ar-
rivals from other planets. The bag ladies and derelicts uni-
formly gave the impression they were sleepwalking. The petty
criminals and random thugs propped against the buildings all
looked dirty and gray.

Daniel walked a little faster, simply for the harmless pleasure
of keeping the girl in view. She wore a loose blouse that hung
halfway down her back pockets. Under its hem, the bounce and
shift of the tight denim was as entertaining as any show she
could have put on in a strip joint.

But even with a distraction of such potency, it was impossible

not to notice the big guy in the leather vest. His sneer alone was
worth a second glance, and the total effect of his appearance
was positively artistic. He looked like a parody of a vicious
bully. Daniel found it difficult not to stare as he passed the man,
but he managed. He kept his eyes occupied with the dancer until
she turned off a block later. Daniel figured she had worked an
extra set. Just for him.

Three blocks further on, now out of the busy part of the
downtown area, he gave up looking for a cab. He turned north,
away from the waterfront, and walked past the darkened store-
fronts in the deserted part of the business district. It was when
he paused to look at a window display that he noticed the man
in the leather vest.

He was a couple of blocks behind him on the deserted street,
but it was unmistakably the same man. Daniel watched him for
a moment. He was moving with a shambling stride that, though
not graceful, seemed to be propelling him forward more quickly
than might have been expected for one of his size and shape.

Daniel turned from the window, no longer interested in the
adult toys it displayed. Until this moment he had seen no indication that Charlie was having him followed today. Now was his
chance to find out. He set off up the street at his fastest walk. He
was confident that he could outwalk the man behind him, or
outrun him if necessary. He had carried his boyhood hobby of
rock climbing into adulthood, with the result that he was both fit
and very strong. If it came to that, he might well be a match
even for such a bruiser except, he reminded himself, that the
bruiser could very well be armed.

Daniel strode along the wide street. Surely this could have
nothing to do with Charlie. It was hard to imagine the dapper
gangster having dealings with such a disreputable-looking thug.
The guy probably just happened to be taking the same street as
Daniel. After two blocks of hard walking, he stopped in front of
another store and glanced behind him.

Impossibly, the man had gained on him. He was now hardly
more than a block behind. Daniel took the next side street. As
soon as he was out of view he sprinted lightly to the next corner
and turned north again, now on a smaller commercial street devoted to vacuum cleaner repair shops and other businesses un-

likely to make their owners wealthy. He felt silly, a thirty-one-year-old poker player running down a deserted street wearing a sport coat. At least, he thought, I'm not wearing a tie. He had a mental picture of himself running down the street in a three-piece suit. Except that he did not own a three-piece suit.

Despite his feelings, he ran another block, then slowed to a walk again. His pursuer, if he was in fact following Daniel, had to be at least three blocks behind by now. No one with a belly like that could possibly be a runner. He checked behind him. The street was empty.

It was two blocks further on that he looked down a side street toward the avenue. There, shambling in his direction, was the thug.

Daniel broke into a run. Someone with a car must be helping him, he thought, without bothering to check his logic. He moved at top speed, covering the distance to the next corner in no time at all. He angled across the street and turned without slowing down. The thug must have a portable phone or something, and be coordinating with a car, and Daniel did not want to be in his sight.

The next corner was an alley. Before he turned into it, he checked behind him. The last thing he wanted was to be cornered somewhere. There was no one in view. He ran silently on the broken asphalt. He was scarcely breathing heavily. He knew he could run for a long time if he had to. But he could not outrun an automobile. From somewhere nearby he heard the sound of a motorcycle engine.

This was getting serious. Was there a net tightening around him? He stopped. Opposite was a building that eighty years ago had probably been a workshop or small warehouse. The sound of the motorcycle was getting closer. Daniel took a deep breath. He peered across the alley at the two stories of stone between the pavement and the roof of the building. He quickly noted every windowsill and crevice, plotting a path to the top as easily as if it had been marked with painted arrows. He started to remove his jacket, then thought better of it. He was not in a position to leave clues.

He checked the alley once more, then darted across and began to climb up the stone wall. He moved lightly and with prac-

ticed ease, reaching the wide sill of the second-floor window as
quickly as he would have on a ladder. As he had seen from below, the second story was going to be trickier. He wished he had
a few basic climbing tools with him. His path to the roof de-
pended on getting an adequate fingerhold in a shadowy horizontal gap between two stones. Unfortunately, and as he had
foreseen, it was necessary to commit himself to the rest of the
ascent without knowing for certain that his grip would be secure.

This, however, was a pot he had already decided to bet on.
Like a good gambler, he was playing the odds. Like a professional gambler, he had considered the possibility that the odds
might let him down. He was confident that if he went down instead of up, he would be no worse off than he had been. The
pavement where he would land was level and unbroken, and a
fall would not surprise him. He could take off down the alley
again and hope to find another hiding place. In any event, there
was nothing to be gained by delay.

Hugging the wall like an insect, he committed himself, sliding the fingertips of both hands into the crevice. It was deep and
roomy. Having gained purchase, he felt more secure than he often did crossing a busy street. Moving as slowly as he had to
and as quickly as he could, he felt his way up the path he had
laid out in his mind, making his climb, as he had known he
would have to do, purely be feel, since to move his cheek from
the cold stone would be to drop like one to the pavement below.

Less than one minute later, he was pulling himself over the
ledge and onto the flat roof. He went carefully. He could see little point in gaining the roof only to fall through a hole or a weak
spot and break his neck. The roof, however, proved to be sound.
He lay there, safely out of sight, and listened for the sounds of
pursuit. Hearing nothing, he peeked over the edge. The alley
was empty. He lay back, smiling. He could stay on this roof all
night if need be. He certainly had no plans to leave for an hour
or two.

In fact, he realized, staying all night was just the thing to do.
If, as seemed likely, though inexplicable, this had to do with
Charlie, he could not return to his apartment. They would be
watching it. And the idea of walking back through the deserted

streets to get to a hotel held little attraction. Anyway, getting down from the roof would be easier in the morning, when there would be some light on the subject. Descents were always more troublesome than ascents, and jumping or dropping from the roof when not absolutely forced into it would be irrational, as well as just plain dumb. He moved carefully back from the ledge and settled himself as comfortably as he could, leaning against an ancient stone chimney.

Five minutes passed before he was startled by the noise. From the alley he could hear footsteps. They sounded as though the person was not picking up his feet, but shambling along. Daniel was sure it was the man in the leather vest. He wished he could have a look, but did not want to take the slightest chance of revealing himself. A rational gambler did not bet his life on any odds. He was perfectly secure where he was. There was no action he could take to improve his position. He sat quietly against the chimney and listened.

When the footsteps stopped, Daniel almost jumped. He could not have left a sign below. He quietly checked his pockets. Everything was there. He felt like a fugitive pursued by bloodhounds. He listened intently. The local silence of the alley was intact. Only the basic noisy hum of the city could be heard. He pictured the man standing below, probably wondering where he had disappeared to.

When he heard the next sound, it was not a footstep. It was a slapping sound, as though the man in the alley was hitting the side of the building with the palm of his hand. Daniel listened without great attention, content to wonder what the man might be doing. He only realized that the noise had been getting closer the moment before the man pulled himself, belly and all, over the ledge and onto the roof.

He did not pause, but headed straight for the chimney. Daniel only gained his feet in time to grapple with him. His thoughts were clear and calm. He must surprise the fellow with his strength, knock him down, preferably slipping in a good kick to the gut, and then get off the roof toot sweet, as Charlie would say.

The man clamped one hand on his forearm. Daniel struggled to pull away, only to feel the grip tighten painfully. He put his other forearm against the man's neck and pushed, hoping to twist away and break free. He didn't—the flesh was cold and unyielding, the man immovable. It was like trying to wrestle with a statue.

"Baldersnarp." The voice had been a whisper.

"What?" Daniel said. His voice sounded high and shaky.

The man was not looking at him. He had turned his head to the side as though listening to someone. Daniel looked around to see if there was anyone else on the roof.

"Rassaddersnatt!" Daniel jerked his eyes back to his captor. The man seemed to be looking right through him. Daniel felt the granite hand relax a bit on his arm.

When the next word was pronounced, Daniel was looking directly at the man. The sound of the word hung in the dark air, yet the man had not uttered a syllable. It occurred to Daniel, absurdly, that his attacker was a ventriloquist.

Yet another incomprehensible polysyllable came from nowhere. The grip on his arm lightened, became almost companionable. The man still seemed to be in a daze.

Every few seconds, another strange word was in the air. The man had not moved since they began. Daniel decided to pull himself free while he had the chance. He braced himself, then cried out in pain as the grip on his arm became tighter than ever. He felt as though the bone would be crushed.

Without any warning he was seized by panic. He heard himself scream in anger and pain as he began to fight with unrestrained fury, striking out wildly with his free arm, kicking with feet and knees, and even tearing with his fingernails and teeth at the arm that held him.

Finally the man seized him with both hands and shook him like a child, lifting him completely off his feet. When he stopped, Daniel could scarcely get his breath. The man had released him. He held him only with his eyes, which seemed in the night shadow to be lit from behind by a dim yellow flame. Daniel's arm throbbed with a deep ache. He could taste blood on his lips.

"Baaldersnaaarp . . ." It was a distant wail.

The man's sneer contorted itself into a sort of smile.

"He has my names on his lips as you have my blood on

yours," he said. He laughed softly as Daniel wiped his lips with his sleeve and spat on the roof.

Daniel could hear the strange voice pronouncing the names as though it came from inside his head. The big man moved closer to him and stared deeply into his eyes. Daniel tried to step back, but found he could not move. The night air seemed suddenly dark and heavy, as though a black mist had settled on the rooftop. Daniel could not tear his gaze from the man—could see nothing but the burning yellow eyes.

It was the ache in his arm that awakened him. He was facedown on a surface that was cold and hard. He willed himself to lie motionless, listening as he tried to gather his thoughts. His last conscious memories were of the eyes and of the chanting voice in his head. Now the voice had stopped. Yet still he seemed to hear its echo, like the memory of a bedtime story transmuting itself into the fabric of a child's dream.

He heard no other sounds but distant ones. He struggled to think rationally. Was he alone, or was the man with the yellow eyes standing over him, waiting for him to move? How long had he been unconscious? Had it been seconds—or hours?

He was chilled. It was hard to imagine that the day had been scorching. He forced himself to calculate, to draw conclusions. If he was cold, enough time had passed for him to get that way. It was silent, save for the night sounds of the city. The man had left him on the rooftop, bruised but alive.

Or would he find, when he moved and opened his eyes, that the yellow stare he remembered was fixed on him still?

He sat up and looked around in confusion at the trash cans, telephone poles, and ramshackle garages. He was in the alley, next to the old building he had climbed. He pulled himself painfully to his feet, leaning against the stone wall. Had he fallen? Had he climbed down and forgotten? He closed his eyes and tried to concentrate. He had no memory of getting down from the roof; no memory of anything after the chanting of the names had entered his head. He remembered the rooftop and nothing more.

He walked three blocks before getting a taxi. He shivered with cold all the way home, and was in bed under a pile of blan-

kets for twenty minutes before the chill began to drain from him
and let him fall into a heavy sleep.

On Saturday Daniel was too sick and weak to try to work out
what had happened to him the night before. He spent all day in
or near bed. His arm was badly bruised and scratched. The fever
that had plagued him through the night, awakening him with al-
ternate sweats and chills, persisted into the afternoon. Late in
the evening he became ravenously hungry. He had pizza sent in
and drank almost an entire bottle of Chianti with it on the
grounds that it would be good for him. Afterward he watched
television for as long as he could stand it, and then went back to
bed feeling rather good, all things considered.

The chanting of the names disturbed his sleep profoundly
without awakening him. When he awoke early in the morning
he had vivid memories of the dreams that had troubled him. Besides the names, which had seemed to strike him with physical
force, he recalled a heavy mist, and in it, a bright circle that
sometimes approached, sometimes receded.

His fever was gone and his arm greatly improved. Feeling
positively cheerful despite his restless night, Daniel showered
and then went out for his favorite Sunday-morning breakfast of
lox and bagels and fresh orange juice, for which he paid far too
much in the dining room of a downtown hotel.

On his way back home, he had the cab driver swing by the
block where he had first seen the man in the leather vest. There
were a number of seedy and disreputable-looking characters
roaming the neighborhood, but Daniel saw no sign of his assail-
ant.

After breakfast he went back to bed and slept till noon. He
awoke refreshed and with no memory of dreams or other annoyances.

For a while he tried to piece together what had really happened to him two nights before. His memory of the events was
obviously unreliable. The number of patent impossibilities was
sufficient proof of that, as far as he was concerned.

Nothing fit. For anything resembling what he recalled to
have happened, there had to have been more than one other person involved. That strongly suggested it had to do with Charlie.

But if it did, then how was it he had not been bothered since? Charlie certainly knew where to find him.

That meant it wasn't Charlie. But if not Charlie, then who? He had been attacked by the strongest gutter bum on the planet and his wallet hadn't even been lifted.

The only thing he could think of was the Russians. He had been mistaken for a brilliant nuclear physicist with important knowledge, and the KGB had sent their secret Bionic Biker to kidnap him. Except the Russians didn't even do those things in books and movies anymore. Daniel spent the rest of the day watching baseball on television and went to bed early.

He had been asleep for four or five hours when the names started. This time he woke up.

". . . vile propensities. Rassaddersnatt the unremittingly vicious . . ."

Daniel was on his feet, his heart pounding, before he had been awake long enough to remember who he was. As the sound of the voice died away, he sighed with relief. He wondered if a drink would help him sleep without further bad dreams.

He didn't remember closing the heavy drapes before going to bed, but the bedroom was completely without light. He couldn't see so much as an outline of a piece of furniture to guide him to the door. He thought he would go to the kitchen and have a glass of wine to help calm him down. He took a careful step forward.

"Baldersnarp!"

Daniel froze. His heartbeat seemed to be located in his throat.

"Who's there?" he said in a startled shout.

"By all thy names and all thy traits and all thy sins I summon thee."

The voice stopped. Daniel listened intently in the silence that followed.

"This is a dream," he said aloud. He took a deep breath. "This can only be a dream."

"With this spell I bind thee and charge thee come! Appear before me!"

"Right," said Daniel. He had had vivid dreams before in which he had suddenly become aware that he was dreaming. In a moment now he would awaken, still in bed. He decided that when he did, he would get up and have the wine anyway.

He put his hands together in the dark. He felt a twinge from his bruised arm. It was amazing how realistic and undreamlike this dream was. The air seemed damp; he could almost feel a mist around him. In fact, he realized, he could see a faint mist in the air, despite the deep darkness. He recalled his fevered dreams of the night before.

"Mine is a summons that must be obeyed! The power of the circle cannot be denied!"

Beneath Daniel's bare feet, the floor was cool. He moved his right foot. He smiled. It was not his bedroom rug he was standing on, but a floor of something hard and smooth and uneven. This was definitely a dream.

He could not tell how far away the circle of light was. Like a star in a dark sky, it could have been inches from his eyes, or miles.

"Now I call thy blood come to this circle. Thy blood and form I will thee bring to stand before me in this circle I have made. Here the circle and the lamp and the Law all bid thee come. Here thy blood must draw thee now!"

Daniel had not noticed when he began to walk, but only knew that he was walking. With every step the circle loomed closer and larger, as though each pace were covering a great distance. He willed himself to stop, but kept walking. He had the strong impression that even if he could stop his feet, he would pitch forward and be drawn ahead by the force that gripped him.

The voice continued, but he didn't listen to the words any longer. He was surrounded by a white mist, made ever more visible by the growing light of the circle.

As he had walked without willing it, so he stopped. The circle now lay at his feet. He could see the stone he stood on, and the circle before him. He breathed as though by conscious effort. The air felt damp and cool. The voice had stopped. The silence was complete.

Daniel felt a presence behind him. Knowing what he was going to see, he looked over his shoulder. In the darkness was a large form, indistinct but for a pair of burning yellow eyes. Daniel stared for a moment, then turned away.

He stepped into the circle.

"Aha! Aha!" Daniel stared at the man. He was wearing a high pointed hat decorated with sickle moons, stars, and a variety of other symbols. Daniel was dressed in a Saint Christopher medal and nothing else.

"I knew it would work!" The man waved a large sheet of heavy paper excitedly. "Now let them bring their wizards! Now let them sneer at Rogan the Obscure!" He laughed in a wild, high-pitched cackle. Daniel decided to buy a book on the interpretation of dreams.

"Just a moment," the man shouted at him. He got a bottle and a glass from a table. Daniel looked around the room. Except for a lamp burning in front of him, there was no light, but he could see stone walls and the shadowy forms of chairs and tables scattered about. The man in the funny hat was trying to pour from the bottle. And pouring he was, but with such violent shaking of his hands that the inside of the glass remained completely dry. When he noticed, he gave up and drank from the bottle, wiping his lips on his sleeve.

The room was cool, the floor positively cold. Daniel wished he had put on some pajamas. He began to shiver. He would have to wake up and adjust the air conditioner soon. He must have set it too low before he went to bed. In a way, he thought, it was a shame to leave such a crazy dream. He knew he would regret it when he woke up. It would be nice if you could come back and finish a dream, he thought.

"Why are you naked?" The man took a step toward him. "Don't you have clothes in the Lower Regions?" He looked him up and down.

"Baldersnarp?" He lit a candle from the lamp and raised it above his head, peering at Daniel from beneath it. He took another step.

"You don't look like Baldersnarp. Baldersnarp is a demon. He's thousands of years old. You don't look thousands of years old, and you don't look like a demon, either." Daniel smiled.

"In fact," Rogan said, his voice rising indignantly, "from the look of you, I would say you're not from the Lower Regions at all!"

"That wouldn't be wine, by any chance?" said Daniel, stepping out of the circle.

Rogan shrieked and leapt backwards with agility astonishing in one of his years. His pointed hat fell to the floor and occupied the spot he had vacated.

"What are you doing out of the circle?" he shouted. "You get back in there!" He stumbled over a chair while attempting to walk backward.

"I command it," he screamed from the floor.

"I'm cold," said Daniel.

CHAPTER
• 5 •

As Marcia rode the elevator to the ninth floor, she felt like a high school girl arriving after classes had begun and walking guiltily through the empty hallways. Not only was she late for work, she was almost late for the carefully timed coffee break that Mr. Figge grudgingly allowed the staff.

She checked her watch again for perhaps the tenth time that morning. There was hardly more than two hours left before lunch.

"What on earth could persuade you to wear such a thing?" Hannah had asked on the first day they had met. "The sun and your stomach can tell you everything you need to know about the time of day."

Marcia had described Mr. Figge and his ideas about strict punctuality, strict tidiness, strict formality, and the other strictnesses that Mr. Figge espoused.

Hannah had gestured to the wristwatch. "So that device is to dictate the length of time we may speak together?" She shook her head. "I must remember to bring you a cure for this little problem."

And on Friday, for she had finally shown up in midafternoon, the first thing Hannah had done was present her with a tiny brass box, the contents and use of which she had patiently explained.

"I wouldn't ordinarily start you with something like this," the older woman had said, "but we must be practical. You just follow the instructions I have given you and everything will be fine."

And now, on Monday morning, Marcia was actually planning to follow those instructions. A month ago, they would have seemed either absurd or insane. Considered from the perspective of everyday common sense, it was profoundly disturbing that now they did not. After only a few meetings with the strange woman, Marcia was increasingly prepared to believe things that contradicted what she had thought of as incontrovertible facts.

But whatever else could be said or thought about Hannah and her stories, it was certain that she knew some very good tricks. On Friday they had walked back to the place where Marcia had seen the man with the nasty aura. The spot where he had stood was empty. Hannah was interested, though, and insisted on combing the neighborhood in search of him.

For the next forty-five minutes they walked up and down streets Marcia had never thought of visiting. If Hannah noticed the appalling seediness of their surroundings, she didn't mention it to her companion. She seemed to be unconscious of the fact that the two of them, particularly Marcia in her prim business outfit, were radically out of place among the hookers, drunks, and petty criminals that populated the locale. Marcia, always accommodating, tried to maintain a positive attitude, expressing her misgivings only with nervous sidelong glances as they picked their way through the broken glass and rubbish.

Finally, though, Hannah went too far. Ignoring Marcia's protests, she had struck off down the kind of alley mothers warn their children of. Marcia lagged behind, hands clenched, mouth open as though to present another argument. She would not have dreamed of walking in such a place, but she liked Hannah, and couldn't bear to see her go on alone. After an anguished moment of hesitation, she hurried after her.

Marcia had been brought up to believe that if she ever dared step into an alley like this she would at least be robbed, probably raped, and possibly murdered. She found she believed it still, judging from her sensation of surprise, almost shock, when the predicted consequences were not immediate. But then, she reminded herself as she caught up with Hannah, she was the person for whom Sunday mornings meant a late breakfast, a thick newspaper, and twinges of religious guilt at the sound of every pealing bell. Her mother was in her grave, but her lessons were imperishable.

And so it happened that when they did run into trouble in an alley that ran between windowless brick walls, Marcia was very sorry and very frightened, but not at all surprised.

Like some creature of the forest or the desert that has undergone an evolutionary adaptation to blend in with its surroundings, the man was invisible until he stepped into their path. In one hand he held a knife that Marcia found the more horrifying because it was so small. It had a short, broad blade with a curved edge—a perfect instrument for slashing.

"Don't make any noise." The man's voice was flat and harsh. It matched his aura. He flashed an ugly, joyless smile as he walked toward them.

"What do you want?" asked Hannah. She did not sound friendly.

Marcia put her hand on the older woman's arm. "Hannah . . . ," she began in a shaky voice.

"Please be silent, my dear," said Hannah without taking her eyes from the man. She waved the fingers of her left hand nervously in the direction of his feet. Marcia wondered if her friend was going to become hysterical.

The mugger had stopped six feet from them. Marcia was painfully conscious of the fact that he, and his little knife, were only two quick strides away. How could they be standing here? How had she permitted Hannah, who was obviously unused to the city, to fall into such a predicament? It seemed to Marcia that in all justice there should be a way to undo her error, that they should be allowed to unwalk the steps that had brought them here.

"What do I want?" said the man. "What do you have?" He was tall and stood with his knees bent slightly. He seemed relaxed, as though enjoying himself. "Let's start with your money."

Marcia began to open her handbag. Hannah did not move.

Marcia supposed she was more badly frightened than she appeared to be. She noticed, though, that Hannah's posture remained impeccable. To look at her standing so straight with her funny little hat adding inches to her height, one would think she felt no fear at all.

"I suggest you put your knife away," said Hannah.

The man grinned down at the knife resting in his palm. "I don't think so, Granny," he said. "I suggest you find some money for me"—his grin vanished—"while you're still healthy." He shifted his weight and raised the knife from his side, staring hard at Hannah.

Marcia felt detached, as though she were in a dream. If he went after Hannah, she was not going to stand and watch. She looked around for something to use as a weapon. If she had something to hit him with, they might get out of this yet. There was nothing nearby but scraps of paper and plastic.

Hannah stared back at the man. "I am only required to warn you once," she said in a voice so changed and tight with anger that Marcia jumped. "I shouldn't have to warn you at all. Any vicious dog would know to keep away from me."

The city seemed to have become completely silent as the mugger narrowed his eyes and focused his angry stare on Hannah. She returned it with a look of utter contempt. If there were sounds from the streets and buildings in the area, Marcia did not hear them.

"Time's up." The man spat the words and started toward the women. Marcia tensed, her eyes focused on the blade that protruded from the clenched hand. She felt ill. She knew that when she tried to help Hannah the man was going to cut her.

With his second step, the man's legs went out from under him as though he were walking on a patch of wet ice. He fell back and to the side with an astonished cry and hit the ground hard. He sat up shouting curses, then stopped abruptly and stared at the bloody slice in his jeans where he had cut his thigh as he tumbled to the ground.

Hannah spoke softly. "Put the knife away."

The man jerked his head up and stared at her with bulging eyes. "What?" he shouted, almost screamed. He looked at his knife—reached across with his other hand to grasp his thigh. From where he stood, Marcia could see him trembling.

"Lady, say a prayer," he whispered, slowly rising to a crouch. He stared at Hannah as a stalking cat stares at a bird. When he made a quick feint with the knife, Marcia gasped in fright. He laughed softly without taking his eyes from the older woman. He swayed and hunched his shoulders, gathering himself like a runner at the block.

When he fell he pitched forward too suddenly and was too close to the ground to get his hands in front of him. He broke his fall with his chin instead. He lay so still and silent that for a moment Marcia thought he was unconscious. She began to tell Hannah they should run, but was interrupted by a stream of ugly profanity.

The man rolled over and raised himself on one arm. There was a spot of blood on his shirt. His chin was scuffed and raw. He got to his knees, glaring at the two women. There was blood on his knife. He examined the pavement in front of him with his hands and eyes like someone looking for a lost earring.

When he suddenly leapt to his feet without warning, Marcia jumped backward. Hannah remained where she was and watched calmly as he nearly performed a split when he fell again. He landed heavily on a section of broken curb and lay there moaning. After a few moments he ran his hands over the soles and heels of his shoes and then with great care tried to get up, ignoring the women and giving all his attention to the pavement and his feet. As he planted his hands and pushed, his feet skidded from beneath him as though they had been yanked away by a rope. He landed flat on his back and lay panting and staring straight up.

Hannah glanced at him with distaste before turning to Marcia. "Let us go on, my dear."

As they walked away, the man called after them. "I can't get up," he wailed.

Hannah turned and walked back a few steps. "I suggest you pray," she said.

The man looked at her with an expression of disbelief. He clutched at his injured thigh and shook his head as if to clear it. "Are you nuns?" he asked in a hushed voice.

Although, or perhaps because, the violence and blood had unnerved her, Marcia was overcome by a fit of giggles that came and went until dinnertime.

They never did locate the man with the bad aura, but for the rest of the search, Marcia had followed her unusual friend to the most unthinkable places without the slightest hint of worry.

But Hannah was not with her now, as she was about to arrive in the office late, very late, for work.

When she saw Marcia, the receptionist rolled her eyes.

"Figge's looking for you, girl. I think he's going to scalp you this time. In fact, he might just cut your head off."

At her desk, Marcia took from her purse the little box Hannah had given her and dropped it into the pocket of her jacket. Then she carefully folded a clean sheet of paper twice and put it in the same pocket.

She was not at all surprised when Colette rushed over to her.

"I'm afraid the boss is really mad at you, Marcia," she said, obviously relishing the thought. "I mean, we're talking Major Trouble here. I mean, when you didn't show up this morning, I was, like, uh-oh, we're talking Big Problem." Marcia wondered how Colette's dates could stand an evening of her chatter. Even Mr. Figge, who had shown no indication that his capacity to absorb her persistent and incessant flattery had a limit, seemed sometimes to notice the annoyances of her diction.

"Anyway, I wanted you to know that when I was in his office this morning"—Colette often found it necessary to "meet" with Mr. Figge—"I told him it wasn't like you to inconvenience everyone else like this."

"I'm very grateful, Colette."

"Well, you know, I mean, he's got a lot on his mind. I mean, we're talking Very Busy Man. He's literally buried in work. I mean, the man needs, like, an assistant. To help run things around here."

Marcia smiled, wondering when Colette would feel she had gotten in enough gloating.

"I mean, someone said I could do it, since I work so closely with him, but I was, like, no, I've only been here eight or nine months; it should be someone like Marcia, who's been here for years. Of course, I guess if he was going to promote you, he would have already done it." She smiled insincerely and got up from the chair, moving in a way that emphasized her ample bust. It was as though she were reminding Marcia, who really didn't have a noticeable chest, how much more qualified in one important way she was for advancement.

"Well, I have a lot of work to catch up on. I'll probably go right through lunch. I guess you will, too."

Marcia watched her as she returned to her desk at a high-speed flounce.

In Mr. Figge's office she had to go through the usual routine of standing in front of his desk while he pretended to be working on something much more important than anything an underling could possibly have to say. She waited patiently if not calmly until he raised his eyes.

"Marcia," he began in the stern tone of a high school principal lecturing a truant, "this is the second—"

"Excuse me," she said, cutting him off. He looked up at her in disbelief. Mr. Figge was not used to interruptions from his staff. As he stared, Marcia had the sudden thought that it was not too late to back out. This—Mr. Figge's dull office and Mr. Figge's dull aura—was reality. Hannah's little brass box was out of place here, and she, Marcia, was simply late for work.

"Well?"

Marcia reached into her jacket pocket. "I have something very important to show you," she said. She unfolded the piece of paper onto the desk. Mr. Figge's desk was invariably tidy, so there was plenty of room. Next she produced the brass box and, placing it in the center of the paper, opened its tiny hinged lid with great care. Mr. Figge was following every movement of her hands with close attention. Marcia emptied the contents of the box onto the paper.

"You see this powder?" she said. She found herself wondering how she was ever going to explain what she was about to do.

"Yes, of course I do." Mr. Figge was not fond of answering such questions. They wasted time. He leaned forward to have a closer look.

Marcia leaned forward, too. She inhaled slowly. She wondered idly if she could have perhaps lost her mind. Then she blew the powder into Mr. Figge's face.

When Marcia got back to her desk, Colette was waiting.

"Well, how was it?" she said excitedly. "I'll bet we're talking Major Encounter, right? I mean, he can really be tough. Of course, he does have to keep things going. You know."

Marcia dropped a folded piece of paper into the wastebasket.

"He decided I should change jobs."

Colette's jaw dropped and she assumed an expression of sympathy and concern, the effect of which was seriously compromised by the sparkle of her eyes. "Oh, that's what I was afraid might happen. I mean, you know, like, when you didn't come in, and I had to take over some of your work, he was, like, really upset."

"He's calmer now."

"Yeah, but what about you? Where will you go? I mean, what kind of recommendation can you expect?"

"Oh, I'm not leaving. I'm just going to work on a consulting basis from now on."

Colette looked more blank than usual.

"Consulting, Colette," Marcia said emphatically. "I'll be setting my own hours from now on."

"But they pay consultants . . ."

"Well, of course it works out to a higher rate of pay. But it's just a different arrangement," Marcia said with a reassuring smile.

Colette actually said the word *you* five times in a row before she could find a way to continue a sentence that expressed her delight that Marcia had not only not been fired, but had been given what amounted to an unheard-of promotion.

After a trip to the personnel office, Marcia worked through lunch to catch up with her backlog. She did not have company, though, Colette having gone home with a headache.

After work, Marcia did not go directly to the bus stop. For one thing, she thought, she could now afford to take a taxi home anytime she pleased. Also, she had to check on the man with the dark aura. Hannah still wanted to have a look at him.

She wished it were later in the week. Hannah would not visit again until Friday. ("You're wishing your life away," her mother would have said.) Of course, Hannah did not have to be reassured about the powder, she had known all along that it would work. But Marcia was anxious to tell her about using it, probably because she had proceeded with such heavy doubts.

Six blocks of walking brought her to the edge of the neighborhood she and Hannah had visited on Friday. She stepped over a broken bottle and peered ahead. Uncomfortable, she advanced, wary as a soldier going behind enemy lines. From the next corner, she had a view of the place where she had seen the man leaning against the wall. The spot was empty. Marcia gave a small sigh of relief. She looked around for a cab. This was no place, as the saying went, for a lady.

It wasn't until she was scanning the street for a taxi that she saw the man in the leather vest. He was almost a block away, but even at that distance Marcia could tell by his unmistakable shape and clothing that it was the man she had seen before. She could further tell, even at that distance, that something was badly wrong with his aura.

As she drew closer, she felt both fear and fascination. Physically the man looked the same—large, dirty, pugnacious. But his aura, impossibly, had completely changed. It had been, before, an aura unusual in its dark portent—one of the worst she had ever seen. Now she was directly across the street from the same man and his aura was unspeakable, impossible, inhuman. What traces of color there were in the gloomy emanation were lurid opacities—clots of red that were almost black; a purplish blue that might have disfigured a bludgeoned corpse; oozing yellows that shone with a repellent glow. Never in any nightmare had Marcia ever imagined such a sight.

She stared in horrified wonder. The fear that gripped her was sickening in its intensity. She would not have been more acutely aware of the danger on the street if a tiger or a grizzly bear had suddenly appeared. She felt as though she should shout a warning; there were people walking within a few feet of this thing.

As she stared, he turned his eyes to her. She could see the dull yellow fire burning behind them. Marcia was sensitive to more than auras, and she knew that the man—the thing—recognized her ability to see him as he was. She felt sick and dizzy, and then panicky at the thought of losing consciousness.

"Lady, you want a cab?"

Marcia bumped her head, both elbows, and her left knee getting into the taxi, then sat with her eyes closed for the first dozen blocks of the trip.

She rarely drank, but the first thing she did after locking herself into her apartment was to pour a stiff measure of cognac into a water glass. She drank it standing at the sink, then made another and took it to the living room, where she sipped it while staring at the wall from her chair.

She did not sleep well that night.

As soon as Renzel was certain the priestess was well away from the house, she put aside her work in the kitchen. She could easily finish it later, and this was likely to be her only chance to attend to matters in the shrine. She hurried across the garden path, not daring to linger and enjoy the mingling scents of the flowers. That pleasure would have to wait for another day, probably after the royal wedding was over and all the visitors had gone home. Renzel knew from past experience that while the priestess had guests she would not be invited to join them in the garden, nor would she have time to do so, since she would be acting as servant to the household.

She entered the shrine by the little side door. Though the sun was high and the day warm outside, inside it was cool and rather dark. Renzel waited for her eyes to grow accustomed to the shadows before ascending the five worn steps to the altar room. The priestess had curtailed the former generous use of candles in the shrine. She thought it an extravagance except for holidays or other times when more visitors than usual could be expected.

All the more reason, thought Renzel, as she started up the steps, to welcome the wedding of the Incomparable Iris. That and the return of Modesty, her missing niece. Renzel stopped on the second step, arrested by the happy thought that always accompanied her thoughts of the wedding of the Matchless Princess. With the princess married, Modesty would be free to marry as well, ending her unnaturally prolonged maidenhood. Although she herself had never married, Renzel thought it scandalous that her niece should have reached the age of twenty-four and yet languish a virgin.

Now, of course, since Modesty had been companion to royalty, her aunt would not be permitted to have a hand in the arrangement of the girl's marriage. The king, meaning, Renzel supposed, some royal flunky, would find her a husband, and find him in the ranks of the nobility.

She chuckled to think how proud her late sister would have been at this elevation of her daughter. Renzel's view was different. It seemed to her that as there were so many more commoners than aristocrats, there must also be a much greater chance of finding a good bridegroom among them. She was prepared to displease anyone of mortal flesh, howsoever royal, who offered an unworthy husband, be his blood ever so icy noble, to her innocent niece.

When she reached the top of the stairs, she was surprised to find a visitor in the shrine. The girl who had been there before with Mistress Hannah had come back by herself. Renzel was always pleased to see visitors, but this one, as she had before, seemed to Renzel to be interested in the shrine itself, without any feeling of reverence for the altar or the goddess. Something indefinable, perhaps in her posture, seemed to display a complete lack of the proper feeling of awe that the presence, however hypothetical, of an immortal being should inspire.

Renzel greeted her without any fear that she might be breaking a mood of devotion.

"Good day, miss."

"Good day, Reverend Mother," the woman replied, using a form of address that was both rarely used, and reserved for priestesses of particular holiness.

"Please, miss, I am not the priestess," Renzel protested. She refrained from adding that she had told her so two days before. "The priestess allows me to care for the shrine."

"Yes, I remember that you told me. But it is your care for the shrine that keeps it immaculate and keeps it beautiful, and I believe that the one who cares for the shrine is the true priestess."

Not having a diplomatic reply, Renzel said nothing. She wondered what it could be about this girl's eyes that made them look so strange and deep in the dim light of the single candle. Something about her presence made Renzel feel uncomfortable, even here in the familiar surroundings of the sanctuary. It was as though the place itself had been altered somehow. Again she was visited by the image of the feral eyes of a wolf. When the girl left a few minutes later, she was not sorry to see her go. She walked to the entrance behind her and watched until she had passed from view on the dusty lane to the city.

A very short time later, Elise was on the short narrow street of the tavern. She entered, nodded to the barman, and passed from the room through the door at the rear.

Errin was perched in his customary seat atop the bar.

"How are things in the Kingdom?" he called, as she closed the heavy door behind her. "Is the king still fat?"

She seated herself at the bar. "It is as it always is," she said. "The nights are still, the ale is still, and the king is still fat."

Errin dropped to the floor. "And with that answer," he said with a broad grin, "you have told me you are from Ambermere. You have given me the answer to a question I am not permitted to ask. You must never forget that wizards, even apprentice wizards, are tricky."

"Mistress Hannah said wizards are overly fond of riddles."

"And what does she say about magicians?"

"That they are fools and meddlers."

"And witches, then. What does the witch have to say about witches?"

"That what they practice is simply a craft, like knitting or cooking."

Errin burst into laughter. "How fortunate you are to have met a witch before you came to us. From a witch you learn things in one sentence that would take a wizard all afternoon to explain. And it's because of the nature of their gifts."

Errin took the seat next to Elise.

"For instance, it's only natural for a witch to belittle a magician. Magicians do not possess power at all, but simply operate spells. A magician is someone who has learned to use a vocabulary of power. When a magician uses a spell, the power comes from the spell. He is merely using the power in the spell as he might use the power of a draft animal."

He smiled at the young woman. "You should be hearing this from Jackson, since he's in the neighborhood. He is really quite brilliant. That's why he is so impatient with the older Brothers.

But since he is not here, I will be your teacher for the moment. And you may be lucky at that. I, knowing less, will be more brief."

Elise laughed softly. "According to Hannah, it is impossible for a wizard to be brief."

"But still," he protested, "there are degrees." He shook his head. "You must not let me get started on degrees," he said with mock seriousness.

"Anyway, I've mentioned magicians. Let me go on to wizards, and then to witches. And then," he promised, "to the brewing of a pot of tea. But to continue, as I am charged with some small part of your education:

"Wizards are practical. We are the engineers of magic. We incessantly devise. We begin with small powers and build greater ones, usually in concert, sharing and splitting and conniving to make more from less, much from little. We stoke the fires of our talents. We know that even a weakness can be turned into power.

"To the witch, hers may be a craft like weaving or pottery, except that it is a craft that can only be practiced effectively by an initiate, and only the gifted are initiated. Magicians manipulate power that lies outside themselves. This is as true of First-Degree Magicians, who can safely use spells of deep potency, as it is of Eleventh-Degree quacks who play shells and peas at fairs to cheat the gullible of their pennies.

"Witches contain power, are themselves powerful, as wizards are, except we labor to augment and amplify our power, while a witch must strive to tame and contain hers. The cities and towns in the kingdoms are full of incompetent magicians. They can be found readily at every marketplace. But there is no such thing as an incompetent witch. Any lad can aspire to be a magician, and can gain a rating for the level of skill he reaches. Witches add to the Sisterhood by finding the gifted and cultivating them.

"Part of the power of the witch lies in her talents of perception, in the same way that much of the talent of a musician, a true musician, lies in hearing deeply into music. A witch forbidden to act as a witch remains a witch, with her special powers of seeing and hearing and knowing, just as a musician denied his instrument still hears and understands things in music that are hidden from others.

"On the other hand, a magician stripped of his tricks and spells becomes just an unemployed man whose wardrobe happens to contain a number of robes and pointed hats."

Elise laughed again.

"You see?" Errin said. "We are not so bad. And you will go a very long way indeed before you find a witch with a sense of humor.

"And I may also claim to be brief, for I have finished my lecture. I have covered magicians, wizards, and witches. There remain only necromancers and arch-wizards, which are, I think, two names for the same thing, but in any event, about whom little is known; and the various Immortals of the Upper and Lower Regions, about whom I, like anyone else you are apt to meet here, know absolutely nothing."

"But Master Jackson said there was an arch-wizard here once."

"Yes, he told me about it. But I understand he confined his conversation largely to a discussion of the quality of the ale he had encountered in his travels. I think I am just as happy that he came before my time here. To think that one who has walked such paths and possesses such power would speak only of commonplace things . . ."

"Perhaps," said Elise quietly, "mere words are best suited to the discussion of commonplace things."

Errin looked at her for a moment with a bemused smile, then shook his head in mock earnestness.

"You sound exactly like old Gavas." He giggled. "Won't Jackson be pleased."

CHAPTER

· 6 ·

When Daniel awoke it was gradually—a slow, warm rise to consciousness. He lay with his eyes closed, enjoying the soft comfort of the bed and pillows. The air in the room smelled fresh, and carried the faint perfume of flowers. In the distance, the lonely song of a single bird could be heard, accentuating the silence it broke.

He lay, hovering at the threshold of sleep for several minutes before awareness suddenly gripped his brain. He thought: The smell of flowers? Maybe. A bird singing? Possibly. Silence? No chance.

He opened his eyes. He stared at the shadowy ceiling. The bed felt very soft. It would be the easiest thing in the world to go back to sleep, but he had things to do. In a minute, when his head had cleared, he would get up and make coffee. In fact, he thought drowsily, this would be a perfect day to go out for breakfast. He could sit at his favorite table and work out a way to deal with Charlie. His eyelids dropped; closed. Maybe he would end up just marrying Roxy. At least if he were married, he'd have someone to wake him up from his nightmares.

Daniel could still hear the bird. He tried to remember when he might have brought flowers into the apartment. He listened for the sound of traffic, jackhammers, sirens. The bird was beginning to annoy him. It was as though the quiet little song were drowning out the hum and rumble of the city. Somewhere a woman started singing.

He opened his eyes, then closed them again and tried to concentrate. He could still smell the flowers. A distant door slammed. He heard a shout, laughter. Still the bird sang, repeating the same small melody over and over again.

When the bells began he woke up with a start. The room was lighter now than before. The ceiling above him was no longer hidden in shadow. He stared up at the unfamiliar wooden planks as the bells clanged away merrily. He remembered his dream of the night before. Of standing naked on the stone floor with the old man screaming at him from behind a chair. Then later, when things calmed down, of being given a long crimson nightshirt and sharing a quantity of wine before being shown to a warm bed. He remembered that no matter how much the old man drank, he remained ill tempered and churlish, saying little beyond "Hand me that flask," and "Lower Regions indeed!"

Daniel had a strong prejudice in favor of logic and against panic. Since he knew it was difficult to be rational while running around in circles, he resisted the impulse to leap up and do so. Nothing was on fire; no immediate response was required of him. All that was wrong was that he had gone to bed in his apartment and had awakened . . . elsewhere. Either that, or someone had replaced his bedroom ceiling while he slept.

He tossed back the quilt that covered him and swung his legs over the edge of the bed. When he managed to pull his eyes from the crimson nightshirt he wore, he looked around the room. The light came from an unshuttered window on the opposite wall. Next to the window was a stand, a basin and a pitcher, and other substitutes for plumbing. There was a carpet next to the bed, colorful with scenes of the field and the hunt. Nearby, next to a bare stone wall was a chair with clothing draped over it. In the corner on the gray stones of the floor stood a pair of boots. This was not his apartment.

He shook his head in bewilderment as he looked at the candles, lamps, and other anachronisms. He stood up slowly. This room had very much the look of a smaller version of the magician's room in his dream. Except he could no longer tell himself he was dreaming. He did not entirely discount the possibility, but he didn't think it made a useful working hypothesis. Insanity or hallucinatory coma, however plausible, were similarly unlikely to lead to useful conclusions.

He touched the bed, his face; checked the fading bruises on his arm. A few steps brought him to the stone wall. He kicked it lightly with his bare foot. "I refute it thus!" he said, at once quoting, and imitating, a favorite literary figure and satisfying himself that the wall was no illusion.

The stone floor was cold. "Thermal mass," he murmured, very nearly exhausting his knowledge of physics. He moved back to the carpet. He stared at his bare feet surrounded by the colorful designs. He forced himself to remain still. Allowing himself to become frantic would do nothing to improve his situation. He closed his eyes and breathed slowly and deeply. In a moment he opened his eyes. Nothing had altered. An experimental pinch (for the sake of tradition) brought a twinge of pain and a transient red mark but no other changes.

He sat back down on the bed and reviewed the events of the night before. Everything that happened after he stepped into the circle had seemed quite real—as real as what he was experiencing now. But in the middle of the night, exhausted from the events of the two previous days, he had found it, if not easy, at least possible to believe that he was in a bizarre dream. This morning it seemed instead a bizarre reality.

And that reality included a definite chill from the stone of the floor and walls. The sun was bright outside the window, but the room was cool. Asleep or awake, sane or mad—alive or dead, for that matter, he had to get some clothes on. He decided to behave—for the moment, and only provisionally—as though sanity had not deserted him.

"One thing at a time," he said. He collected the strange clothing from the chair and put the boots by the bed. In ten minutes he was washed and dressed, and felt thoroughly prepared to stroll onto the set of a Robin Hood movie.

From the open window he could see a walled garden three or four stories below, and beyond the walls, the brick facades and tile roofs of what appeared to be houses and shops, the latter distinguishable from the former by having signs over their doors. On a distant avenue he saw pedestrians passing in and out of view and one large wagon being pulled, very slowly, by a pair of animals with horns.

He took a seat on a wooden bench by the window. No riddle could be solved, no problem conquered, without information. Daniel was passionately interested in figuring out what had happened to him, but since nothing in his surroundings made any sense, he was without a starting point. It was, he thought, like trying to play a form of poker in which the cards were all dealt facedown, and could not be examined until the betting was over.

He raised his eyes from his boots. On the wall opposite was an unframed drawing. It was of a single figure, drawn as though in haste and with a leaky pen, on a plain white background. Daniel smiled, then began to laugh. The subject was an elaborately dressed man in the process of making a courtly bow that involved a complicated articulation of the limbs and joints. It seemed clear that such a posture could only be achieved by one willing to practice attitudes by the hour. The smirk on the gentleman's face left no doubt that to bow well was his highest ambition.

Daniel wanted to have a closer look, but was laughing too hard to get up from his seat. Successive glances from tear-filled eyes brought successive waves of laughter until he slid from the bench and sat on the floor. Even as he laughed helplessly he wondered in a corner of his mind how much of his reaction to the admittedly humorous drawing was due to disorientation. Not that he cared; laughter was always to be welcomed. He was grateful to the artist.

He crossed the room to the bed and stretched out on his back. Maybe if he relaxed for a few minutes something would occur to him. Or maybe he would go to sleep and wake up in his apartment.

Neither of those things happened. He got up and crossed the room again. The sun was well up in the sky. The bells that had awakened him hadn't been announcing early Mass. Lunch, maybe. He realized that he was hungry.

He stepped up onto the deep sill of the window and, holding on with one hand, leaned out as far as he could. Daniel was in-

different to heights; the view from his vantage point held no ter-
rors for him. He looked down, and then up, studying the stone
walls as well as he could. There appeared to be perhaps three
stories above him, terminating in what looked like a parapet at
the top. The walls themselves were of undressed stone, fitted
crudely, and had many sills, ledges, and vaguely decorative out-
croppings. This building could be more easily climbed than the
garage where he had met with the trouble.

He dropped back to the floor of his room, satisfied that if he
wasn't dreaming, and hadn't lost his reason, but was a prisoner,
escape would be hazardous but definitely possible. He was
about to try the door when the incantation started.

"Demon's blood!" Daniel immediately recognized the voice.
He did not bother looking around to see if the old man, Rogan,
his name was, could possibly be in the room with him. That
would, he knew by now, be far too much to hope for.

"I summon thee hither. Come you now and stand in my presence."

Daniel felt as he had in the dream when he walked without
volition. But this time his steps moved him forward but one
pace at a time. Beyond the door was a hallway and a narrow
flight of stairs, which his feet obediently climbed. Two flights
up he found a door. It opened at his approach. Daniel was not
greatly surprised to find himself back in the room he had come
to last night, nor to find himself standing in the presence of
Rogan the Obscure.

The old man looked up at him with a complacent smile.

"I'm getting pretty good at this," he said. "Care for some
wine?"

Daniel declined, mentioning breakfast.

"Food?" Rogan made a face. "Isn't it kind of early in the day
for that?"

Daniel decided there was no point in going around perpetually flabbergasted. If, after all, this was a dream, it was his
dream; if insanity, it was equally his. And, it suddenly occurred
to him, if it was real it was real. In any event he would have to
eat. Questions and explanations could wait. Breakfast could
not.

"I don't suppose you have lox and bagels?"

"Locks? You're free to come and go as you please." Rogan laughed with a high-pitched cackle that Daniel found particularly irritating. "After all, I can summon you whenever I want to. Go and eat, by all means. Just don't bring any food in here." He sipped from a goblet. "Isn't a bagel some kind of musical instrument?" he said. He refilled his glass and settled himself comfortably on his cushioned chair. After a moment he looked up.

"Still here?"

"I have no money and no idea where to find a meal."

"Well, as for money, you need none. This is a castle, not a tavern. And as for food, it's hard to avoid it in this place. This is the residence of the fattest king now at large." Rogan looked at him expectantly.

"No pun intended," he said finally.

"What?"

"Never mind," said Rogan, then added angrily, "Don't they have humor where you're from?"

"Not before breakfast."

The old man gave him a bitter look. "Fine. Just go down the stairs . . ." He stopped. He stared out the window. "That's not a good idea," he said, as though to himself. He stood up and pulled a bell cord at the wall. In a moment running feet could be heard on the stairs. The door opened and a boy slipped into the room. He was carrying a flask.

"I want some food up here," Rogan said brusquely.

The boy looked stunned.

"Not for me, you idiot! For my . . . guest."

The boy looked at Daniel, smiling with recognition. "Oh, that's the man that was climbing out the window," he said. "I thought he was going to jump," he added cheerfully.

Rogan looked at Daniel with a speculative glance, then waved his hand at the boy. "That's all," he said.

The boy turned to leave. Rogan stopped him with a quick gesture.

"You may as well just leave that," he said, pointing to the flask.

The boy closed the door behind him.

"What's he talking about?" he said.

Daniel thought about it for a moment but he could see no possible advantage in dissimulation. "I was not climbing out the window," he said. "I was leaning out to see if there was a way to climb up or down the walls."

"You must be out . . ." Rogan began in a loud voice, then stopped in midsentence and took a sip from his never-distant goblet. When he spoke again, it was in a quiet, conversational tone.

"And what was your conclusion?" he asked with an unconvincing attempt at a friendly smile.

"That up would be easier than down, and a mallet, some spikes, and a rope would be a big help," Daniel answered promptly. He could hardly wait to see of what possible interest the preliminary escape plans of one who was patently trapped in some sort of magical snare could be to the magician who controlled him.

"You've done this sort of thing?"

"More or less."

Rogan pointed out the window. "Could you climb up here?" he asked in a casual tone.

Daniel looked out the window. As he suspected, it was directly above the one in his room.

"Yes."

"From the garden?"

"With the things I mentioned, yes."

Rogan stepped back and looked Daniel up and down.

"I noticed when you arrived last night dressed, as you were, in only that talisman you wear on your neck, that you looked rather strong. If you climbed up here with your rope, could you take something from this room and carry it back down with you?"

"Something like what?" Daniel asked. This was beginning to sound like a "theft" for insurance. Daniel knew because Charlie had once tried to engage him in a similar conversation, all very hypothetical, of course.

"Something heavy."

"How heavy?"

Rogan looked as though he wished they were talking about the weather. He hesitated before answering.

"A dog," he said. "A big dog."

"I wouldn't be able to hold a dog. I have to have both hands for climbing."

"A monkey," Rogan said quickly, "but big; some kind of ape. It could hold on to you."

Daniel was getting exasperated.

"If the ape were big enough, I could hold on and it could do the climbing. Apes are real good at climbing."

Rogan looked annoyed.

"All right. A woman."

"A human woman?"

The magician nodded.

"Not a very big woman?"

"No, a slender young woman."

"With a good rope and something to tie it to, it could be done."

"By you?"

Daniel nodded. "Yes, by me, but she'd have to hold on."

Rogan smiled and walked to the door with a light step.

"Enjoy your meal," he said. He picked up the flask the boy had put by the door and left the room.

"So you tried to summon a demon. That makes sense." Daniel had finished his meal and was engaged in what he privately considered the most ridiculous conversation he had ever had, or heard of.

"What else was I to do?" asked Rogan. He looked sincerely interested in getting an answer.

"How should I know? What I want to know is how did you end up with me? As you have remarked more than once, I am not a demon."

"I just got done explaining it to you. I saved your life."

"By sending a demon after me; I think I have it now."

"No, you do not. Sending the demon was a mistake. But if I hadn't called him when I did, you would be just a pleasant memory of his. A little rooftop repast. I would think you'd be grateful."

"Okay, I am. Thank you. But how does that get me here?"

"From what you told me, I would say you have a bit of his

blood in you. After all, I did not go to all this trouble for the purpose of summoning a gambler to Ambermere. We already have plenty of gamblers, and we didn't have to use magic to get them, either. What brought you was his blood."

"I'm glad you didn't mention all this before breakfast."

"So you drank a drop of the demon's blood," said Rogan with a cheerful smile. "The only other possible outcome was that he drink all of yours. You should look at the bright side." The magician filled his cup, offering to pour for Daniel, who declined. Rogan settled back into his chair.

"After all," he continued, "you're perfectly safe, for the moment."

"For the moment?"

"Well, there's no telling what will happen when I call the demon tonight. You are going to be caught in the spell, too. I'm afraid you may be trapped in the circle with him." Rogan took a languid sip of wine. "I imagine he will be happy to see you. You know, you may be the first dinner to have escaped him in the last five or ten thousand years, and once I have him trapped, you will be of no further value for deflecting the spell. Of course, I may be able to control him."

"You aren't sure?"

"Well, there is obviously something wrong with the spell, or he'd be here and you wouldn't."

Daniel decided perhaps he'd have some wine after all.

"So the Inimitable what's-her-name is missing, and you want this vicious demon to find her for you?" he said, pouring for himself.

Rogan sat up straight in his chair.

"You are speaking of the Inimitable Iris, Fairest Flower of the Kingdom, the Dazzling Daughter of the king, the Most Stunning Maiden of This or Any Other Court," he said with stiff dignity.

"And," he added, "she is not missing; I know the very room she occupies at this moment." He rose and pointed from the window with a straight and trembling arm.

"She is there, held in captive by the evil king, Razenor," he announced impressively, "locked in the tower of his castle at Ascroval!"

He peered from the window, as though trying to see the distant kingdom. He moved his pointing arm ninety degrees to the left.

"Actually," he said in a softer voice, "Ascroval is more in that direction, I think." He raised his cup to his lips.

Daniel sat quietly. The sun cast a lengthened shadow of the wine flask onto the scratched and dusty tabletop. He looked out the window. From his chair he could see nothing but blue sky and white clouds. He thought, in a detached way, about the fact that familiarity tended to make even difficult things easy. As a professional gambler, he was familiar with the process of making choices from among unpleasant alternatives.

He wondered if there was any chance that Rogan thought he was being subtle.

"In a tower?" he said, finally.

"Yes, yes, a tower," the magician replied absently.

"Stone, I suppose?"

Rogan turned to face him. "What's that you say?"

"I said I'll bet it's made of stone. Like this one."

"What is?"

"The tower at Ascroval. Where the princess is being held."

"Oh. Yes, why, so it is. Just like this one. That's right."

Daniel poured himself some more red wine. He sat for a moment, staring at his reflection in the cup.

"When do I leave?" he said.

Rogan smiled at him.

"Tomorrow," he said. "Tomorrow morning."

After Daniel obediently studied the maps to and plans of the castle at Ascroval that Rogan supplied him with, he and the magician paid a visit to the weaponsmith.

"A small hardwood mallet weighted with lead?"

"To drive the spikes that we'll be picking up in the morning," Rogan said, handing the astonished craftsman the drawing that Daniel had made for him. The man glanced at them.

"Which morning might you be speakin' of, Master Rogan? Some day next week, was it?"

"Tomorrow, three hours after dawn," Rogan replied. "Have

you seen my brevet from the king?" he added, drawing from his pocket a heavy card bearing the royal seal.

The smith gave it a close look. He sighed.

"But what of Baron Sote's dagger?" he said disconsolately, gesturing to a glistening shaft of steel.

"It will make a nice spike," said the magician. "Remember, three hours past dawn. No later."

As they walked from the smithy, Rogan leaned toward Daniel.

"We'll have them by noon," he whispered triumphantly.

Rogan gave Daniel a purse and sent him into the town with the serving boy.

"No doubt you'll be wanting to eat again, and you need to learn the price of things and the value of the coins for your journey." The old man glanced at the sky. "Just see that you're back by late afternoon. I have someone for you to meet, and I wouldn't want to have to summon you." Daniel could still hear his cackle as he and the boy passed through the gate.

By the time they got back to the castle, Daniel had bought, and watched his companion consume, a sample of every confection, tart, and sweetmeat known in the city. Daniel himself had lunched most satisfactorily on cold meats and cheese, a crusty loaf, and the best mug of ale he had ever been cheered with.

They had also visited, at the nearby edge of the city where the boy had taken him for the purpose of seeing the river, a small shrine dedicated to some goddess whose name Daniel had never quite caught. He had entered, the boy remaining on the lane finishing a berry tart, and been impressed by the sense of peace he felt there. It was cool, almost cold, inside, and dark but for the light of a single candle.

He knelt before the altar almost by reflex, a habit from hundreds of early Masses in his boyhood. "Confession on Friday," he murmured to himself. He added to the coins in the bowl an amount sufficient to purchase an entire tray of nut pastries and turned to leave. Only then did he realize that he was not alone. A middle-aged woman holding a broom was beaming at him from a shadowy corner.

* * *

Back in the apartments of the magician, he found waiting
with Rogan a man he was certain was a gambler. Some gamblers, never the best, just looked like gamblers. Daniel had often
tried to isolate the identifying characteristics. The best he had
come up with was an approximation. They seemed to radiate a
mixture of fragile confidence, cunning, and fear. This guy
would have looked very much at home in a cheap green suit and
a clashing tie with a complicated knot.

"The Count Reffex," Rogan announced with a flourish, and
then presented Daniel in the more or less apologetic tone appropriate to the introduction of a commoner to an aristocrat.

The magician brought out a deck of playing cards. Daniel
found their crude beauty intriguing. They appeared to be block
prints, trimmed to a uniform size. The colors were vivid, the
figures and numbers almost hypnotic.

"If you are to go out as a traveling gambler," he said with an
unnecessary wink that was supposed to be surreptitious, but
which Daniel knew Reffex had not missed, "you'll have to understand the games that are played in the inns and taverns. His
Grace has generously offered to instruct you." Rogan smiled
archly, which made him look very silly. "The count is a great
gamester," he said, looking at the two men expectantly.

"No pun intended," he said, laughing lamely, and by himself.

Reffex explained the rules of the most popular game in the
land. Despite the fact that he did so with perfect clarity and
economy, Rogan insisted on adding explanatory comments that
demonstrated a fundamental misunderstanding of the principles
of games of chance, and greatly protracted the period of instruction.

When they were finally ready to play, Daniel watched the
count deal the cards and pick his hand up with a faint smile.
Daniel took up his cards and examined them quickly, at the
same time watching as Reffex rearranged the cards in his hand.

Early in his apprenticeship, Daniel had learned that the ability to detect crooked deals and other forms of card manipulation
was a valuable skill for someone in his line of work. The author-
itative word was, "You can't see 'em if you can't do 'em." Accordingly, and because he turned out to have a flair for it, he had
spent quite a long time becoming adept at every species of

fraudulent sleight-of-hand known to the card table. For him, it was purely a defensive maneuver. Cheating at cards was not to his taste. Besides which, it was totally unnecessary for a competent poker player.

Reffex apparently did not share his sentiments.

Daniel turned to Rogan. "I'm going to need some money," he said.

"What for?"

"Stakes."

Rogan favored him with a blank stare.

Daniel put his cards facedown on the table. "Money to play cards with."

"You don't have to play for money. Reffex owes me pl . . . I mean, His Grace is willing to instruct you. Just learn the games."

Daniel caught the merest suggestion of a smile on the face of the count.

"The game I am trying to learn has no meaning unless it is played for money. If there are no stakes, there is nothing to risk. If there is no risk, there is no game." Daniel stood up. "And anyway," he added, "I don't play cards for fun."

Rogan made a great show of counting out Daniel's dole, then grudgingly handed it over to him, muttering unconvincingly to the effect that he absolutely could not afford to lose so much as a tithe of the sum.

It turned out that Reffex knew only one crooked deal. Every time he tried it, Daniel would simply note the location of the good card Reffex had slipped himself, and play and bet accordingly. Daniel resisted the temptation to ruin the count's afternoon by retaliating with some really high-powered cheating. He reminded himself that he was there not to act as an agent of justice, but to learn some new card games.

The two men played for a few hours, covering all the games that Daniel was likely to encounter. As he had known they would be, Daniel's discipline and money-management skills were as valuable in these new games as they were in seven-card stud. Once he had studied the deck, he was able to make estimates of odds that were as close as he would ever need, and his card memory worked as well with these cards as it did with the fifty-two he was accustomed to. He always knew what cards had been played, always knew the pot odds, and always knew the odds of getting what he needed and how likely it was that his hand would win.

The count was no better than a superior pretzel-contest player. He broke even in each game only in the first few hands, and kept his losses down by introducing new games frequently.

"Well, you've learned enough of this one to get by," he would say briskly, as though taking satisfaction in Daniel's progress. "You can pick up the fine points later."

In fact, the fine points in all card games were essentially the same, and were contained in the set of skills and habits that Daniel had "picked up" long ago. It was for this reason that he could help to further the bridge ambitions of his sister-in-law, even though he rarely played the game except in tournaments she entered. Reffex could teach him no refinements, only rules.

Daniel noted with interest that the aristocrat seemed much more concerned about preserving the illusion of his status as the teacher and the better player than he was about actually winning at cards. Of all the follies of the gaming table, this was one of the most dangerous.

The count left them only after spending several minutes being ludicrously patronizing on the subject of Daniel's progress under his tutelage.

"There were, of course, a number of times when I thought it best not to press an advantage," he explained to Rogan. "But his play was very good. Very good. And very promising. I hope I have been able to help him." He smiled grandly and with great insincerity and swept from the room like an emperor.

Daniel turned to Rogan shaking his head. He accepted the offered glass of wine.

Rogan sat quietly for a few minutes, then leaned forward.

"You see," he began earnestly, "when I say the *count* is a great *gamester*, well, games and counting, you see. That is, all games, well, most games, involve counting. Don't they?"

"Definitely."

Rogan stared at Daniel.

"Apparently you are totally bereft of any trace of humor," he said angrily. "If I sent you to the Lower Regions, they'd probably send you back."

Daniel sat up in his chair.

"Sent me where?"

"Not on purpose, my boy. I was just thinking about how to get you home, after you rescue the Flower of Maidenhood, of course. The problem is, the only spell of that sort I have is the one that returns the demon to his demesne in the Lower Regions, and I doubt you'd like it there."

Daniel spent some time, and energy, questioning the magician about Regions, demons, and precisely where he was now in relation to his own world. The answers he got were inconclusive, but informative in strongly suggesting that the limits of Rogan's knowledge on the subject were narrow. When he had learned all he thought he was likely to, which was practically nothing, he left Rogan to his wine and went to his room.

In bed, Daniel reviewed the events of the day. He no longer thought he was dreaming, or crazy. He had decided to follow the principle of Ockham's razor, which he understood to recommend against seeking exotic explanations when simple ones were available. And in the face of the palpable reality of the day's experiences, the simple explanation seemed to be that he had been transported to another . . . place, and was under the power of Rogan the Obscure, a not entirely sane magician who was immoderately fond of red wine and black puns.

Daniel went to sleep fully expecting to awaken in Ambermere, and not back in his apartment.

CHAPTER
· 7 ·

His night of restful sleep was interrupted, finally, by a noisy dream. In it, the city employees who were perpetually making repairs to the street in front of his apartment building had found use for a large machine whose only function seemed to be the production of a monotonous pounding noise.

But when Daniel awoke, the noise did not fade with the dream. He got out of bed shaking his head, as though to clear it. He looked around, still in a daze of dream and sleep.

The pounding was coming from his door. When he opened it, it was to the sight of Rogan's boy standing in the hallway holding a huge breakfast tray, and with his boot poised for another kick.

He looked at Daniel with an expression of keen disappointment, and then glanced toward the window.

"My master said to bring you this," he said sullenly, stepping forward and thrusting the tray at Daniel.

When Daniel took it and thanked him, the boy did not leave, but stood by the door as Daniel put the tray on a small table.

"Don't bother to wait," said Daniel.

"What about my tip?"

"You want me to give you a tip?" said Daniel, advancing on him.

The boy nodded and held out his hand. Daniel seized him by

the upper arms, lifted him easily from the floor, and set him down in the hallway.

"Okay, here it is: If you ever pound on my door like that again, it will be you that goes flying out the window."

When he showed up at Rogan's rooms, the old man had the charts and maps out again.

"I must admit there's something I haven't quite worked out yet," he said. "I was rather counting on accomplishing this with the demon, who would to into Ascroval, devour a few dukes and earls, generally terrorize the place, knock down a couple of walls, and then grab the girls and bring them back to me."

"Girls?" Daniel said. "Yesterday it was the Royal Knockout, Irene. How did she get to be plural?"

"It is the Peerless Princess Iris," said the magician stiffly. "Of course she has a companion with her, some commoner whose name I can't recall."

Daniel looked at the magician, making sure he had his attention. He spoke slowly and distinctly. "Rogan, listen to me. I cannot carry two women down a rope."

"No, no. Of course not, my boy. You get the Matchless Princess; the diplomats will attend to the other girl in good time." Rogan walked slowly to the window.

"Unfortunately, that is not the problem that is troubling me. My concern is what you are to do once you have her safely on the ground. No one was going to pursue the demon; they would all be busy running in the opposite direction. But now, once the princess is missed, there will be a great hue and cry."

"But by the time anyone notices, we could be across the border. It doesn't look that far on the map. I assumed you would tell her to be ready at a time of night when she wouldn't be likely to be missed."

Rogan looked uncomfortable. "Tell whom?" he said.

Daniel stared at him. "What do you mean, 'tell whom'? The princess, of course." He tried to catch Rogan's shifting eyes. "She is going to know I'm coming, right?"

The old man began a close examination of one of the maps. "Not exactly," he said without looking up.

Daniel dropped into a cushioned chair and leaned back. "Would it be rude to ask why not?" he said in a monotone.

"It's just not feasible," the magician said airily. His manner suggested they were discussing a minor detail.

"But you must have spies or friends there. You said you know exactly where she is."

"Yes," said Rogan, "but our spies work for Lord Rand, a completely unreasonable and incompetent man. If he knew what I was doing, he would find some idiotic reason for objecting."

"You mean like the four-percent chance of success?"

Rogan turned from the window.

"We have a much better chance than you imagine. You see, my boy, you are forgetting one very important thing. We are dealing here with royalty. This is not some hysterical chit of a girl you are going to save. This is the Incomparable Iris, who has grown up at court, with all its intrigues. Since childhood she has been surrounded by noblemen, diplomats, priests, and other deceitful and dangerous people.

"Why, even if I had a way to alert her, I would hesitate to jeopardize the undertaking by doing so. The message might be intercepted; or her companion might betray the secret."

"The other girl? Why would she do that?" Daniel asked, his voice skeptical.

"Not on purpose, you understand. But she is only a poor commoner. Undoubtedly she is by now thoroughly demoralized, and susceptible to pressures to which her royal fellow prisoner would be immune."

Rogan smiled at Daniel.

"Of course, you are right," he said. "With any luck at all you will have the princess back at the Feathermere Inn before those larcenous buffoons at Ascroval know she is gone. From there it will be easy. I can have a horse and a suitable escort waiting for her without arousing suspicions. That close to the border it is necessary to be circumspect, but I am foolish to fall prey to pessimism. You don't by the slightest chance ride, do you? You could pass for an aristocrat and get there two days sooner."

Daniel shook his head.

"Well," said Rogan philosophically, "then you must remain a traveling gambler and use your own feet."

Daniel did not bother to ask about other forms of transportation. From what he had seen of the carts and wagons in the city, walking would be infinitely more comfortable and somewhat faster.

"Besides," the magician added, "this way you will attract no attention at all. There is nothing more commonplace than gamblers at inns."

The spikes and mallet were ready by late morning. The rope Rogan himself provided. Daniel, who had been expecting something suitable for mooring an ocean liner, was delighted when Rogan showed him the smooth, light coil. He tied it to a heavy brass fixture in the fireplace and pulled on it as hard as he could.

Rogan watched from his chair. "I would scarcely go to all this trouble and then endanger the Princess with an inadequate rope," he pointed out. "That comes from the Fishermen's Quarter. When we prepare fireworks, we hoist items much heavier than princesses and card players with it, I can assure you."

He gave Daniel a traveler's bag with a broad shoulder strap. It contained a change of clothes, a few decks of cards, and had enough room for the climbing gear. Daniel put the bundle of spikes, the mallet, and the coiled cord into the bag.

"Don't close it yet," said the magician, fetching a hooded cape from a hook on the wall. "You probably won't want to wear this until later in the day."

Daniel took the garment. "I don't need this," he said. "If I put it on I'd look like the Scarlet Pimpernel."

"Don't you have weather where you're from?" asked Rogan. "Damp, chilly days? Cold nights? Rain?"

Daniel rolled up the cape and put it in his bag.

The old man went to a table and opened a drawer.

"One more thing," he said.

"Mittens?" asked Daniel.

Rogan handed him a purse. Daniel sensed that he did it with great reluctance.

"Remember this when the king rewards you. It is not my intention to finance this expedition from my own shallow pocket." He poured two goblets of wine.

"It would be unthinkable to send you off without a drink to your success," he said, raising his goblet to his lips. "When we next share a glass, eight or nine days from now, all will be well in this kingdom." Rogan poured himself another. "Unless, of course, you are unsuccessful, in which case I shall have to summon the demon after all." He peered at Daniel across the rim of his goblet.

"You don't have to remind me," said Daniel. "A good gambler always knows where he stands. I want the princess back as much as anyone does."

It was not until he had left the city that Daniel felt he was truly on his way. Despite the fact that he could be recalled by Rogan's spell at the magician's whim, he experienced a sense of liberty, of boundless freedom, as he left the city and the castle behind him. The dusty lane he traveled was in fact a highway that stretched, according to the maps he had studied, through four kingdoms before wandering into the mountains at the end of settled lands.

He had been assured that there was no village so mean as to lack an inn, and that he would pass at least three in a normal day's walk.

"You should not have to skip a single one of those meals you are so fond of," Rogan had said with an expression that suggested he was in no danger of forgetting whose purse would be growing lighter at each stop.

"I would not want you to delay yourself, my boy. But there will be no harm if you can manage to win some money at cards while you are traveling," he had said in a tone of great earnestness. "After all, you are posing as a gambler."

When he had hardly left sight of the city, Daniel came to the shrine he had visited the day before. On an impulse, he entered. As before, it was dark and cool inside. And as before Daniel felt the deep sense of peace that seemed to pervade the place. He had the sudden unbidden thought that the power of Rogan's spell would not be able to penetrate the stone walls of this particular little building.

He stayed for longer than he had meant to, feeling the peculiar efficacy of the altar and the room. It was as though the shrine was located at a geographical point where some unknown beneficial forces happened to be concentrated.

He had lunch at the principal inn of the first market town he came to. It was not long after noon, and a sizable crowd had congregated in the public room. He shared a table, the universal custom when space was scarce and customers plentiful. By the time he had taken to the road again, he knew more about the details of cultivating turnips than he had learned in his previous thirty-one years. Until meeting farmer Zernick, Daniel had not realized just how long it was possible to talk about one vegetable. It was all the more remarkable, he thought as he left the town behind, considering that his contributions to the conversation had been confined largely to nods and an occasional "I see," or "you don't say."

Before long, he had left the village and surrounding farms far in his wake. He felt a great sense of solitude as he progressed along the road. The land was flat, and had few trees. Daniel could see a long way in all directions. Behind him, he knew, lay the sea; far in the distance ahead, the mountains. Before lunch he had passed a number of travelers, a few mounted. Now, for all he could see, he might be the only man in the universe. It would be, he thought, a very good time to wake up in his apartment. In the lonely and silent landscape it was easy to imagine that none of the events of the last thirty-six hours had occurred.

Daniel stopped. He realized that the only sounds he had been hearing were his own footsteps. He listened in the silence. It was absolute. The still air carried not so much as the song of a bird, the rustle of a leaf.

Now his sense of displacement was keen. The effect of the silence and peace in the shrine of the goddess had been to give him a feeling of orientation, of focus. The silence and peace here were like those he might have felt adrift in the middle of the ocean.

It was fairly late in the day before Daniel had to resort to wearing his cape. He had noticed that the sky was darkening far in the distance when he had passed through the last village, an hour before, but had given it little thought. When the temperature had begun to drop, he had still been close enough to turn back, but he decided to press on; he had never been fond of backtracking. Now, as the first timid gusts of wind brought the smell of rain, and then the rain itself, he had a vision of himself seated in a comfortable chair by a window with a mug of tea, observing the weather rather than experiencing it.

The cape turned out to be large enough to be worn over his bag. With the hood up, Daniel remained dry, though he could not dismiss the image of the chair and the window. As soon as he came to a tree large enough to give any shelter, he took what refuge it offered. He settled himself on the dampened grass and leaned against the trunk.

He sat there enjoying the sound and smell of the rain for quite some time before reluctantly admitting to himself that this was more than an afternoon shower. The wide and lonely sky was gray on all sides. It was impossible to imagine that there could be a place where the sun was shining. He couldn't be sure how far it was to the next inn, but he was quite sure he wanted to reach it before darkness or wet roads made travel difficult. Daniel had no intention of spending the night out of doors when he had a pocket full of Rogan's money.

It was a muddy and discouraged poker player who finally reached a village just as evening was threatening to become night. The air was turning cold. Daniel was happy to see billows of smoke rising from the chimney of the public house, and the light of many lamps glowing in the windows.

No one but he was abroad. The rain was still falling, though not so hard as it had. Daniel trod the wet and slippery lane between the houses until he stood before the inn. For a moment he paused at the door. From inside he could hear laughter.

The innkeeper's wife took his cape to dry it at the kitchen fire.

"A very handsome wrap," she said. "You'll have it back brushed and dry in the morning, good as new."

Daniel dined on boiled meat and slabs of buttered bread, and thought it an incomparable supper. The ale was dark, and still as water from a well.

At a number of tables there were card or board games in progress. Daniel glanced at them without interest as he climbed the stairs to his room.

He awoke early and was on the road within an hour of sunrise. The rain had stopped at midnight, and the well-packed road was dry enough for travel. Again, once out of the village, he was alone on the highway. But now the air was full of the song of birds. They started from the weeds and hedges at his approach, rising up and settling in waves as he passed their hiding places. Meanwhile, far above in the cloud-strewn sky, great birds of the ocean soared on private errands, wandering their trackless ways aloof and unconstrained.

Despite the clouds, there was no rain. By afternoon the road was dusty again, bearing out what he had learned from farmer Zernick about the deplorable lack of "a good soaking rain" during the current turnip season.

Now Daniel met travelers more often. Most were bound from one village to the next, and were in no hurry judging from the way they loitered along. Daniel felt that he was moving at a comfortable, efficient pace, but the way he passed the country folk on the highway made him look like a one-man army on a forced march.

That day the cape stayed in the bag. By the time the inevitable evening shower arrived, Daniel was indeed seated in a comfortable chair by a window, sampling a concoction of hot wine and spices. He played cards after dinner with the innkeeper and some other local merchants. Not wishing to victimize them, he amused himself by using every crooked deal he knew to throw pots to the other players, and winning only enough to pay his keep.

"We might as well not o' bothered," said the innkeeper as the game broke up. "There's scarce enough money changed hands at this table to buy a bean." He looked at Daniel. "And you a gambler," he said, shaking his head as he walked away.

As Rogan had predicted, Daniel arrived at the Feathermere Inn not having skipped a single meal in the four days he had been on the road. It was market day in the border town. When Daniel arrived, early in the afternoon, the streets were still crowded with merchants, farmers at their stalls, and shoppers. He engaged a room at the largest inn, disposed of his bag, and then strolled aimlessly along the narrow ways.

He stopped at a number of farmers' stalls to inspect the early turnips with a connoisseur's eye and discuss the urgent need for a "good soaking rain." At the stand of an ancient person who looked more like a small, wrinkled tree than an old woman, he purchased a length of coarse homespun cloth. It was meant to serve as a cover for a farmhouse kitchen table, but Daniel had another use in mind. He folded it as carefully as if it had been the finest lace, and carried it off under his arm.

In the morning he had a late and hearty breakfast. On his way out of town he supplied himself with a loaf of bread, a large smoked sausage, a waxed cheese the size of a softball, and two flasks of the best wine.

"Thank you, Rogan," he said as he stowed his purchases among the clothes and gear in his bag.

By late morning he was in the forest. On each day of his journey, he had seen more and more trees. Yesterday he had even passed through a large woods on his way to Feathermere. But now he was within the realm of the forest proper. The map he carried showed that from just before Ascroval all the way to the distant mountains, the forest ruled. From this point farms and villages were only to be found on land that had been cleared by the heavy labor of men and their draft animals. In these lands there were no cities like Ambermere, with its miles of streets and buildings radiating from the harbor. Here the towns were walled.

In Ambermere the residence of the king was in the capital city. In the mountain and forest kingdoms the reverse was true. The walls and towers of Castle Ascroval contained the city, embracing a population of craftsmen and merchants, as well as courtiers and soldiers, and streets and buildings in a planless maze that none but natives could hope to know completely.

By late afternoon he had reached his destination. Daniel did not think that his gear would necessarily be instantly recognized as the tools of a burglar, but he did not risk entering the city through the gate with its keeper and guardsmen. With any luck at all, he thought, he would never see the inside of more than one room in this place. He contented himself with a distant glance at the walls, then continued on the highway between the dark trees of the forest.

As he had hoped, he had many hours of daylight to scout the vicinity of the castle. Rogan had assured him that he would meet with no guards or watchmen outside the walls.

"They have nothing to fear, or so they believe," he had cackled, looking at Daniel as though he wished for a demon still.

The woods were dark, the trees ancient and tall. Though thick and impassable in places, the undergrowth was intermittent and easily avoided, or so it appeared from the road. But Daniel was keenly aware that terrain that presented no challenge in the light of the afternoon sun, however screened and filtered, could be a nightmare of impassability after dark.

When he had traveled a short distance beyond the castle, he left the road. He moved quickly through the trees until he was out of sight of anyone who might pass.

He got just close enough to the walls to keep them in view as he followed a semicircular route back to the side of Ascroval occupied by the castle itself. He was encouraged by the ease with which he was able to make his way through the woods. The ground was carpeted with the leaves of uncountable autumns. Before long he was seated with his back against a smooth-barked tree, picnicking on sausage and cheese, and studying the window of the room that held the prisoners.

It was some seventy-five feet above the ground. The edge of the forest was fifty or sixty feet from the walls. Daniel, keeping well back among the trees, could not get a close look at his goal, but he could see from his hiding place that with the spikes and mallet the ascent would be straightforward enough, always assuming he didn't fall and break his neck, a possibility when climbing without a secured line. It was only when compared to his chances in a rematch with the demon that making an unmoored vertical climb became attractive. He rather hoped, in fact, that he would never be called upon to make another.

The trip back down on the rope, of course, was going to be quick, easy, and without any real danger, but he could hardly expect his passenger to view it thus. Daniel had had plenty of time to think about the rescue. He had decided that it would be pointless to engage in any long-winded attempts to persuade the Envy of Every Maiden that departing by way of the window made sense. He was going to enter the room prepared to carry the Royal Abductee down the rope by force, then discuss the points of etiquette with her later.

He finished his lunch and began to walk in the direction of

the road. He was determined not to suffer the risks of the climb
and then wind up wandering lost in the forest until morning
came and Iris was missed. "Whom the Flowers Cannot Hope to
Rival," he said, feeling guilty for having even thought of the
Royal Name without an attending epithet.

When he found the highway, he retraced his steps carefully,
and then made the trip two times more, until he was sure he
could do it on the darkest night. On his route, it was necessary to
cross a small stream, along one bank of which was a narrow, but
well-defined path. With hours remaining before it would be late
enough to climb, he decided to follow it.

The path followed the flowing water deeper and deeper into
the forest, leaving the bank only occasionally to skirt heavy
growth or tangled brush that grew there. In a little over an hour,
he came to a small clearing, where he found a building made of
logs. It had a few windows, which were shuttered, and a door at
each end, both latched but not otherwise secured.

He entered, calling out, though he was sure the place was
empty. Inside was a stone fireplace and chimney, two large tables with benches, and a number of wooden platforms that,
judging from the stacks of neatly folded blankets, were meant to
serve as beds.

Daniel was satisfied he had found a winter shelter for aristo-
cratic hunters. Though it lay less than an hour from the castle on
a summer afternoon, he supposed that in bad winter weather,
the shelter of the castle might be half a day from this spot. He
opened the shutters. He imagined that the place might be quite
cozy on a cold day, with a roaring fire, and wine and hot food
laid out on the tables. He unfolded several blankets and made
them into a mattress for one of the beds. He removed his boots,
improvised a pillow from another blanket, and lay down to
compose himself and rest for the excitement that the night
would bring.

CHAPTER

✦ 8 ✦

Having little else to do, Daniel napped. He slept lightly, opening his eyes every once in a while to check the approach of night. At dusk he got up. Within a few minutes the cabin was closed and he was on the path to the castle.

As the daylight was dying, he reached his spot near the wall. While there was yet a little light, he retraced his way to the road, coming to within sight of it before turning back. When darkness had completely fallen, he made the trip once more. It was, of course, more difficult in the dark than it had been before, but he had done it enough that he was in no danger of losing his way. Feeling rather proud of himself, he returned to his place by the tree to await his moment.

The tower was windowless except for the one he was to climb to. On either side he could see high windows, some of which were lit, as was the princess's, with the flickering light of candles or open lamps. As time passed, one window after another went dark. Finally he felt he could wait no longer. If the princess was asleep when he made his entrance, things would be even more complicated than they promised to be already. About to embark on the scheme, Daniel realized, as though for the first time, how truly insane it was. But the fact that he was here, in a place called Ascroval, and at the bidding of a magician who had summoned him (by mistake) from a high-rise apartment building in another world, made all else seem sane by comparison.

He took from his bag the bundle of spikes, the wooden mallet, and the neatly coiled rope. He placed them on the ground in front of him. Then he brought out the homespun tablecloth. He unfolded it, then refolded it lengthwise and, working with great care, knotted the two ends together securely, making a loop, which he put over his right shoulder so that it fell across his chest and low against his left hip. The rope he arranged similarly in the other direction.

It was not until he was twenty feet above the ground and had placed his first spike, driving it home in a narrow crevice that could not have afforded a finger- or toehold, that he figured out the right way to go up and down the wall. The material the smith had used for the spikes was much stronger than he had guessed. The first one he drove seemed to find a path to the heart of the crack between the stones. Daniel was sure that it would remain there until the next earthquake. Clinging to the wall like an insect, he paid out the rope, then knotted it onto the spike right next to the rock. He quickly lowered himself back to the ground. There he sat against the wall of Razenor's castle and recoiled the rope so that he could use it in the way he had just devised.

Soon he was standing on one foot on the first spike. He left it, climbing only while the placement of the heavy stones made it easy for him. Again he drove a spike and secured the rope to it, not failing to leave a fair amount of slack between the spikes. The mallet he promised himself he would keep forever. Used properly, it was virtually silent as it wedged the pins of steel into the wall.

It did not take him twenty minutes to ladder himself to the window, and at no time had he been in danger of plunging to his death. Lacking any fear of heights, Daniel was relatively happy to find himself perched on a spike seventy or eighty feet above the ground tying a knot onto the stonework of a windowsill. Although he was sure that the pins would stay put, it was no longer vital that they do so. Taking great care to move silently, he shifted his position so that he could see inside the room.

Seated in a large cushioned chair was a woman so pretty that

Daniel stared for several seconds before remembering that he had business to attend to. He felt that finally he could understand how the princess had managed to accumulate all the hyperbolic epithets that were cemented to her name. At her feet was another young woman—a girl, really—in tears and with an expression of stricken hopelessness knit into her features. Her head rested against the thigh of the seated beauty, who was smoothing her hair with a gentle hand, and speaking to her softly.

When he suddenly opened the window and entered the room, the weeping girl shrieked and then slumped to the floor. The young woman did not hesitate for a moment, but jumped from the chair and came straight at him. The look in her eye left no doubt that as far as she was concerned, he was going back out the window. The girl on the floor raised her tear-streaked face and screamed. The woman turned at the sound.

Seeing that the situation could only deteriorate, Daniel moved quickly and decisively. Without regard for her high birth he seized the young woman roughly and used all the force necessary to manhandle her into the tablecloth sling.

"I'm a friend," he whispered implausibly as he dragged her through the open window. He did not have to tell her to hold on as they went over the edge.

Her gasp on the sill he was certain was the last breath she drew until they reached the ground. For Daniel, on the other hand, the descent was simply a matter of keeping his head and paying attention to his feet. He had room in his brain, he was startled to notice, to be intensely conscious of the Royal Thighs clamped to his hips, the arms around his chest, the soft breasts pressing against him, the cheek on his shoulder. It was little wonder, he thought again, that they spoke of this princess in the extravagant way they did.

On the ground, he did not wait for her to recover, but lifted her unceremoniously and ran for the shelter of the trees. Only when they had reached his bag did he stop to untangle her from the twisted sling.

The moon had come out in a cloudless sky. Some little of its light reached them beneath the trees. He watched her quietly as she recovered from the shock of the last two minutes. Breathing deeply, she looked disheveled, confused, and unbelievably beautiful. She stared at the wall and the window above, then closed her eyes and took three slow deep breaths. When she opened her eyes, she looked more or less as she had when she sprang from the chair. Daniel found himself wishing that it was someone else who was fixed in that angry gaze.

"Thank you for rescuing me," she said. She spoke in a low, even voice. "Now what are we going to do about the princess?"

Daniel was confused. It was as though he had just laid down four aces, only to have them beaten, somehow, by a pair of fives.

"You are the princess," he asserted, but without confidence.

The young woman did not reply.

Daniel waited. The woods, he noticed, were very quiet.

"Where is she?" he asked finally.

"She is up there where we left her," she replied, pointing to the tower window. "Except now she is alone."

Daniel sighed. "You're her companion."

"My name is Modesty," said the young woman.

Daniel listened in the silence for sounds from the castle.

"She screamed," he said. "Will someone come to the room?"

"No," said Modesty, "Iris . . . the Princess Iris has been very upset every day. No one pays any attention."

"Then I can go and get her," said Daniel, picking up the sling.

Modesty put her hand on his arm. Daniel instantly recalled every detail of the feeling of her body against his.

"Can you bring her down unconscious?" she asked.

"Impossible," said Daniel immediately and with great conviction. This was something he was quite certain of.

"Then you can spare yourself the climb. She fainted at the sight of you. Try to imagine her coming out the window."

Daniel started to put the sling in the bag.

"Wait," she said, still touching his arm. He waited. For a moment she said nothing. Most of Daniel's attention was focused on the part of his arm where her hand rested.

"Can you carry me back up?" she asked, brushing away a straying lock of dark hair.

He resisted the impulse to lift her on the pretense of judging her weight. She was a little above average height and, though she looked very fit and lean, was not in any way petite. He could carry her down a rope or run with her in his arms, but he was not strong enough to pull them both up the tower wall.

"No," he said simply.

Modesty nodded. "Then I have to climb it myself," she said. She started toward the castle.

"Wait!" said Daniel.

She turned. "I can't abandon her there. She won't be able to stand it by herself."

"You want to go back?"

"Of course not," she said calmly, "but I'm going back just the same."

"Listen to me," he said. "I know what I am talking about and I am telling you the truth. You look pretty strong. You might be able to climb high enough so that when you fell you'd break your neck. But you will never get even halfway to the window." He gestured in the direction of the forest. "Right now we have to get away from here. I know a place we can go. If you want to come back, I promise I will help you."

Modesty looked directly into his eyes.

"All right," she said.

They had not walked far before Daniel halted.

"We're going to have to stop here," he said. "I can barely make out the path. There's not enough light."

Modesty brushed past him. "I can see it. My aunt says I must be part cat."

They reached the cabin when Daniel would have thought they had some way yet to go. It seemed to him that he had had his eyes locked on the graceful motions of her body for only fifteen or twenty minutes.

Modesty found candles and something to light them with in the dark room. Once there was light, Daniel closed the door. When he turned back, she was sitting on his bed with her head in her hands.

"Are you all right?" he asked.

She looked up at him. Daniel missed the sarcastic expression on her face, his attention being entirely occupied with the details of her eyes, the turn of her lips, the shape of her chin, the hint of color on her cheek.

"No, I am not," she said.

Daniel said nothing. Modesty turned away from his stare.

"Oh, I'm sorry," he said. "What did you say?"

Modesty straightened her lips to remove from them the traces of a smile, then turned to face him with a serious look.

"I said, no, I am not all right. Not after that trip down the rope. I am not fond of heights."

"But you asked me to carry you back up."

"I must get back to the princess. I thought that would be better than showing up at the city gate in the morning."

"Is that what you are planning?"

"I have no plan. I am going to return to the princess. If she does not have a friend to support her, I truly think that she might die." She brushed away the tears that came to her eyes.

"But that's a worry for tomorrow, not tonight." She looked at Daniel speculatively. "Where do you come from that you could mistake me for the princess?"

Where he had come from was a far more complicated question than Daniel was prepared to discuss, but he was sure he could deflect it simply by being frank and honest about the mistake he had made.

"When I looked through the window in the tower, I saw a woman so beautiful that all those outlandish compliments about shaming the flowers and so on almost started to make sense. It never occurred to me to doubt that you were the princess."

Modesty turned away quickly. Her eye fell on Daniel's traveling bag.

"You didn't by some chance bring food with you?" she asked after a moment.

While Daniel laid the food and wine on one of the tables, Modesty located platters and cups. They sat together on a bench.

"Wait," she said, before they began. "This is most improper. If I am to dine alone with you, I must at least know your name."

Daniel introduced himself.

"And another thing," she said, starting to laugh. "What do you mean, the compliments 'almost' made sense?"

Daniel couldn't help laughing with her, despite his suspicion that she was making fun of him.

"Real food," said Modesty, inspecting the table with approval. "I wish the princess were here to share this. I'm sure she'd feel much better if she had a proper meal. At Ascroval they've been feeding us like rabbits. Dainty food is all right if you don't have to live on it," she said, cutting a piece of sausage.

"You don't have to go back," said Daniel. "I can take you to Feathermere before morning."

She stopped eating and turned to him with a serious expression.

"I know where Feathermere is. If I wanted to go there, I would already be on my way. In the morning, I am going to Ascroval." Her dark eyes caught his and held them. "There is no reason for us to talk about this. None at all." She returned her attention to her meal.

Although he had not eaten since his afternoon snack, Daniel found that his interest in food was slight. He sipped wine and watched as Modesty attacked the little feast with warm enthusiasm. He was not quite sure how it was, but this woman, dressed in a plain shift, wearing no trace of makeup, every hair out of place, eating a piece of rather greasy sausage from her fingers, presented to his eye a picture of stunning beauty. He felt as though he could be completely happy just watching her for hours.

She glanced over to him.

"Yes?" she said with a lazy smile.

When Daniel answered, it was with the eerie feeling that he was listening to someone else speak. He knew it was not polite to stare, and his intention was to mutter some excuse and change the subject. But when he opened his mouth, that is not what came out.

"I know I'm staring," he said, "but I don't think I can stop." He paused for a moment, then continued in an unpremeditated rush of words. "Modesty, I would climb that wall a hundred times just to be allowed to look at you. I have never met anyone like you; I have never seen anyone as beautiful as you. I have been with you for two hours, and I seem to be in love with you. I'm sitting here watching you and I can hardly remember to breathe."

Modesty lowered the sausage to her place. The color rushed to her cheeks. The knife slipped from her fingers as she brought her hands to her face.

For a moment she said nothing.

"Excuse me," she whispered from behind her hands, "but I thought you were just going to ask me to hand you the wine."

Daniel felt a rush of embarrassment. "I'm sorry," he said, "I didn't mean . . . I didn't say that to upset you."

Modesty removed her hands from her face and spoke facing straight ahead, as though addressing someone seated across the table from her.

"You free me from a prison. You tell me I am beautiful. You say that you are in love with me." She looked at him, moving only her eyes. "Shall I now demand an apology?"

She turned to face him. "Do you think I hate to hear you praise me? I can see that you are not some courtier using compliments like coinage. You have proved that you are strong and daring and"—she smiled faintly—"except for the first moments of our acquaintance, you have treated me with respect. I cannot despise your compliments. Besides," she added with a pretty grin, "you are a very handsome man. Perhaps if I had followed you on the path I would have stared at you in the way that you stared at me."

Modesty laughed at the expression on his face. She put her hand on his shoulder.

"This is not a time for you to speak of love, but I am flattered that you like me, and that you like to look at me." Her smile faded. "I don't know what is going to happen at Ascroval," she said. "Yours may be the last compliments I am ever to hear in this life." She smiled at him again. "So don't regret them; not on my account. But please, you must share this meal with me. Or else in time you may just remember me as the girl who ate so much."

After their picnic supper Modesty seemed distracted. They sat by a window and talked, but she did not ask Daniel any awkward questions about his hometown. She seemed satisfied with his rather ambiguous description of his dealings with Rogan.

"That makes sense," she said. "It didn't seem like the sort of plot Rand would have worked out." She finished the sip of wine in the bottom of her cup. "On the other hand, it's awfully direct for Rogan the Obscure," she said absently.

For a few minutes neither spoke. The silence was broken only by the intermittent bursts of song from a nocturnal bird somewhere nearby. Daniel was content to sit quietly and observe his beautiful companion. The beautiful companion herself seemed to be off somewhere in a private world. Once or twice she raised her eyes to meet his for an instant and then looked away, smiling to herself.

From the beginning of their brief acquaintance, Daniel had noticed that when Modesty's eyes caught his, he was unable to see anything else. Now that they were lowered, he was tracing the lines of her features, mapping her every charm.

With her eyes averted still, she rose silently and paced to the other end of the room. It occurred to Daniel to wonder if he was making her uncomfortable. He reminded himself that she was, after all, hardly more than a girl, and caught in very difficult circumstances. As a companion to a princess, she had undoubtedly led a sheltered life. Her seeming self-possession might be only a fragile veneer. He tried to pull his eyes from the mesmerizing sway of her hips, the line of her thigh against the thin cloth of her shift. What she needed was not lecherous stares, but whatever comfort he might be able to offer her.

She walked back to the table and poured herself some more wine. She drank it quickly, then turned with an abrupt motion and walked the length of the room again. She stood in the shadows by the far wall for the space of a dozen heartbeats, then walked slowly back. She seemed to be in a state of agitation. Daniel tried to think of something he might do to calm the fears she must be feeling.

His reaction when she bent suddenly and kissed him on the cheek was surprising in its intensity. His face tingled and he felt a wave of dizziness pass over him. Modesty stepped back as he got to his feet. She fixed him with her dark gaze.

"Daniel," she said in a soft voice pitched low, "I'm ready for bed. Are you?"

Daniel was.

A while later they lay in a quiet embrace. Modesty's eyes were closed as she whispered to him.

"Now I know something about the future that I didn't know before," she said with a soft smile. "I still don't know what may happen to me, but I know I will not die a virgin." She laughed mischievously. "It was very kind of you to assist me in this way. And now Iris can stop worrying about her wedding night. She will be so relieved when I tell her about this."

"Tell her about it?" said Daniel, shocked.

"Oh, I must. She's very worried. No one at the court will tell her anything. One old countess has talked to both of us, but only to say we must 'submit,' and that she fears I lack pliancy, as if I am to make myself pliant for some mincing courtier or blustering lord." Modesty began to raise her voice indignantly.

"Peace," whispered Daniel. "You're perfect the way you are."

"Am I? I think you must be perfect, too. I will say nothing of love, but I like you very, very much."

They lay together silently for a while. Finally Modesty put her lips next to his ear.

"I don't want to be greedy," she whispered, "but . . ."

The plan came to Daniel in his sleep. He awoke instantly, fearing that it might already be too late, but the night was still dark. Modesty lay facing him, her dark hair mingling with the shadows, one hand resting on his shoulder. He woke her with a kiss.

"Oh," she said, with a sleepy smile, "I remember you."

Daniel explained his idea to her.

"But what can we do, even if we are within the walls?" she protested.

"We can try to get the princess out of there."

"I don't see how."

Daniel smiled at her.

"Neither do I," he admitted, "but you're just going to join her again. Anything is better than that."

"You will be captured. That's not better.

Daniel could think of no good reason to trouble Modesty with stories of his summons, the danger from the demon, or anything about Rogan. Besides which, his reasons for wanting to free the princess now had more to do with the woman who lay beside him than with the "practical" considerations of danger from supernatural beings.

"Modesty, I love you."

"Please don't talk of love," she said. "We must take the joy that the moment gives us, and be grateful."

"All right. I will just say I want to help you. There's no reason why I should be captured. It's a big place, Ascroval; there must be many strangers there. There will be no harm in looking around."

"I fear there may be great harm to you, but I cannot stop you."

"Are you sure you will not be missed until midmorning?"

"Quite sure." Modesty stretched slowly like a cat, and with devastating effect on the staring Daniel. She smiled. "We have lots of time."

CHAPTER

· 9 ·

Daniel and Modesty arrived at the gate within two hours of dawn. At her insistence, they entered the city separately, Daniel going first. He watched from a public well as she passed the guards among a crowd of farmers with their carts.

They wandered the twisted alleys for a time, familiarizing themselves with the neighborhood of the castle. The ways were lined with stalls and shops. Daniel noticed that, as they walked, Modesty was paying close attention to the wares of the clothing merchants.

"Do you want something?" he asked. "I have money."

"Good," she said. "Give it to me."

Daniel handed over the purse with a grin. Modesty removed a few coins and returned it to him. They were at the edge of a small square with a fountain. She pointed to a cafe opposite.

"Wait for me there," she said, and was gone before he could answer.

Daniel took a table under a tattered awning and sat there sipping strong tea and thinking about his lover and his predicament. Modesty was unwilling to leave the princess alone for more than perhaps another day, and that grudgingly.

"The princess is a lovely person. There is much in her to admire. But she is fragile. She cannot endure this captivity alone." So Modesty had told Daniel in answer to his arguments against her return. Arguments with Modesty, Daniel had already learned, were apt to be brief and unsatisfying. As far as he could see, the old countess had a point—pliancy was not a quality his new friend had cultivated.

Daniel caught himself drifting into a reverie on the virtues of his lover. Very pleasant, but not of any real use in the present situation. He had to find a way to rescue the princess from this citadel, despite the fact that rescuing princesses from citadels was not his regular line of work.

Although, he reminded himself, the original harebrained scheme had actually succeeded. He had rescued a stunningly beautiful, cool-headed, and courageous young woman from her prison. She would be halfway to Ambermere right now if only she had been the princess. Daniel, of course, had ample reason to be thankful that she was who she was, but it did complicate matters.

"Why," he had asked Modesty on the way to Ascroval, "is she spoken of as a great beauty? You would think there had never been a woman to compare with her."

"It's a custom. It wouldn't matter what she looked like. But she is very beautiful. When she's at her best, she is most impressive. This prince—Hilbert, his name is—is making no bad bargain."

Daniel ordered more tea. A boy stopped on the cobbled pavement outside the awning. He wore a turban and baggy clothing, and was singing a song with incomprehensible words in a hoarse alto. Daniel flipped a coin to him, hoping he would go somewhere else. The boy stopped singing. That's a start, thought Daniel.

"Master, you need a serving boy?"

Daniel shook his head.

"A guide? I can guide you everywhere." The boy spoke as he sang, in a voice hoarse and raucous.

Daniel smiled. "No," he said, hoping he wouldn't have to repeat that syllable a dozen times, but expecting to.

"Master, I think you need me to serve you. If you look at me, you will see what a good boy I am." He stepped to the table. Daniel glanced at him and shook his head again.

"But, master, you didn't really look."

Daniel looked, and felt his pulse quicken as his eyes were trapped in the familiar dark gaze he had known only since yesterday.

They found a room above a public house not far from the castle gate. Inside, Modesty twisted from Daniel's eager embrace.

"That was for last night, my beautiful lover," she said, blushing deeply. "Now the princess frets and worries without me to help her. We must find a way to enter the castle, or else I must simply surrender to the guards."

Daniel resisted the impulse to protest, contenting himself with a more or less innocent question.

"Are you related to the princess?" he asked.

"Goodness no. I am a commoner."

"Then how do you come to travel in such high and mighty company?"

"Daniel, you must speak of her with respect," said Modesty in a sober voice.

"Because she is a princess?"

"Because she is my friend." Modesty took his hand.

"As for how that can be, we met when she was a girl of seventeen. She noticed me one day at the shrine where I lived with my aunt, and came to the garden to talk to me. I was nineteen at the time. She wouldn't let the great ladies who were with her come near us. We talked for a long time. Then she invited me to the castle. The ladies didn't know what to do. Then they were offended because my aunt didn't like the idea any better than they did, while they expected a common working woman to be thrilled at the great honor of it.

"At the end of the day, the princess sent a footman to ask my aunt's permission for me to remain a few days. You understand, she didn't inform her of the royal intentions; she asked her permission.

"I will tell you, because she is my friend, and I want you to like her, what made her seek me out in the garden. Despite the pampering and spoiling she has always lived with, she is very sweet and modest." Modesty paused, looking uncomfortable. "She said that she wanted to have a companion so pretty that people would stop saying all those silly things about the very flowers in the garden suffering by comparison with her. And she begged me that first day at the palace not to use her titles when we were alone." She brushed a tear from her eye. "She was so desperate to have someone call her by her name."

They returned to the topic of getting into the castle. When Modesty learned that Daniel was a gambler, she became optimistic.

"Why did you not tell me this before?" She laughed. "Of course, we have not spent much time in conversation since we met." She sat on the edge of the bed. "I suppose I must expect that if I ask a man to lie with me." She giggled. "You must think I am very poorly named."

She questioned him about his skills, how well he played, what games he knew. Daniel told her of his evening with Count Reffex.

"He cheats," she said indignantly. "I have seen him do it."

"I believe it," said Daniel. "Anyone who can see in the dark the way you do must have a quick eye. But Reffex is not so clumsy that he could not fool most people." He got out a deck of cards and demonstrated a number of phony deals.

"But," she said in a troubled voice, "I can't catch you at it."

"That's because I know how to do it right," laughed Daniel.

Modesty didn't say anything for a moment. She walked the length of the room twice while Daniel put the cards away. She knelt down in front of his chair to bring her eyes level with his and stared at him with a sober expression.

"Why do you know these things?" she asked finally. Daniel thought she looked as though she would burst into tears.

"If you don't know them, you can't protect yourself against them," he replied. He took her hands in his. "I don't cheat at cards," he said.

She nodded contritely. "I'm sorry," she said. "I didn't think you did, but I suddenly realized I do not know you at all, except . . ."

She kissed him lightly and smiled at him. She stood up and unwound the turban from her head.

"Now I have an idea of how we can get inside the castle. You must draw attention to yourself at the gaming houses in the neighborhood, demonstrate the techniques of cheating. I will rush around the streets and talk of it, as though of some marvel. Some passing lord or other is bound to invite you to show these things to the court." She sat down on the bed and removed her sandals.

"Of course," she said, sending a glance toward him, "no one will be at the tables until afternoon." She stretched, flexing every muscle in her body. "How ever shall we occupy ourselves in the meantime?"

A few hours later Modesty, dressed as Daniel's servant boy, darted down a narrow street lined with shops, attracted by the sound of angry voices. She found a richly dressed man shouting at an old fellow in an apron outside a modest shop.

"You will be paid when I see fit. I am not to be dictated to by a wretched tradesman."

"But you have the merchandise, my lord. Am I not to have my fair return?"

"Of course I have the merchandise. I ordered it. Who would have it?" The nobleman pointed an angry finger at the cringing merchant. "I suggest you return to your shop and find something better to do than pester your betters. If you spent more time working and less time whining, you'd be even richer than you are already."

He wheeled and nearly ran over Modesty.

"My lord, my lord," she cried hoarsely, "you must come and see this wonder." She dodged a halfhearted kick in her direction.

"No, truly," she persisted, following him down the street, "it is a marvel."

"It will be a marvel if you survive the beating I am going to give you. Be off!" He turned and continued on his way.

"Nay, but listen, my lord," she called after him, raising her voice as he departed. "The man is a magician with the cards. He is a virtuoso of cheating," she wailed in a hoarse shout, "and is showing his tricks in the taverns."

The nobleman stopped and turned. He took a coin from his purse and beckoned, smiling.

"Perhaps I should have a look," he said. She ran after him, being careful not to get too close. He flipped the coin to her. She caught it without taking her eyes from him. "There's a good lad," he said, "show me where to find this fellow."

Daniel did not fail to notice the arrival of his serving boy and the overfed young man with the florid complexion. He shuffled and dealt the cards with rapid deftness, giving himself an unbeatable hand, which he then displayed.

The lord moved up to the table. Those crowded around gave way, stepping on each other's feet and bumping into chairs. Having been coached by Modesty, Daniel got to his feet and managed an obsequious nod.

"You'd best come with me, my man," said the nobleman. He made it sound like an arrest.

"We will be delighted, my lord," Daniel answered, gesturing for Modesty. The nobleman sniffed. He turned and led the way without waiting to see if he was being followed.

When they had left the vicinity of the tavern, his aloofness disappeared.

"You must dine with me in my apartments," he said eagerly. "I find your skills fascinating. I myself am interested in cards. You might say it is a sort of intellectual hobby I find amusing." They walked along in silence for a block.

"Not really the sort of thing, though, to demonstrate to just anyone. In the wrong hands, such tricks could be misused, don't you think? How much better if they are known only to a few."

Gaining entrance to the castle took no more than the wave of His Lordship's hand in the direction of the guards. Once inside, he turned to Modesty.

"You'd best go to the kitchens, boy. I have my servants to wait on us upstairs. You tell the cooks Lord Scropp says to feed you."

Daniel's protest was drowned out by his servant's hoarse protestations of gratitude.

"Yes, sir. Just the thing for me, sir. Thank you, sir. Don't you worry. I can find it, sir."

Daniel's mouth was still open when the turbaned head disappeared around a corner.

In no time at all, Modesty was busy making a nuisance of herself in the vast kitchens. She opened pots and lifted the cover of every dish she could get to. But she seemed such a likable and pretty boy that the cooks tolerated her and answered her silly questions. They whispered to one another what a charmer this lad would grow to be with his beautiful dark eyes, smooth skin, and nimble, flirtatious ways.

And flirt she did, with every serving wench no matter how plain, and exerted herself to befriend the boys as well, gathering them in a corner to make jokes at the expense of the cooks, bakers, and any adults who passed through.

And while Daniel and Lord Scropp were lingering over dessert, she had spent her last coin for the privilege of carrying lunch to the lady in the tower.

"Mind you tell no one," said the serving girl, pocketing the coin and dazedly touching her cheek where the soft quick kiss had surprised her.

The guard unlocked the door for the turbaned boy with no show of interest. He was of the king's personal guard, and had only today been put here in place of the much less exalted trooper whose job it had been to keep awake in a lonesome hallway far from any amusement. Some trouble had occurred, apparently, but not of a sort to enliven a dull assignment.

Inside, Modesty looked at the familiar room cautiously. The princess lay on her couch.

"Thank you, I want nothing."

"You must eat, miss," said Modesty in her hoarse serving-boy voice.

"Must I?"

Modesty did not want to shock Iris, but neither did she want to waste precious time.

"Miss, I want you to take a deep breath and remain calm."

"Go away."

"Iris, please don't scream," she said in her own voice.

To her very great credit, Iris did not scream.

She stared at her companion, dressed as an urchin, without moving. Modesty came to her, pulled her to her feet, and hugged her. The princess was crying silently.

"I thought you must be dead," she whispered. "What happened?"

Modesty told her, including every detail that modesty did not forbid.

"Iris, you mustn't be shocked; he is so . . . Anyway, I am going to free you from this place, if I can. And if I can get to you so easily, what may Daniel and I together not be able to accomplish?" She hugged the princess again. "Courage!" she said from the door. She smiled conspiratorially. "And remember the sweet secrets I have told you."

It took her the better part of an hour to find Lord Scropp's rooms. The nobleman had taken unto himself a fair measure of wine, and did not appear to be following with complete success the intricacies of cheating at cards.

Daniel extricated himself with a promise to return the next day. "I'm afraid I am not able to explain this with the necessary clarity after such an ample repast," he said, shifting to himself the blame for his pupil's stupidity with the adroit insincerity of a seasoned diplomat.

"Well, here then, my man," mumbled Scropp, producing a small purse with an air of reluctance reminiscent of Rogan.

Daniel's polite protest was anticipated by his serving boy, who nimbly plucked the purse from the noble fingers and began a barrage of profuse thanks that did not cease until after the great man's servant had put them through the door.

"You are a marvel," said Daniel back in their room above the tavern. "I couldn't see what we were going to accomplish with this nobleman beyond adding another clumsy cheat to the gaming tables. But while I'm watching him drop cards on the floor, you are talking to the princess. I am amazed." He shook his head bemusedly. "Again."

"Well," she said, "your servant is about to perish from hunger. I suggest you feed him."

Daniel had eaten his fill at Scropp's. At a back table of the nearest cafe, he sipped tea and watched Modesty be so true to her masquerade as to eat with the appetite of a teenage boy.

They didn't tempt fate by talking where they might by some chance be heard. It was not until they were back in their room that they tried to formulate a plan. The best they could devise was for Modesty to spend the next day trying to learn something that would be of use.

"But I must see her as well," she said. "She is being very

brave, but if I can't visit her and give her reassurance, she will become frantic." Modesty drew back the curtain to look out the window. "My poor princess," she said. "She would feel abandoned when I visited my aunt for a day or two. Now she is locked away in a room no bigger than this one." She turned to Daniel.

"But here, I have you. She has no one. While I lie in the arms of my lover tonight, the princess trembles on her couch alone."

Since Daniel had only a vague agreement to join His Lordship sometime after noon, he and Modesty allowed themselves the lazy luxury of sleeping late. But they were awakened and greatly alarmed in the midmorning by a loud knock at their door. Reacting faster than Daniel, Modesty sprang from the bed and began to hurriedly wind her turban as she called through the door in her servant's hoarse shout.

"Who disturbs the master gambler at this early hour?" She jumped into her baggy disguise on the way to the door. "My employer is not a maker of bricks to be at his kiln at dawn," she bawled.

"A message from the castle," said a voice from the hallway.

Obeying Modesty's whispered order, Daniel lay yet among their rumpled bedclothes. Modesty disengaged the heavy latch and opened the door partway. From where he lay, Daniel could see her take a note from an invisible hand.

It was a summons in the form of an invitation. Lord Scropp wished Daniel to present himself sooner than they had agreed, for the purpose of being displayed before some guests who were expected to arrive before noon and could be assumed to be interested in Daniel's arts.

Daniel and Modesty had a quick breakfast and a whispered discussion, and then presented themselves at the castle steps. Once they were inside, Modesty set off for the kitchens. They had agreed that she would look in on him when the opportunity offered itself.

At Scropp's apartments, Daniel found his pupil in the company of three other men, one of whom was dressed in so outlandish and extravagant a costume that Daniel could scarcely refrain from staring. The man wore robes that would not have been out of place on a wealthy bride. His hat was an enormous pointed contrivance decorated with a galaxy of arcane symbols vaguely reminiscent of astrological runes. It was only after having been presented, in the customary apologetic manner, to this personage, introduced as "the great wizard, Remeger, who has consented to view your tricks," that Daniel realized that of the other two men, out of all the multitudes of all the kingdoms of this world, he was acquainted with one.

"Your grace," he said, nodding with appropriate humility to his erstwhile teacher, Reffex.

The good count launched into his impersonation of gracious condescension, greeting Daniel with something approaching familiarity, and being very jovial with his pal Lord Scropp.

"You see, Scropp, I've bested you again. I know the man from Ambermere, where I think he'll tell you he learned a few things from me, if I say it myself."

The third man was another aristocrat from Ambermere, a Baron Sote, whose name Daniel thought sounded familiar, though he couldn't imagine how it could be.

"How is it, then, Reffex," he said with an affected drawl that Daniel hoped he would not hear much of, "that I don't know this fellow? I'm no stranger to the gaming tables at home."

"No, no," said Reffex, with a languid imperial wave, "he came to me for instruction, you see."

"But he's not of the court, certainly?"

Daniel found it interesting to be the subject of a discussion that did not acknowledge his presence. He wondered if these noblemen would be so foolish as to play cards with him for money.

"Oh, didn't I mention, the wizard will be interested in this, he was a guest of Rogan's."

The great Remeger pretended not to know who Rogan was until Reffex reminded him.

"Oh, yes," the wizard said, "it is he who fashions himself 'the Obscure,' is it not?" He uttered a "ha-ha-ha" that was evidently meant to be taken as a disdainful laugh, the reaction of an eminent wizard to the predictable follies of a mere magician.

Daniel, not being part (except as subject) of the conversation, had leisure to wonder at a trio of grandees in whose company even Scropp began to look like a fellow of wit and charm.

Baron Sote turned to Daniel.

"So," he said, "then it is you I have to thank for the fact that my dagger was not ready on time?" Without waiting for Daniel's reply, he turned to the others.

"The weapon smith told me that Rogan had turned up with a stranger and authority from the king, and had made him drop everything to fill an order overnight. What was it again?" he asked Daniel.

"I'm not quite sure, Your Grace. It had something to do with magic or fireworks, I believe."

"Oh, I remember. The smith showed me the drawing when I thought he was lying. Spikes, he said they were. Thin, not terribly long. I can't imagine what they were for." He patted an empty sheath at his belt. "I still don't have my dagger."

In no face did Daniel, whose occupation involved reading facial expressions, see signs of trouble. Remeger, unfortunately, had been looking toward the window when the spikes were mentioned. He turned to them and took a step toward Daniel.

"Well then, sir," he said with an empty smile, "let us see these tricks of yours."

The wizard left before long. It was only by calling on discipline that Daniel was able to keep his mind on what he was doing. He was painfully conscious that as long as Baron Sote was at this court, there was a chance, perhaps a good one, that the wrong person would hear of the spikes. Daniel was still trying to work out a way of ensuring that the subject of spikes would not arise again when a servant came to say that he was wanted in the corridor.

He excused himself and went to the doorway hoping for a moment of privacy to consult with Modesty about the complication. Perhaps, he thought, she would know if Reffex and Sote could simply be informed of the situation. It was even possible, though hard to imagine, that they might be of some help.

But instead of Modesty in the corridor, he found the wizard with half a dozen guards waiting to seize him. They marched him quickly to a windowless room off a narrow inner hallway. Before locking him in, the wizard sent the guards from the door.

"Do you think we are fools?" he hissed. "The lady you kidnapped is back with the other guest. Everything is just as it was before you came with your rope and spikes to commit this outrage." Remeger favored him with an ugly grin. "Except you are locked in this room now, guilty of a crime against this kingdom and its sovereign." He started to close the door, then opened it again.

"Fool! I am not some palace magician like Rogan the Obscure. How dare he send you here to challenge me? How could you think to breach the defenses of a castle protected by the magic of a wizard?"

Daniel could not see how his situation could be improved by pointing out that he had been breaching those defenses for days, and had only been caught through the agency, not of magic, but bad luck. He did his best to look contrite, sitting with his head bowed until the door slammed and the bar dropped into place.

CHAPTER
⋅ 10 ⋅

Jackson was in a cab crawling through city traffic three blocks from the bar when he saw Elise. She was standing in front of a cigar store next to what was certainly the last wooden Indian in the city, possibly in the state. As she gazed off in the direction of the harbor, four or five blocks away, she appeared to be totally lost in thought. Jackson was used to seeing adepts of all sorts, especially those of his own Order, exert their powers of concentration. Errin, for instance, seemed always to be trying to penetrate some mystery by staring at something. But whatever Elise was doing, it was something quite different. Jackson himself had suggested tricks she could use to improve her concentration. Elise, though, looked almost as if she were not really standing there, or was someplace completely different at the same moment. As the cab moved on, Jackson glanced back at her. She looked as though she were entirely alone. As though the street, the traffic, and maybe the planet itself did not exist.

He shrugged. Her talents, her interests, were not really his concern. He had been asked to give her instruction when the opportunity arose. To show any further curiosity about her would be not only pointless, but improper. Unless of course he could trick her, as Errin had done. That was not curiosity; it was instruction. Jackson thought it odd that she would be so unguarded. Total innocents were not sent to places like the bar. This could not be her first brush with the Order.

When he got to the bar, finally abandoning the cab in despair, he mentioned seeing the barmaid.

"She could be standing on the moon," he said.

"Nothing wrong, surely?" asked the bartender.

"No. She probably looks distracted to anyone who notices her, but there's nothing amiss. I saw it because I know how to look, and I know who she is."

"Oh?" said Errin, eyebrows raised.

"You know very well that I mean I know she is one of us, not a meter maid or a lawyer."

"And she's a local from Ambermere."

"Probably. Assuming she wasn't just being more clever than you. Remember we don't really know each other in the Order, especially when we are young. Maybe I am really"—he raised his eyebrows and twisted his features—"a necromancer," he said dramatically, making complicated motions with his fingers and hands.

The other young man laughed. "Or the new conductor of the philharmonic."

When they stopped laughing, Jackson looked around the room. Gavas was in the corner, asleep or awake, Jackson could not tell.

"He hasn't left here for weeks, has he? He never does anything. I have never seen him study, and he never offers to teach, unless you count the occasional incomprehensibility he bestows upon us." He stood up to remove his jacket.

"You know," he continued, "I have books in my room. . . ."

Errin raised his eyebrows.

"It's okay. Mervin and Gavas both approved. Anyway, when I am there I am usually studying. And when I come here, I end up sitting with Elise. Not that I mind, exactly"—he lowered his voice—"but Gavas doesn't even do that, and to tell you the truth, I get the impression Elise would rather I didn't bother. She's polite, but she could not be called an eager pupil."

Errin nodded. "She is always telling me not to trouble myself. But I assumed it was because you are a better-informed teacher." He laughed. "Or, of course, an arch-wizard."

The street door opened, letting in the usual din along with a blast of hot city air. Elise waved to Gavas and the others as she passed, and joined the two young men at the bar.

"Did your taxi ever get here," she asked Jackson, "or did you give up and walk?"

The back door opened with a groan, admitting Hannah. She chatted briefly, stopped to talk to Gavas for a moment, then left the quiet sanctuary of the bar by way of the street door.

Marcia had been waiting for Hannah for over an hour, never remaining seated on the bench for more than a minute. She had walked every path of the little park a dozen times. It had been ten days since she had seen Hannah. It was then that the witch had given her the little box that had proved so effective on Monday morning, just one week ago. But on that same day, after work, she had seen the monster, as she thought of him for lack of a better term.

She had stayed at home on Tuesday; it wasn't really until Tuesday morning that she had been able to get to sleep. On Wednesday she had returned to work, though she regretted it when she got there; the bustle of the office seemed almost intolerable to her frayed nerves.

Marcia would have gone back home, except the thought of sitting alone all day was less attractive than staying at the office, even if it meant enduring the sudden sycophantic friendship of Colette, who had discovered that her work often required the "input" of the newly created consultant.

After work, Marcia did something that she had been sorry for every moment since then. She got a cab outside the office, but instead of going directly to her apartment, she asked the driver to go by way of the street where she had seen the man in the leather vest.

He was not where she had last seen him. Marcia was relieved. She had made herself come back to this place, but she had not wanted to endure again the sight of the monstrous aura. She settled back in the seat as the taxi stopped in a line of cars waiting for a red light.

The focus of another person's dislike or ill will was something Marcia could detect as an almost physical sensation of weight pressing against her. Sitting in the cab, she felt the sudden weight of concentrated malevolence bearing down on her.

She was gripped by an icy fear that seemed to come from somewhere deep inside her. Knowing what she would see, she forced herself to turn her eyes to the near sidewalk. There, not twenty feet away was the monster, his yellow stare burning into her. Marcia would have screamed if she had been able to breathe. She saw the booted foot step off the curb in her direction. The light changed. One by one the cars ahead of them began to move. The thing, whatever it was, came closer.

With nightmarish sluggishness, the cab drifted ahead. Marcia was sure the light would change, trapping her. She saw the green give way to yellow, then felt the sudden jolt as the driver pushed the accelerator to the floor and roared through the intersection with a muttered curse.

In front of her building she handed her pocketbook to the driver.

"Pay yourself," she said.

The driver hesitated. "Are you all right, lady?" he asked. Marcia's hands were trembling violently.

"Yes," she said. She managed a brittle smile. "Give yourself a good tip."

The man insisted on showing her what he was taking, counting out the bills deliberately and calculating the tip with niggling precision. Marcia forced herself to be patient, rather than yielding to her earnest desire to scream and run into the building.

On Thursday she had gone to work, though late, and worked until the office closed. She told the receptionist she wouldn't be in until Monday and took a cab directly to her apartment.

She awoke in the middle of the night, certain that if she went to the window, she would see the monster on the street below, looking up at her. The longer she lay there, the more certain she became. Finally she got up and sidled to the window, disturbing the heavy drapes just enough to get a view of the street.

The fact that it was totally empty gave her comfort, but not so much that she had any hope of further sleep. She sat up till dawn, then slept half the morning. She followed this routine until Monday, sitting up most of the night and sleeping at odd times during the day. On Monday she slept through half the morning, and did not leave the bed until time to go to the park, though she had been awake for some time.

When she saw the now familiar dark dress of the witch she ran to her. Hannah's smile at seeing the shy and reserved Marcia running toward her like a twelve-year-old faded when she saw the expression on her adept's face.

When she had heard everything that Marcia had to tell—the aura, the fact that the monster was aware of Marcia—Hannah insisted on taking a quick walk through the park and the streets immediately surrounding it.

Back at the bench, Marcia was horrified when Hannah said she had to leave.

"It is only for a very short while, and only because I must get help. There is no danger near, but this is very serious. Do not leave this place."

The trays from the tavern in Ambermere had arrived and Elise and Errin were being kept busy. The three locals who had taken to frequenting the strangely silent little bar with the rich amber ale and platters of bread, cold meats, and cheese, were relishing their peaceful lunch. They had shared a solemn vow not to tell anyone else about the place, for fear it would be spoiled by crowds of vice presidents and accountants.

At the big table in the corner, every chair was occupied. Jackson was seated with the others, earnestly disputing a point with a bearded man who looked roughly three times his age.

Errin had vaulted over the bar to transform himself from waiter to barman and had just given Elise fresh glasses for the locals when the door opened to admit the witch.

"What an honor," he said as she approached. "You've not taken a meal with us since . . ."

Hannah passed him as though he wasn't there. He watched as Elise, carrying a tray of food and drink to the locals, turned to face her. It was most unobservant of him, he thought, that he had not noticed until that moment how very odd her eyes were.

When she reached the waitress, the witch crossed her hands on her chest and bowed.

"Forgive me, Holy One; my adept has seen a demon."

With a gesture, Elise stopped the wizards in the corner from leaving their chairs.

"When?" she asked, at the same time placing the tray on the table of the gaping locals. Hannah told her.

"Where is she now?"

The witch gave her directions to the park. Except for her voice, the room was utterly silent.

"You will stay here," Elise said to Hannah. "I will see to your adept."

The witch nodded.

"Master Errin," said Elise, turning to the bartender. She gestured to the locals. "These men may not leave until I return."

Errin had been staring in openmouthed astonishment. He remembered himself in time to bow. "Yes, Holy One," he murmured hoarsely.

The young woman strode to the door, nodding to Gavas as she passed. When the door to the street closed behind her, he raised his hand.

"Let us continue our meal," he said quietly. "Mistress Hannah would have noticed if there were any danger near. We will talk when it is time to talk."

No longer in a mood for leaping, Errin walked around the bar and went to the locals.

"Gentlemen," he said with an effort at a smile, "do you have everything you need?"

"What's going on here? What does she mean, we can't leave?"

"Just until she comes back," said Errin.

"And just who is she?" asked one of the men.

Errin shook his head slowly. "I'm sure that if I knew, I wouldn't be allowed to tell you."

As intently as she had been watching for Hannah's return, Marcia couldn't imagine how she had failed to see the woman who was walking toward her, but she had no leisure to dwell on the question. The effect of the aura she was seeing was perhaps similar to what an unusually sensitive listener would experience in the presence of the most exquisitely beautiful singing. She rose to meet her, then sat back down, confused. The woman took a seat next to her.

Marcia found her voice. "Who are you?" she asked.

"My name is Elyssa. That is my true name, for you, but you must call me Elise. What it is needful for you to know of me, you can see."

Marcia nodded.

"Good. Now tell me what has happened."

Marcia repeated her story, exactly as she had related it to the witch.

"What you have seen is a demon," said Elise, "and the demon has seen you, and knows you."

Marcia gasped.

"I don't mean the demon knows where to find you, but you are in great danger nonetheless." She removed a ring that she was wearing and, taking Marcia's right hand, placed it on her finger. "Do not take this ring off for any reason. It is mine and it will help protect you. You must wear it until I take it back. Remove it for no one else." She paused. "And if anyone asks you whose ring it is, you must tell them it is Elyssa's ring."

Elise released Marcia's hand.

"Whose ring is that?" she asked.

Marcia looked down at her hand.

"This is Elyssa's ring," she replied softly.

"And so you must say when the demon asks you."

A look of horror replaced the smile on Marcia's face, and did not depart when she heard what Elise had next to say.

"The demon seeks you, and will find you in time. I want you to seek him as well. He should not be here. He must not stay here. The sooner he is found, the sooner he will be gone. When you find him, I will know it, and I will come. If you can find the strength, it is my will that you become the hunter."

Elise touched the ring on Marcia's hand.

"Whose ring is that?"

"This is Elyssa's ring," said Marcia. She looked at it where it glistened on her finger. It seemed to pull her eyes to its beauty. When she looked up, Elise was gone.

* * *

When Elise returned to the bar, she walked directly to the locals. "You must leave. You may speak of this only to one another. You may return, but may never bring any other person with you, or send another here."

The men looked at each other. One of them folded his hands on the table and peered up at her over his glasses.

"Now, look here, little lady, we're—"

"You will not speak," said Elise in a monotone. She pointed to the door.

The three men rose together and filed out without a word.

Elise turned to Gavas. "Where is this Old One, this free necromancer? I want you to go to him, and if this is his work, you will bring him to me."

The old man bowed. "I am sorry, Holy One. He is on the other side of the continent."

"Then I must go." She beckoned. "Come tell me the place, then while I am absent, you and your wizards can prepare this door in case the demon should come upon it."

The old man and the young woman walked to the door in the back and spoke quietly. When she passed through, he returned to the others. He beckoned to Errin, forgotten behind the bar.

"Come, Master, lend your strength to this magic we make, for it must be strong indeed."

As Jackson joined the circle the men were forming, he looked bewildered. He peered at Gavas. "You *know* an archwizard?" he said in a subdued voice. "A necromancer?"

It was morning in the garden. Alexander leaned on the stone parapet and let his gaze wander. Far below was the ocean, hidden just now beneath thick fog, making it, he supposed, more of a proposition, or perhaps a hypothesis. . . .

"Necromant!"

He glanced over his shoulder.

"My, my," he said in a dry old voice that sounded like the rustle of silk. He straightened up and turned to face Elise.

"I must be getting careless," he whispered. He gathered the fingers of his right hand and pressed them to his forehead just above the bridge of his nose. He made a sudden gesture at Elise as though swatting a fly. For a moment he gave every appearance of being unaware of her continued presence.

"What," he said, "still here? How unusual. Begone," he said lackadaisically. He peered at her from beneath nonexistent eyebrows. "Look here, sweetie, I don't want to make you uncomfortable. Why don't you just scrim? Or is it scram?" He looked puzzled. "Anyway, don't force me to be dramatic."

"Have you loosed a demon?"

"What?" For one who scarcely spoke above a whisper, Alexander sounded outraged. "Who are you anyway?" He walked closer to Elise. He raised his voice to conversational volume. "Listen," he said, advancing on her, "how would you like to spend the next five hundred years . . ." His voice trailed off. He stopped one yard from his visitor.

"Oh, dear," he said in a very small voice.

"Have you loosed a demon?"

"No, Holy One." Alexander made a deep bow that would have done credit to a far younger man. "Nor have I ever, nor would I."

"But you summon them." It was not a question.

"I do, yes. But rarely, and only for talk. They know so many . . . ," he began. "But of course I needn't tell you."

Elise nodded. "You know the proverb about cats, do you not?"

"Yes, Holy One," he replied, bowing again.

"Who else could accomplish this? This is an old, powerful demon, not one to be summoned by triflers."

"Besides the holy men in the mountains, only one called Gavas, that I know of, but he would not."

"I have just left him," she said. "You know nothing of this?"

"Nothing."

"Then I leave you as I found you."

"But you leave me the knowledge of your visit, Holy One?"

"Of course."

"And may one know the name that . . . ?"

"You have been threatening Elyssana."

The old man looked stricken. "Holy One, I never meant to, I mean, knew . . ."

"That was meant in jest, necromancer. Be at peace; we are not so easily offended."

Alexander bowed. When he looked up, he was alone. He passed through the French doors to his study and went to a lectern where a large book of obvious antiquity was open. "Elyssana," he repeated as he leafed carefully through the brittle pages. He found what he sought and read, stopping at intervals to look through the doors to the spot where Elise had stood.

After a time he returned to the garden wall and stared at the fog below.

Elise stood at the back of the bar. The wizards were gathered at the front door.

"But surely, Gavas," Jackson was saying, "we may do more than hide in here and defend a door. I was reading that demons are only . . ."

Gavas turned and bowed to Elise. The others followed suit.

"Pray finish your instructions, Master Gavas," she said.

"The demon must not have the freedom of the passage," he said, "and until we know what we face, Master Jackson, we dare not risk more. This could be a demon of a hundred names. You must not be tricked into contending with a potent being. Simply hold the door against the demon. Try to perform more, and while you are artificing together, you may be struck with irresistible force."

"Good," said Elise. "These stout wizards, Master Mervin and the rest, can protect the way here, but you know, Gavas, that your place must now be on the streets."

The old man nodded. The others stared at him.

"And I want Master Jackson to go with you; he is local here and must know the city well." She turned to the young wizard.

"Master Jackson, listen to me well. Do not leave the side of your companion for any reason." Jackson bowed, smiling. Elise continued in a voice that, though it was no louder, had suddenly become sharper. "You must understand this clearly, young one." Jackson's smile disappeared. Elise gestured to Gavas. "The arch-wizard cannot protect you from the demon unless he can put his hand on you. Do not stray beyond his reach. Beyond these doors it is only in the ambit of the necromancer's power that you are safe." She turned from the dumbfounded Jackson to Errin.

"Master Errin, this demon has been summoned from Ambermere, probably by a magician or someone else who didn't understand the forces he was using. Go and find the one who has done this thing."

"And return with him, Holy One?"

"No. By no means. You are a wizard. Deal with him as you see fit. This is a wizard's problem; I leave it to you. And I will not be here. I have other paths to tread."

Rogan was beginning to worry. Six days had passed since Daniel had left. He should have easily arrived at Ascroval two days ago. If he had accomplished the rescue that night, the princess could have left the inn at Feathermere on a fast horse by yesterday morning. This, then, was the day on which she should arrive, and she might have managed it by last night if she had made any effort at all.

Still, there were several hours of daylight left. He turned from the window. He was just in time to see his chamber door open quietly. A young man stepped into the room.

"How did you get in here? I have a spell on that door."

Errin closed the door behind him.

"Doesn't that suggest anything to you?" he said. Errin walked to the chalk circle on the floor.

"Keep away from that!"

"Where is the book?"

"What book?" said the magician, looking at the book where it lay open on the table.

Rogan and Errin worked together to efface the circle of chalk. In a quarter of an hour, the stones that had borne it carried only the marks of age and wear.

"All that work," said the old man in a despairing tone.

"All that mischief," said Errin.

"Are you going to take my book?"

"Have a look at it," suggested the wizard.

Rogan walked to the table slowly, as though he was afraid the book would explode or burst into flames. With a suspicious last glance at Errin, he bent over it. He began paging through it, slowly at first, and then with greater speed, until he was flipping through the pages at a terrific rate. He slammed it closed and turned to his visitor.

"Very amusing," he said sourly. "I paid a lot for that book."

"Well," said Errin, "now you can write your own. You have all those blank pages you can fill. If you're really lucky you might be able to sell it." He joined the magician at the table.

"Now tell me exactly where you sent this victim of yours, and what you hoped he would accomplish."

CHAPTER
· 11 ·

Night had fallen by the time Errin had prepared himself for his journey to Ascroval. He had sat, motionless as a brass effigy, through the evening, while Rogan drank wine, paced, and muttered out the window, watching for signs of the return of the princess.

When finally the wizard stood up to leave, Rogan hastened to open the door for him.

"If you encounter the princess on the road, you will see her safely home, will you not?"

"I will not meet your princess on the ways I pass tonight," was the reply.

At dawn the heavy battle gate at Ascroval was raised with strain of cables and creak of wheels. The wood sang and rumbled against the polished stone of its ancient track, ceasing only when the timber braces were laid in place upon their sills of granite.

A short distance away, Errin watched the operation from where he lay with his head pillowed on the bole of a flowering tree. When the keeper and the troopers had completed their work, he rose lightly to his feet and strolled in the direction of the city.

* * *

Remeger stood, dressed only in a nightshirt, before a closet stuffed with gaudy robes and a number of enormous pointed hats. On this day did he want to appear especially magnificent. He could picture the scene now. The room would be filled with the most important aristocrats of the court. The page would announce him in a loud, clear voice that everyone would hear: "The famous and great master wizard Remeger." He himself would be outside the door. He would wait just the right amount of time, then make his entrance to gasps of admiration.

He frowned. He could picture the scene, but not his robes and hat. He paced back and forth in front of the closet, stopping occasionally to pull the hem of a robe across his arm and study the effect.

When he turned at a slight noise and saw the young man standing in the middle of his bedroom, he said "Yeep!" and jumped high enough to win a prize.

"What are you doing in here? Who are you?" he screeched. "I have a spell on that door."

Errin looked genuinely surprised. "That door right there?" he said, indicating the one he had just passed through. "Are you sure?" He shook his head. "At least I noticed the rebuff Rogan had working. It was actually pretty good."

"Rogan? At the palace at Ambermere? He is a mere magician." Remeger struck a pose of supercilious menace, the effect of which was seriously weakened by his bare feet, lumpy ankles, and wrinkled nightshirt. "I warn you now," he intoned, "you are in great peril. I am Remeger the wizard!" He accompanied his announcement with a haughty, wide-eyed glare and much waving of his hands in Errin's direction.

Errin, remembering Jackson's arch-wizardly antics in the bar, dissolved helplessly into a fit of giggles.

Remeger watched with his hands hanging uselessly at his sides. He looked bewildered, like a raving lunatic in the grip of a sudden fit of lucidity.

"In strict point of fact," the young man said when he stopped laughing, "you are Remeger the magician, I would say of about the seventh degree. That's two or three grades below Rogan's rank." The older man opened his mouth to speak, but was stopped by a gesture from Errin.

"You are also Remeger the uncommonly lucky imposter," Errin continued. "Rogan was very nearly successful in summoning a demon." Remeger looked ill. "Guess where he was planning to send it."

The magician slumped into the nearest chair, paying no heed to the carefully cleaned and polished shoes he sat upon.

"Now," said Errin, "you will tell me about the Princess Iris, her companion, and any other person connected with them."

Remeger stared silently from his chair. Errin came and stood over him.

"Remeger," he said in a conversational tone that nonetheless carried a note of menace, "I am not pretending to be a wizard. I am one. I suggest that you not force me to demonstrate my power over you." He turned and walked to the other side of the room.

Remeger sat staring disconsolately at the floor. "The princess is locked in the tower with her companion. The man who climbed the tower is also a prisoner, in an inner room not far from here. Today they are to appear before the king to answer for their crimes."

"Their crimes?"

The magician nodded. "Yes. Treason, for one. Slander of the monarch."

At a questioning look from Errin he elaborated. "The actions of all of them have made it appear that the king holds the princess captive."

"And so he does."

"But to charge the king with such behavior is slander, which is treason, of course. And anyway, the man, the one who climbed the tower, kidnapped the companion of the princess. And then he and the girl were apprehended within the castle, she in disguise, obviously plotting some mischief."

"Rescue of the princess or some such?"

"It would not surprise me," the magician said with a bleak look expressive of world-weary cynicism.

Errin extracted from Remeger the time and place of the meting out of royal justice before turning to the door.

"Remeger, you will see me soon again, and after that meeting you will have cause to remember me." Errin caught the magician's eye. "But now, when I leave this room, you will have no memory of me or of anything that has passed between us."

Remeger leapt to his feet. "No!" he shouted. "Wait! What is to become of me? What are you going to . . .?"

Errin passed through the door without answering.

As Remeger turned to his closet, he noticed the light ballroom shoes crushed on the seat of the chair. He picked them up, turning them over with a puzzled expression. After a moment, he tossed them aside, reflecting that he had much more important things to worry about than shoes.

He walked pensively across the soft carpet. On his face was an expression of intense concentration. Gold, he thought, was a very impressive color, but was it perhaps too gay for proceedings of such gravity? The green robes were sober, yet not without their highlights. . . .

Errin pondered the question of what to do. He did not have the power of a demon, to simply round up the captives and walk out the gate with them. Even an arch-wizard—like Gavas, he thought with a sudden whispered laugh, remembering his own astonishment and Jackson's incredulous stare—would have difficulty managing such a trick without the benefit of fairly elaborate planning. It was one thing, and a fairly easy thing, to get yourself where you wanted to go without interference from guards and the like. It was quite another to do it in a party.

If Elise were there . . . Errin had not allowed himself to think about Elise. "Holy One" was an ambiguous and general term that did not tell him who or what she was, only that she was exalted in some remote degree. But clearly her powers, whether her own, which, it occurred to him, was an almost terrifying thought, or bestowed, were far beyond anything within his ken. Judging from her conversation with Gavas about the other necromancer, she had crossed the continent and returned in moments. The ability to do that sort of thing did not come from wizardry or necromancy, but was found at some higher source of power. Like the demon, she could without doubt simply do what she felt like in this situation.

But it was only the wizard Errin who was here, and he had not much time to prepare himself. He banished idle speculation from his mind and concentrated on the problem at hand. His only legitimate concerns were for the man Rogan had displaced with his botched spell and with the bogus wizard Remeger. Rogan he had dealt with already, though leniently. But even though wizards were not primarily in the business of righting wrongs and correcting monarchs, magic not being required for those chores, Errin thought it only reasonable that he make some effort to relieve the distress of the damsels while he was in the neighborhood.

The problem was that wizards were very good at doing one thing at a time, sometimes quite marvelous things, but not particularly good at juggling many problems at once. Errin could protect himself from virtually any mortal danger, and could be of great help to a single companion. But to do more was going to require trickery, and trickery, though part of the wizard's stock in trade, could be tricky.

Yesterday Marcia had waited for as long as she dared after Elise had left her. She had hoped that Hannah would come back to tell her what to do. But the longer she remained in the little park, the more convinced she became that the demon would find her there if she did not leave.

In the twenty-four hours since, she had been in her apartment with the curtains drawn. More than once she had begun to take the ring from her finger. She wondered if wearing it might draw the monster to her. Perhaps if she were not meddling in these things, not meeting with these strange people, she would not be in the terrible danger that so clearly threatened her.

Witchcraft, she thought. She tossed her head as though to dismiss such a silly thought. Which in itself, she knew, was silly. What of the powder and its indisputable effect on Mr. Figge? And if not that, what of Hannah's disposal of the mugger? And more than any of those things, what of the woman who had come to her in the park? And what of her aura? Marcia was not a skeptic on the subject of auras. Elyssa's aura told her things that she understood, yet could not define, even to herself. Like a word hidden on the tip of the tongue, the message of the aura was known in some deep place, but not open to analysis.

And yet the woman that wore this aura, Elyssa—Elise—had told her she should go out and look for the demon. Elise wanted her, Marcia, to be the hunter. Marcia shuddered. She had a vivid memory of the monster as she had last seen him . . . it. The thing had been bad enough as a man. She would not have cared to face him when he was nothing more than a particularly nasty-looking thug. The idea of facing, not to mention discussing the ownership of the ring she wore, with a demon, whatever that was, was pretty nearly unthinkable.

Except that Marcia had thought of little else since she had left the park. She had been able, surprisingly, to sleep during the night, and had not been troubled by the dreams of the monster. She had dreamed, in fact, of pleasant things that had slipped beyond the reach of memory when she woke up.

She checked the time. She decided to go out for lunch. She would even walk. It would do her good, she thought. It certainly beat hiding under the bed.

By the time she had passed, first the closest restaurant to her building, then her favorite of those nearby, and continued walking to the verge of the downtown area, she had stopped trying to fool herself.

I'm doing it, she thought, then repeated the words aloud, not caring if people saw her talking to herself. *If you can find the strength, it is my will that you become the hunter.* Those were the words Elyssa had spoken to her. Marcia looked down at the ring, thin against her finger. A flood of misgivings engulfed her. It was a little, ordinary ring of heaven-only-knew-what metal. For all she knew it would turn her finger green. She raised it closer to her eyes, stopping on the sidewalk to look at it. It was, she decided, a beautiful ring. Small and plain, but beautiful nonetheless. "This is Elyssa's ring," she said as she began walking again.

She had lunch, finally, at a little place in a declining neighborhood. It was a bar and grill left over from two generations ago, had a great deal of ramshackle charm, and served food that was very nearly inedible.

After her meal, she turned in the direction of her apartment and took a different route on the return trip. Back home, she read her mail, such as it was, took a long soaking bath, and then followed it with an official nap—in bed, wearing pajamas, blinds drawn. She drifted into sleep conscious of the ring on her finger.

She awoke to the thought of food. "Good," she murmured as she got out of bed. She was glad she had slept the afternoon away. She opened the blinds and looked down on the early-evening traffic while she dressed.

Marcia got a light sweater from a drawer. It was summer, but she expected to be out late, and the nights were usually cool. She got her biggest handbag from the closet. As she refolded the sweater to fit in the bag, she felt as though she were watching a stranger. This skinny woman in the slacks and flat shoes, taking a sweater so she wouldn't get cold walking lonesome streets of the city after midnight, this couldn't be Marcia.

She felt a strange combination of elation and fear. The feeling was probably, she imagined, just what she would feel if she were setting out to commit a robbery or take part in a military operation. Except that this was more like setting out to be the target of a robbery or raid, she reminded herself. She forced herself to conjure up a mental picture of the monster as she had last seen him. She held the image in her mind, concentrating on it and on holding back the accompanying sense of panic.

She ate a quick meal in a restaurant not far from her office. In the taxi on the way to the street where she had seen the monster before, Marcia realized she had no idea what to do if she found him. She didn't have a chance to experiment, because the man was nowhere to be seen. The driver categorically refused to drive down the alleys as she timidly asked. Marcia watched him adjust his rearview mirror so that he could keep his eye on her in the backseat.

"You got a destination, toots?"

"No," she said, embarrassed. What must the man think of her? "Just, um, just let me out here," she said.

"I hope you find what you're lookin' for," he shouted after her as she crossed the street.

Marcia felt, and was, completely out of place on this tough and ugly street. All the other women in sight were either prostitutes or bag ladies. But this was the logical place to begin. She walked along, trying to behave naturally, as though she were accustomed to spending evenings in such surroundings. A block ahead she saw a scandalously dressed girl lounging by a parking meter. Marcia picked up her pace a bit. It only made sense that a streetwalker would know the neighborhood regulars. Marcia had never knowingly talked to a prostitute before. She was working up her courage when she saw the aura.

It was the original dark pall that had marked the man in the leather jacket. She recognized it as easily as she would have recognized his face or shape, except that she saw she was clearly mistaken. The man slumped against the building was a sick old wino. As she walked past, he stared at her with eyes that were glazed and dull.

When she was not more than a few steps from the prostitute, who appeared to be in her mid-teens, a car pulled up. The girl wobbled hazardously from the curb on her impossible heels and leaned into the window. As Marcia walked past, she was inserting her tightly wrapped torso into the front seat.

Marcia looked back at the wino. He was struggling to his feet, clawing at the wall for support. She started to walk back in his direction, watching him stumble his way up the street. As she crossed an empty intersection against the light, she saw him enter an alley and disappear from view. When she reached it, she peered into the shadowy way. She did not intend to walk down any alleys without Hannah, but she thought the man could not have gone far. It had suddenly come to her that if the big man with the sneer and the tattoos could become a demon, then the wino could be the thug. Either it was all absurd and impossible, or none of it was. Marcia reminded herself that if she was to function, she was going to have to change her ideas about rational thought and what was and was not possible.

She took a few steps into the shadows of the alley. She wondered how a man that was barely able to keep his feet could have gone far enough to be out of sight. Feeling rather brave, even daring, she made herself go a little farther as she peered ahead looking for the old man. Marcia felt an echo of the carefree spirit with which she had followed Hannah on their recent expedition through this place and others just as bad. The two of them had been completely free of constraints that were matters of unreflective habit with Marcia.

She heard the noise behind her too late. Before she could move, a hand covered her mouth with the force of a blow. She could taste dirt and sweaty skin as the rough fingers pulled her lips painfully out of shape and wedged against her nose. She was yanked backward, felt her heels bouncing on the pavement, saw dark walls rush past. Her mother's warnings seemed to scream inside her head.

When she was released, she nearly fell, but was caught and set ungently on her feet. Her vision cleared; her heart began to pound. The man before her was not, as she had momentarily imagined, the wino who in any event could scarcely drag himself along. Nor had she been seized by the demon, which she only thought of after she could see it wasn't so. Breathing in her face was a hard-looking man dressed in rumpled clothes and wearing an angry frown.

He pushed her roughly against a brick wall. When he tried to take her handbag, and she did not immediately let go but held on to it in a stupid daze, he smacked her, knocking the back of her head sharply against the bricks.

"Jewelry," he said in a quiet, businesslike tone. He might have been a surgeon asking for a scalpel.

Marcia shook her head.

"Watch."

She held out her arm. He dropped the watch into his pocket. He took her wallet out of her bag, removed the cash and credit cards, and tossed it over his shoulder. He glanced toward the street, then began pulling things from the bag and throwing them to the ground. Marcia stared at her sweater lying crumpled at his feet. Her eyes filled with tears. She was trembling. She felt a sick fear crawling inside her.

She hardly felt it when he slapped her again.

"The ring," he said. "Take it off."

Marcia looked at him stupidly. The man grabbed her wrist and yanked her arm up. The back of her hand rapped against the bridge of her nose. She felt his fingers on the ring, twisting at her finger. With a convulsive movement, she balled her hand into a tight fist.

She did not feel, but only heard, the angry scream that seemed to originate at the balls of her feet. She had the sudden vision of making a noise loud enough to knock down a wall. The mugger jumped away from her, raw shock in his face. Marcia felt the fear inside her changing to cold, hard anger. She had a sudden sense of expanded time, as though things were happening very slowly. The clenched hand that protected Elyssa's ring felt like the carved fist of a statue, impossible to open.

She saw the man's knobby fist as he drew it back with implausible languor.

"You stupid bitch! I'm gonna smash your stupid face in!"

She watched his look of furious concentration and his approaching fist. She wondered if she was seeing things in microscopic detail and glacial speed because this was a deathblow, and the last sight she was to see. The fingers and knuckles were growing, filling her vision. She stared, fascinated by the sight, then moved her head out of the way in time to observe the details of the collision between the fist and the brick wall.

In undistorted time, the man turned quickly to her with an expression of offended surprise that vanished from his face as suddenly as it had appeared.

She looked indifferently on his suffering as he screamed and rolled on the worn bricks that paved the alley. She coldly retrieved her belongings from his pocket. The handbag, sweater, and other things were too filthy to bother with. She picked up her wallet and brushed it off. Marcia wondered if the deep anger that she felt would ever entirely leave her again. As she stepped around the writhing man, she had to restrain herself from spitting on him.

Back on the lighted street, she was not able to loosen her fist until she made a conscious effort to do so. She rubbed her aching hand, feeling the ring secure at her knuckle. Of the few cabs she saw, none would stop for her. By the time she had walked to her apartment, she was too tired to undress. She fell across the bed with her clothing and her bruises and slept till morning.

It required little attention to cook up a spell for entering the audience chamber. Errin wandered in with the titled gentlemen that were taking part in the business. No eye of guard or noble rested on him; glances slid from his features, unable to stop. Anyone counting the occupants of the room would have been able to reach an accurate total. But if he had then listed the names of those present, and counted the list, he would have met with a puzzling discrepancy.

Most of those in the room had entered by a door from a great hallway, some few from inner doors. From one of them now entered a page.

"The great and famous master wizard Remeger," he piped in a boyish soprano. A few nobles glanced in his direction, then resumed their quiet conversations. Errin watched the door, but saw no sign of the magician. After enough time had passed that his entrance seemed unconnected with the announcement, Remeger, wearing a fiercely dignified scowl, made a gradual entrance, first a sleeve, then a boot, and finally the entire personage, adorned in a robe of a blinding color for which Errin did not know a name, and a hat the size of a small building.

He stalked across the room looking neither left nor right and settled himself in solitary glory behind the throne. In a few moments another man, dressed modestly, entered quietly by the same door. He walked to the throne and stood next to it.

The king was announced by a herald who possessed a deafening basso that he inflicted on his auditors with evident relish.

"His most puissant highness, monarch of all Ascroval," he intoned, raising his voice at each measured syllable, "protector of the poor"—a bejeweled duke standing next to Errin laughed into his hand, feigning a cough—"father to every maiden, benefactor . . ."

"Enough," said the king, breaking in as he seated himself. "We're all friends here."

The herald bowed deeply and backed out of the room. Errin restrained an urge to tangle his feet in a spell. When the door had closed behind him, the king directed a stern gaze in Errin's direction.

"Just how is it," said the king, "that you laugh, Mikkermill? I do defend the poor. So do we all." The royal gaze wandered the room. "We see that they are defended from the dangers of accumulating too much money." The king rushed to end his sentence and was overtaken with laughter almost before he could finish. Every nobleman laughed with the king, and none stopped before him.

"And as for being a father to every maiden," the monarch went on, "perhaps that is saying too much, but I do give my attention to every maiden who merits it. My undivided attention." The king laughed uproariously. By some coincidence, so did everyone else in the room, save the three members of the royal guard, who could not have been more silent if they had been stuffed or carved soldiers.

"The royal wit is sharp today, Your Highness," said the man next to the throne.

"And when is it not, Femigris? As my adviser, you can testify to my love of gaiety, of a light heart."

"Indeed, Highness. So can we all."

"Well, let us see if this doesn't prove diverting." The king nodded to the guards. "Bring in the prisoner."

CHAPTER
· **12** ·

Daniel was brought from his cell by half a dozen taciturn guards. They halted before a door in a dim hallway and knocked. When the door opened, Daniel was escorted in by two of the soldiers. There were twenty or thirty men in the room. Scropp, he noticed, was not among them. In fact, the only person he recognized was the wizard, dressed in an outfit that in its inflated grandeur would have satisfied the most exalted leader of the most childish fraternal order ever known.

The king was, by comparison, dressed conservatively, though the cost of his silks and jewelry could have fed and housed a peasant family for a generation.

Daniel was brought to a position in front of the king. He did not resist when he was seized by four guards and placed, not gently, facedown on the floor. He lay there listening to the laughter from the gallery behind him. When it subsided, the king spoke.

"A very pretty curtsey. Let him rise." Daniel got to his feet.

The king stared at him, looking him up and down.

"So this is the kidnapper?"

"It is, Your Highness," agreed his adviser.

The king had not taken his eyes from Daniel.

"How is it," he said, "that you came to my castle to commit this vicious crime?"

Daniel knew he had a hand consisting of only one card. Folding was not an option, and he couldn't see a bluff in the situation. He played his hand.

Having thought it out beforehand, he was able to answer the king's question with admirable brevity. And that is precisely what he did. He told the king in outline how and why he had come to scale the tower wall, leaving out little that had passed before Modesty's rescue, and most of what had happened after it, and emphasizing the fact that if he failed, the demon would be sent.

The king turned to the wizard.

"Well?" he said.

The magical one more curtsied than bowed, being encumbered by his headgear.

"Preposterous, Your Highness. Not even I would call a demon. Not that I do not know how to," he said with an ominous glower, "but that is reserved for necromancers. Rogan, the Obscure, he styles himself, is a mere magician. I doubt he has the skill to summon a rat to a garbage heap."

His remark was greeted with uproarious laughter from the king and gentlemen of the court. Finally everyone was quiet, except for the wizard, who seemed unable to overcome the effect of his own witticism until a pointed glare from the monarch silenced him.

"You must think we are children here at Ascroval," the king said, returning his attention to his prisoner. "You think to frighten us with tales of demons and necromancy. But when I pronounce your sentence . . . and your punishment, you will alter your view, I believe." The king raised his eyes to look beyond Daniel to his gathered gentlemen.

None was giving him closer attention than the smallish chap whose face he couldn't quite make out, but whose eyes trapped his for an instant with a gaze of concentrated intensity. For a king, Razenor was a man of few words, but he felt suddenly that this was perhaps an occasion upon which one might indulge in a bit of eloquence. Some slight display of philosophy might not be out of place.

"Patience, nobles. I know you are angry," he said. A contagion of frowns and scowls spread through the room. "But justice will prevail here, as it always does in the end, I promise you." The royal finger pointed to Daniel. "This miscreant will pay for the crimes that have infuriated you." The king turned to his adviser.

"Femigris, is this not the criminal who abducted the companion to the princess, our guest here at Ascroval?"

"Your Highness is correct, as always."

"And has he not broken our laws, insulted our sovereignty, and violated the security of our royal guest, setting her life at risk?"

"He has, Majesty."

"Did he not, under cover of darkness, creep to our walls, like a duck, to rob us?"

A puzzled expression crossed the face of the adviser.

"Just so, Your Royal Highness," he said after hesitating the space of a breath.

"But our walls are not made of feathers, are they, Femigris?" Razenor raised his eyebrows and favored his adviser with a smile that managed to be both condescending and conspiratorial.

"Indeed they are not, Your Most Royal Highness," replied the adviser, sure of his ground.

"Nay, our laws are stone," proclaimed the king. He paused for a moment, staring over the heads of the assembled aristocrats. "That is, our walls are like our laws . . . and vice versa, so to speak. That's it. The wall is a law."

"Your Majesty exceeds the philosophers," said Femigris.

"As the ducks exceed the fishwives, wouldn't you say, Femigris?"

"I . . ." The adviser cleared his throat. He pulled a handkerchief from his tastefully embroidered sleeve. "I suppose I might, Your Majesty," he said without great conviction.

"Then must I not, bound by the law as I am, pronounce the just sentence of that law, that all may know the king is not a fishwife?"

"Certainly not. I mean, you must, Your Highness, and are not, too . . . either . . ."

"Well, then," continued the king, "is it not meet the fishwife wait upon the duck?"

"Ah," said Femigris with a panicky smile, "I see what Your Majesty means. Of course."

"What?" roared the king.

"I mean, of course not, Your Puissant Majesty, as all must agree." Femigris looked at the stony visages of the nobles out of the corner of his eye.

"The ducks and tailors all must yield to sausages," announced the king with a wink.

"Your . . . Your Majesty's wit is ever apt," said Femigris, emitting a series of rapid yelps meant as laughter. He sent a wild-eyed look to the wizard, who seemed to be studying the toe of his left boot.

The king rose, pointing at Daniel.

"All the bells of all the ducks will waken the fishwives with their sausages, lest the yards of tailors shall be heated," he intoned solemnly.

The silence that followed was intolerable, especially to Femigris, who finally spoke in a flood of words.

"Sometimes the . . . the . . . the . . . the . . . royal wit goes beyond the ability of lesser men to fathom. Your Majesty must forgive us our mean abilities."

The king turned a withering stare on Femigris.

"Previously!" he hissed, with a dangerously darkening eye.

Femigris groaned.

The king stamped his foot like a gigantic out-of-temper six-year-old.

"There are ducks in every chair of contrast!" he screamed. He turned to the soldiers.

"Slim ducks will be entered by the portico," he shouted in a tone of angry command.

The guards, left in doubt, did not move.

The king snatched a mailed glove from his belt and aimed a dangerous swipe at the nearest soldier. The soldier remained motionless as the blow missed his cheek but not the king's, where it landed with enough force to draw blood. Razenor cried out. He dropped the glove and brought his hand to his injured face. With a howl of rage, he drew his dagger and raised it over his head to strike at the trooper, then looked up to see the point turned in his direction. He moaned, dropped the knife to the floor, and collapsed onto his throne.

"The ducks," he said, then continued in an inaudible mutter.

The duke that had stood next to Errin pushed forward.

"Hold the prisoner," he said to the guards as he joined Femigris beside the throne. Others came forward, standing nearer to or farther from their deranged monarch as their rank and nerve dictated. As the king remained quiescent, the crowd near him grew. Daniel watched everything in the room, particularly the small man who was deep in conversation with Remeger in a corner. Daniel thought it odd, but he couldn't really focus on the fellow well enough to get a look at his face. The face of the wizard, on the other hand, was plainly visible beneath his monumental hat, and it was the face of a badly frightened man.

"Gentlemen," called the duke, "please be calm. We must not allow this momentary . . . indisposition to deflect us."

"It is a spell!" said Remeger portentously, joining the crowd.

Femigris looked up. "Oh, I wondered where you were," he said, using the diplomat's gift of mixing sweet courtesy and naked contempt in his voice. "Well, spell or not, and that's your department anyway, the duke and I have thought of a strategy to deal with this little . . ." He trailed off.

"In any event," he continued brightly, "this is not a kingdom where learning is unknown." He produced a pen and paper and placed them in the hands of the king.

"Please resume your customary places, nobles, and the king will make his will known despite this trickery or whatever it is, which," he continued with a hard look at Remeger, "we will soon be masters of. Please write your wishes down, Your Most Gracious Majesty."

The king, though still bleeding from his cheek, gave some appearance of being in command of himself. He did not try to speak, but scribbled away with the look of intense concentration. When he had completed his message, he handed it with laudable calm to his adviser.

Femigris struck a pose before the throne and raised the paper with a flourish, casting a stern eye on Daniel before beginning to read.

"The ducks," he said with an air of triumph followed quickly by a close squint at the document. The king smiled and waved at him to continue. Femigris cleared his throat. ". . . are watching in the porticoes of the . . ." He was interrupted by laughter. He quickly raised his eyes to Daniel, whose face presented a picture of perfect sober calm. The king leapt to his feet. The duke once again came forward.

"Nay, nay, Royal cousin, it is more trickery." The king sat down slowly. The duke approached the throne. "You understand, Your Majesty?" The king nodded.

"Aha!" cried the duke. "Now we shall see how far these tricks will get the tricksters." He bowed in the general direction of the king. "I believe I know Your Majesty's intentions concerning this matter." The duke snapped his fingers at the guards to get their attention. "Will Your Majesty permit me to speak for him in this matter? If I speak Your Majesty's mind, you may approve my words with a nod." The king nodded eagerly.

With a condescending smile at Femigris, the duke replaced him beside the king. He straightened up to his full height and beamed at his audience.

"I am a relative of our king, and though some"—he emphasized the word—"may be unaware of it, we speak sometimes of matters of state. It is not only in the halls of power that consultations are . . ."

His preface was interrupted by the king, who began kicking the base of the throne with his heel and gesturing for his noble relative to get on with it.

"To the matter at hand, then." He smiled at the monarch, avoiding the complacent look of the adviser. He extended an accusing arm in Daniel's direction.

"Speaking for His Majesty, most puissant lord of Ascroval, protector . . ." At the sound of the royal heel, he stopped in midsentence as though he had planned to all along. He cleared his throat. His arm still was aimed at Daniel.

"Subject to his approval I speak thus for the king: First, you are not a fishwife, nor a skillet either, and so the ducks"—he paused as though for effect—"may not crow in chorus for your bootlace." The duke turned to the king and was gratified to see him nodding enthusiastically. He shifted his complacent gaze to

Femigris, but the little smile that sat upon the lips of the adviser told him that all was not well. He reviewed in his mind the words he had just spoken. His face fell.

"I didn't mean the ducks," he said hurriedly, appealing to his audience. "It was the bootlace that the fishwives, you see, were . . ."

Femigris stepped in front of him and faced the aristocrats.

"Anyone else?" he said with a smirk.

The silence that followed the invitation was broken, finally, by Remeger.

"This is the work of a mage too powerful to be challenged," he said.

The adivser whirled to face him. "Where is your counterspell? You call yourself a wizard. It is time you earned your keep."

Remeger removed his hat. He held it at his side for a moment, then let it drop to the floor.

"I am undone," he said. "My powers, what powers I have been permitted to keep, are inadequate to any such battle. It would be like a lapdog fighting a mastiff. From now on, my magic will be performed at fairs and markets." He slipped out of his heavy robe. It fell to the floor by his hat. "My last duty is to give you the terms dictated to me."

"Dictated by whom, and when?" said the adviser furiously. "I see no mage."

Remeger straightened up and pointed a trembling finger at Femigris.

"Fool!" he cried. "While the duke stood and prattled like an idiot about ducks and bootlaces, the mage was here, in this room among us, speaking to me. You may do battle with him if you like. Defy him, if you wish. In a week, the court may all converse together of ducks and fishwives." He strode to the door in his undergarments. No one attempted to stop him. Before leaving, he addressed them.

"These are the terms: This prisoner is to be freed at once, set at liberty outside the keep. The two maidens in the tower are to be escorted, with all the courtesies due to royalty, to Ambermere, where you are free to employ any lies or other tools of diplomacy you may care to. For every day they remain captive, the king will be a week in his present condition. And hear this: If any prisoner comes to harm, there will be a daily funeral at this court until the last survivor must dig a hole for himself to fall into. So I was told by the mage. Tempt him if you like." He turned and left.

The discussion was brief. Daniel and the guards waited in the hall. When Femigris emerged, he did not look at Daniel. He addressed the guards. "Escort him from the castle. Do not allow him to come to any harm, and under no circumstances allow him back inside."

In a matter of minutes, Daniel was alone in the street before the gate. The guards had told him that this was where the ladies would emerge, but not before a proper escort could be assembled.

Daniel hurried to the inn to settle the bill and gather his belongings. His plan was to be absent from the gate for no more than five minutes. During the period of his captivity, he had thought of little else besides Modesty. He now knew what it was to ache for the sight of someone.

When his door opened, he thought for a moment that somehow she had been freed already and come to find him. His visitor, though, was a small sandy-haired fellow that he thought looked familiar. It wasn't the face, but the size of the man and the way he dressed that Daniel recognized. It was not until he began to lose consciousness that it came to him that this must be the mage.

He had an interminable dream in which he and the mage walked in a shadowy landscape where everything was distorted in the way objects are when viewed under water. They were surrounded by a palpable, muffling silence in which no thing was audible, not breath or footfall or sigh of wind. Sights of the everyday world—trees, hills, villages—appeared and disappeared in the aqueous atmosphere, passing with a noiseless haste suggestive of flight. After hours of tiresome travel, Daniel realized they were in Ambermere, or some city so like it as to be a twin. The tile roofs, stone lintels, and brightly painted doors were as he remembered them from his single day in the city. They entered a tavern, still enveloped in the silence of the dream, and passed through a door in the back to a room almost completely dark. Leaving that room, they were again in a tavern, but a different one. It was there that they were joined by others, and there that his dream became sleep.

When Daniel awoke to the sound of jackhammers and traffic, his first thought was of his sanity. The ceiling he stared at was without question the one in his apartment bedroom. The sounds he heard from outside were without question not the sounds of Ascroval or Ambermere. With a paroxysmic effort of will he forced himself to remain in the bed. He would not yield to the impulse to run wildly around the apartment confirming the evidence of his senses. Nor would he admit, yet, the despairing thoughts of Modesty that clamored to take him over.

He reviewed last night's dream in his mind. It seemed that rather than an imaginary magical journey from Ascroval to Ambermere, it had been an actual journey, though equally magical. He was determined to think about his situation in a coldly logical way, regardless of how idiotic it might appear to be on the surface. It was like betting one hundred dollars for a chance to win a two-thousand-dollar pot when the odds were nineteen to one against you. The fact that something seemed crazy didn't mean it was.

Rogan the Obscure, in whose existence he was not prepared to disbelieve, must have found a way to get him back home. Daniel closed his eyes. He reviewed the events since his encounter with the demon. He counted the number of days he had been "away." He knew, was utterly certain, that those days had actually elapsed, and that the events that he recalled had actually occurred. Either that or he was as insane as any inhabitant of any asylum in the history of lunacy.

He got up and looked around his familiar bedroom. He was dressed as he had been for his journey to Rogan's apartments, wearing his father's old Saint Christopher medal and nothing else. He saw no sign of the clothing he had been wearing in Ascroval. From the window he could see the crowded street below, with its impatient traffic and inevitable contingent of the city's corps of jackhammerers. He wandered to the kitchen. Opening the refrigerator released the smell of soured milk. In the living room he turned his television on and tuned it to the weather channel to see the continuously displayed date and time in a box at the top of the screen.

He had been gone ten days. He slumped wearily to the couch and rested his head in his hands. Of all this—the magic, the supernatural beings, the other world—only one thing seemed to him to be of the slightest importance. Dozens of images of Modesty crowded into his mind.

After thirty seconds had passed, he got up and turned off the droning television. He strode back to the bedroom and began to dress. A climber in trouble dare not hang on a rock thinking about his predicament and hoping help will come, for while he hopes and worries, his strength ebbs away and he loses the ability to help himself. It did not seem to Daniel that he was in any position to wait for help to arrive.

His only connection with Modesty's world was through the demon. Rogan, or someone, had found a way to return Daniel. If they had not already dealt with the demon, they would certainly be working on it. If the demon was not already back in the Lower Regions, he might well be catching the next bus.

Daniel did not check his mail on the way out. He hit the sidewalk at something approaching a run, looking for cabs as he turned his steps in the direction of the harbor.

A large black car with heavily tinted windows rolled slowly to the curb next to him. The back door opened. Daniel did not recognize the man that beckoned to him.

"Okay, Danny boy, get into the car," he said with a smile that was not meant to cheer.

Daniel had to forcibly remove his mind from his lover, the demon, magic, and the practitioners of magic. He stopped and looked into the car stupidly.

"Come on, kid. Hurry it up."

When Daniel remembered his trouble with Charlie, it was as though he were recalling something from years ago.

"No time," he said, starting to walk again. "Tell Charlie I'll call him."

The car followed him along the curb.

"I said get in!" The man sounded like someone who was about to lose his temper.

Daniel was not in a charitable or kindly frame of mind and he

did not have time to waste with Charlie and his . . . employees.
He vowed to himself that if the guy came after him, he was going to hit him as he was getting out of the car, and with as mur-
derous a blow as he could manage. It only made sense to treat
this as a threat to his life, especially considering that it might actually be one. In any event, he was not going to allow anyone to
keep him from trying to get to Modesty. Probably for the first
time in his life he was prepared to make an honest effort to hurt
someone. He faced the car.

The man was pointing a snub-nosed pistol at him. Daniel
found he didn't much care. His mind was entirely focused on
finding the demon without being ripped apart like a kitten in a
kennel. Guns just made little holes in you.

"See this, Danny? This is a thirty-eight. A chopper. Now get
in!"

Daniel approached the car. The man smiled and made room
for him on the seat. Daniel grasped the door. He nodded toward
the gun.

"Shove it," he said without much feeling, and then slammed
the car door and strode off. A moment later the car roared past
him, cutting across traffic to glide down a one-way street the
wrong way.

But confident as Daniel had been that Charlie had no immediate intention of having him gunned down on the street, he
knew the next car that came for him would get him. It was just a
matter of sending a couple of extra men.

When his cab dropped him off on the block where he had first
seen the demon, he called Charlie from the first pay phone he
saw.

"You got a lot of nerve, kid." The way Charlie said it didn't
make it sound like a compliment.

"That's because I'm desperate."

"Who cares? What I want to know is where's my daughter?"

"Roxy?"

"You gonna play dumb with me?"

"Charlie, listen to me. I've been away for over a week. The
last time I saw Roxy—"

"Kid, if you're not at my place in a half an hour, I'm gonna send some people after you which you'll be sorry you met them."

Charlie hung up without waiting for a reply.

Daniel was convinced that he was in a race against time. If someone thought it was worth the trouble to put him back where he belonged, they would certainly be concerned about removing the demon. He couldn't know when, or how, he was returned to his apartment, but it was sometime during the last eight hours.

The demon, in the form of the oversize guy with the leather vest, was not difficult to describe. Daniel learned immediately that his name was Ferris. Keeping an eye out for big black cars with opaque windows, he hurried through the neighborhood asking everyone when they had seen him last. "You a cop?" was the most common response, but he did learn that Ferris had not been seen since someone named Marsh had been killed, more than likely by Ferris, according to most people on the street who had any opinion at all, which was not many.

Daniel was attempting to talk to a woman who might have been anywhere between the ages of thirty-five and eighty, and who muttered to herself while he spoke, then surprised him by answering intelligibly.

"Probably dead," she said. "That would be my guess."

He gave her a couple of dollars and was walking away when a man with his right hand wrapped in a cast hurried up to him.

"You looking for Ferris?" he said. Daniel told him he was.

"I got hurt on the job," the man said. "Now I can't work."

Daniel didn't care; he had lost all interest in other people's troubles. It occurred to him to wonder where Roxy might be. If he wanted to think about anyone else, at least it would be someone he knew. He had a sudden, unbidden image of Roxy slouching on a couch watching television, growing fainter as the hours devoted to vapidity passed, and finally fading to complete invisibility.

"That's too bad," he said finally.

"Yeah, some woman . . . some bitch just . . . just . . ." The man trailed off. "Then she comes down here again," he continued, "and just looks right at me like I'm nothing!"

"What about Ferris?" asked Daniel. He didn't feel he had time to watch this guy work himself into a frenzy.

"That's what she was down here asking about." The man was practically shouting. "Do you know her? Do you know her?" he demanded.

Daniel's sense of urgent excitement was greatly tempered by fear. He was going on the assumption that there was a good chance that anyone looking for Ferris was a magician or wizard or something like that. But had they already found him? Had the race ended before he had had a chance to enter?

"Someone was looking for Ferris? When?"

"Right the day after she messed my hand up. She looked right at me. Just like I'm just nothing."

"So when was that?" said Daniel, forcing himself to keep from sounding anxious.

"Do you know her?"

Daniel got out his wallet and found a twenty-dollar bill.

"I don't know her," he said, holding the money in front of him, "and I don't know Ferris. When did she come here?"

The man looked confused. "I already told you," he said. "To-day. A few hours ago. It was just last night I got hurt. Last night." He reached for the twenty. "My hand hurts bad," he said wearily.

Daniel felt a great sense of relief. He couldn't have hoped for more. A few hours ago. He pulled the bill back.

"What about Ferris?" he said.

The man looked at him suspiciously. "You going to give me the money? I'm losing a lot of work on account of your friend. She owes me a lot."

"What about Ferris?"

"I saw him last night. This morning, really. He didn't even look at me, and he was right across the street."

Daniel gave the man the money. "There?" he said, pointing across the street to a strip joint.

"No. It was a couple of blocks from here, where I have a room." He told Daniel the address. "You see him, you tell him Jaybee saw him. Tell him I got hurt. He didn't even look at me."

"So how did you get hurt?"

The man looked at the sidewalk. "I don't want to talk about

it. That stupid bitch!" He put his good hand on the cast as though to protect it. "She took things out of my pocket when I was laying there in the alley. She didn't even care that I was hurt. You know how many bones I broke in my hand?" He saw that Daniel was holding another bill, a ten.

"Okay," he said. He took the money between his thumb and forefinger. Daniel held on to his end.

The man sighed. "I was just going to hit her . . . slap her, like. She was giving me a hard time." He looked at Daniel as though he wanted to make sure he understood. "She screamed at me. But it was so loud, it hurt my ears. You know, she could damage someone's hearing," he said piously, as though he were in the habit of concerning himself with the general welfare. He sounded like a grade-school teacher warning of the terrible dangers of pencil throwing.

"I used to box," he said, "you know, in a gym, for a little money. Help out, like. I know how to punch, and I know how people move. This bitch, it wasn't natural. She should have been nailed, and then she wasn't there." His voice was that of a man describing a tragic accident. "I hit a brick wall with my fist," he said with great feeling.

Daniel let go of the ten.

"So what did the doctor say? How long before you can get back to punching women in alleys?"

He noted, as he walked away, that the guy looked positively hurt.

Daniel spent a little more time trying to find out something about the woman who was looking for Ferris. She, not the demon, was the one he needed most to find.

A teenage prostitute in clothes so tight they distorted her figure told him as much as anyone, which was nearly nothing. When he left in a cab, he knew that a skinny woman who looked like a schoolteacher had been asking about Ferris a few hours before.

He had the driver drop him near a downtown car rental agency. In a few minutes he was driving to the place where Jaybee had seen Ferris.

After cruising the city streets for hours, Daniel napped

through rush hour at a comfortable hotel that was not downtown and not fashionable. He didn't want to meet anyone who might be looking for him. He had supper sent to his room. By early evening he was back in the car, with a full tank of gas and the night ahead of him.

CHAPTER

· 13 ·

The first thing Daniel did was to make a complete circuit of the places most likely to harbor the demon. The young prostitute he had talked to before was still at the same corner. When he stopped and rolled down the window, she came and leaned in. Daniel had the distinct impression that she didn't recognize him.

"Looking for something?" she asked with a pout that made her look like a caricature of a harlot. To Daniel's eye, she seemed more like a ninth-grader dressed up in someone else's clothes.

"I'm still looking for Ferris and the lady that was asking about him."

Her expression changed as though she had just that moment managed to focus her eyes on him.

"Oh, yeah," she said without discernible enthusiasm. She eyed Daniel up and down.

"Don't you want me to get in?" she asked.

Daniel ignored the question.

"Have you seen them?" he asked.

"Who?"

"Ferris, or the woman that looks like a schoolteacher?"

"Oh. No." She started to leave.

"Wait a minute," said Daniel.

She paused and looked at him, adjusting her pout to maximum power.

"Get in," he said.

She was more expensive than he would have imagined, but he had withdrawn plenty of cash from an automatic teller at the hotel, and was not in a mood to haggle. She rode with him while he combed the streets and alleys. He would have no trouble recognizing Ferris, but he had never seen the woman. And the woman was the one he was most interested in finding, since she was clearly some sort of magician, presumably from the other world.

If he found the demon, after all, he could scarcely just walk up to him and ask for his help. He had an admittedly vague plan of finding him and then keeping him in sight until something developed. Besides locating the pursuers, that was the best idea he had been able to come up with.

If it came to it, he thought he might approach Ferris if it were in some public place. He knew the demon talked; maybe he would tell him something. Daniel, after all, had diverted the spell from him. There was clearly a way, or ways, to get to Ambermere from here, but once the demon and his presumed pursuers were gone from the city, Daniel would never find those ways.

From time to time as they drove, the girl, Brenda-Lee she called herself, spelling it for him, would reach over and put her hand on his arm or his thigh and suggest that since he had paid, they should do more than ride around in a car.

When he replied, finally, that she was too young for him, she asked the perennial question of those still young enough to wish themselves older.

"How old do you think I am?"

"I'm afraid to guess," he had said. "Keep looking for the schoolteacher."

Marcia was getting very tired. She had spent hours in taxicabs during the afternoon before deciding that anything, including walking, would be an improvement. It was extremely tedious to sit in the backseats of dirty cars and ride up and down the noisy, congested streets of the city. The drivers could not contain their curiosity, and insisted, when she would say no more than that she was looking for someone, upon making guesses concerning her errand. That had finally convinced her that, lacking a driver's license, she must resort to walking.

Her last driver had held his peace for so long that she had begun to feel positively grateful. Then, at a red light he had turned in his seat and looked at her with great compassion.

"It's your husband, right? How long has he been gone?"

His eyes were sad, as though he could not help sharing the hurt he was convinced she was suffering. Marcia looked at his large wrinkled face; his rather clownlike, bulbous nose. It was not difficult to imagine that his sympathy was entirely genuine, but answering him, she found, was simply too much trouble.

"I'll just get out here," she had said, unable to suppress the feeling that she was guilty of shocking rudeness.

When night had fallen, she had stopped at a modest restaurant despite her lack of appetite. She relished the rest, if not the food. She had lingered, trying to talk herself into going home. But a strange will to persist asserted itself, convincing her to look around just a little more. It was as though she were forcing herself not to shrink from continuing her search in the dark. Since her experience with the mugger, she had stopped giving any thought to that sort of danger. Not that she felt herself to be immune, but the normal hazards of the city seemed to have become irrelevant.

Now she was feeling numb. She walked the dark streets of a section of deteriorated houses and small apartment buildings. She would go, she decided, back to the street where so many things had happened—where she had first seen the demon, where the man had tried to rob her, where she had started the day's search. Then she would allow herself to go home, where she would sleep and sleep and sleep.

She turned at the next corner in the direction of the avenue one long block away. From an alley two and a half blocks behind her, a big man in a leather vest and T-shirt shambled out of the shadows and stared after her with hungry yellow eyes.

Daniel turned off the avenue onto the sleazy street where Brenda-Lee's corner was. He dropped her off and watched as she wiggled her immature body back to her spot. She turned and waved, shooting him a parting pout and lowering her eyelids as though trying for a part in a kiddie-porn movie. Daniel waved and made a U-turn, ready to continue looking.

Up the street he saw a woman hailing a cab. She was skinny, looked to be over thirty-five, and by the standards of the street was definitely dressed like a schoolteacher.

Daniel blew the horn and cranked the window down. When Brenda-Lee sent a languid glance in his direction, he stabbed his pointing finger toward the woman. Brenda-Lee looked up the street, holding on to a parking meter and stretching her neck. She nodded vigorously and then sent him an unpremeditated little-girl smile. Daniel vowed to come back and see if he could find a way to get her off the street.

When he looked back, the woman was getting into a cab. The driver pulled away and before Daniel could reach them had gone through a yellow light and turned the corner. Daniel roared to the intersection. Without hesitating, he went around the left side of the car ahead of him, nudged between the pedestrians crossing with the light, and inserted his rented car into an angry chorus of horns and shouted curses. He passed half a dozen cars on the avenue, using his horn more than his brake to avoid collisions.

By the time he had caught up with the cab, the blinking lights of a police car were in his mirror. Daniel blew his horn at the cabby and gestured for him to stop. In the rear window he could see the blurred features of the woman turned to face him. The cab picked up speed. Daniel stayed with it. The policeman was directly behind him now and had begun flashing his lights. The siren gave little grunts to catch his attention.

Daniel didn't bother to look back. He focused all his attention on the taxi. Although the street was open in front of him, the driver had slowed down to a speed well under the legal limit. The woman's face was in the window again. Daniel mouthed the words *stop* and *demon* a number of times before remembering to turn on the lights inside the car so she could see him. He couldn't see her well enough to read her expression. The cab suddenly sped up, pulling away from him.

Before he had time to react, the police car gave a sudden

surge and smoothly pulled out beside and slightly ahead of Daniel's small, underpowered car. As though he had done it a hundred times before, the officer maneuvered the big cruiser in a way that forced Daniel to pull over.

The policeman checked Daniel's license.

Daniel wondered if the woman in the cab understood, or cared, that he was involved with the demon.

"All right," said the officer with a friendly smile. "Please don't leave your car." He made a call on his radio, then stood leaning against the cruiser, beaming at his prisoner.

"Aren't you going to give me a speeding ticket?"

"Not today." He kept smiling. "Must be your lucky day." He walked around the front of his car to the driver's side.

"You just sit there a minute," he called to Daniel before sliding behind the wheel.

Daniel couldn't believe it. Only a few minutes had passed. There was still a remote possibility that he could catch the taxi, although it would entail speeding again. Still, as the officer had said, it seemed to be his lucky day. The cruiser was still blocking him. The policeman was sitting behind the wheel looking into the rearview mirror. After another minute, he put the car into gear and made a wide U-turn. He waved to Daniel as he drove up the street.

Daniel started his car, turned on the lights, and then watched as a long black car pulled into the spot just vacated by the police cruiser. Before he had time to swear properly, let alone do anything constructive, two large, mean-looking men were opening his door. As he got into the backseat of Charlie's car, he caught a glimpse of a cab at a curb a block or so up the avenue. For all he knew, it was the one he had chased, back from dropping off the woman he might now never find.

The cabby talked into the rearview mirror as he and Marcia watched Daniel get into the black car.

"Of course he's in trouble. Who do you think drives around in big black cars like that with the Frankenstein twins in the backseat? That's not the Salvation Army, lady. These guys even got the cops working for them."

Marcia watched the car make the same U-turn the police car had.

"Follow them," she said.

"Hey, this isn't a movie. I don't follow gangsters. You give me a destination, I'll drive you there. That's all."

The big car was on its way down the street. In a moment it would be lost, and with it the handsome young man who had some connection to the demon. Marcia felt a cold sensation akin to the icy anger she had felt toward the mugger last night. She clenched the hand that wore the ring. When she spoke it was in the voice of a stranger.

"I tell you, follow that car. Now."

The cab pulled away from the curb at once. "You want me to stay back?" There was a quaver in the driver's voice.

"Just don't lose them." Marcia exhaled as though she had been holding her breath. She opened her clenched hand slowly. She stared at the taillights of the car a third of a block ahead, and wished she were in her apartment.

In a few minutes they were back on the street where she had caught the cab. The big car turned down an alley in the middle of the block.

"That's a dead end. Blocked by construction," the driver said timidly.

"You're sure?"

"A hundred percent."

"Then I'll get out here."

She paid the fare, then walked to the alley in time to see the men escort Daniel through a door near the back of the strip joint on the corner. The car sat empty in the shadows next to the building. She waited to see if anyone came back out, then walked into the alley. Farther along she could see the dark outlines of construction equipment and piles of debris.

She reached the door, a metal one covered with a mixture of rust and flaking paint. The ring, it was becoming evident, had power. But though she had recognized it after escaping from the mugger, her sudden ability to dominate the cab driver had been completely unexpected. She wished she knew the extent of the powers she could call upon, and how reliable they were. Elise had said only that the ring would help protect her from the demon, and had mentioned no powers or virtues beyond that. For the hundredth time, Marcia wished that Hannah were with her. Having no idea what she would or could do if it opened, she tried the door. It was locked. She looked up. Above, on the second floor, a window that had been dark a moment before showed a faint light.

Back on the street, she stood in front of the neon-encrusted strip joint. She took a deep breath and entered. Out in the alley, the unmistakable shadow of Ferris emerged from the construction site.

Inside the bar, a few boys of college age ignored their beers to watch raptly as a pretty girl on a platform behind the bar performed an obscene dance. Marcia had expected to find an artful, if lamentable, striptease in progress. One that tantalized the onlookers with delights gradually and perhaps never fully revealed, teasing their imaginations with what they might hope to see.

This dancer, however, was naked, and was engaged in a frank effort to see how utterly and completely she could expose her nakedness. She shuffled in time with the monotonous recorded music, turning herself like a steak on a grill so that the shifting, jiggling flesh of her front and her back sides were equally exposed to the hot attention of the spectators. As a finale, she bent her knees and slowly lowered herself backward until she lay writhing on the bare wooden stage with her legs spread as wide apart as she could get them. Marcia was impressed with this display of athleticism, but found that she couldn't keep herself from worrying on the girl's behalf about the danger of splinters.

Behind the bar was a generously proportioned middle-aged man who showed no interest in the dancer. Instead, he was giving his attention to Marcia, favoring her with a very fishy look. She took a seat at the bar.

"If you came here for trouble, you can just turn right around," he said without any particular malice. "All these girls are past the age of consent. Now which one are you looking for? And please don't tell me what a good girl she's always been."

"White wine, please," she said.

The bartender raised his eyebrows. He poured from a very large bottle into a very small glass.

"That'll be four dollars."

"Montrachet?" she asked, handing him a five.

"Huh?"

"I said, where is the ladies' room?"

He pointed to the back.

At the far end of the room, next to the rest rooms, was an unmarked door. Marcia fumbled with her handbag and looked back at the bar. The bartender was facing the front. She tried the door. The knob turned. As she opened it she glanced over her shoulder, then stepped quickly through.

The hallway was lit by a single bare bulb hanging from the ceiling. The outside wall was bare brick, decorated with clots of dried putty and scraps of wood and plaster. Opposite were four or five doors, each separated from the next by only a few feet of wall covered with cheap paneling that was dirty and scarred. A glance past a partly open door showed a tiny cubicle with an unmade cot and a folding chair. From behind another door came the noise of creaking springs and other sounds that Marcia would have preferred not to hear.

Across from the door to the alley was a narrow staircase. Marcia was on the third step when she heard a telephone ringing somewhere upstairs. Boards creaked under a heavy step. She heard muffled voices, then loud laughter and chairs scraping on a bare floor. She retreated to the hallway. From upstairs came the sound of a door opening, and then the noise of many feet on the steps.

Behind her, the door from the bar opened. The girl who had been dancing entered, followed by two of the college boys. She looked calmly at Marcia, as though fully clothed women who were skinny and wore no makeup were a common sight in that hallway. She draped her naked arms over the shoulders of her escorts. The short robe she was wearing fell open, exposing the voluptuous curves of her breasts as well as the rest of the intimate folds and dimples of her nakedness.

"Sorry, honey," she said in a low-pitched, husky voice, "but these two are both for me." The young men laughed more loudly than the circumstances warranted. Their faces were flushed, whether with excitement, drink, or embarrassment Marcia could not judge. They were still laughing nervously when the dancer shepherded them into one of the cubicles and closed the door behind her. The last Marcia saw of her was the unexpected, almost sisterly wink of a heavily mascaraed eye and the smooth round flesh of her inadequately covered bottom.

The men the cab driver had referred to as the Frankenstein twins were the first down the stairs, a pair of fairy-tale giants dressed in business suits. They both looked at Marcia briefly but rudely, as though she were a painting they weren't interested in. The next man down the stairs was talking to Daniel.

"So we're gonna take you elsewheres, like. You know what I mean?" He looked at Marcia. "Take a hike, sister. You know what I mean?" He looked at his watch. "Wait a minute. I gotta make a call. Just put him in the car, Mikey. I'll be back in a couple of minutes." He was up the stairs before Marcia could say a word.

She addressed the man called Mikey.

"Excuse me, but I have to talk to this man," she said, nodding to Daniel. Daniel shook his head at her almost imperceptibly. Mikey was less subtle.

"Excuse me, but no you don't. Beat it, lady." Mikey and the other man took Daniel's arms and hustled him through the door.

It slammed behind them. Marcia clenched her ring hand, looking for the feeling of power that she had felt before. She felt nothing. She waited a moment, then opened the door and stepped into the alley.

She saw Daniel pushed into the backseat of the big car. Mikey was about to get in after him when the other man called him.

"Hey, Mikey. Get a load of this punk."

Mikey walked around the front of the car. Marcia was looking to see if Daniel was going to take the chance to try to escape. Instead, he was gesturing to her through the window. She looked past the men in front of the car. There, standing twenty or thirty feet away, was the demon. He was ignoring the men. His yellow eye was on her.

Mikey looked over his shoulder to check on Daniel, then turned to the other man.

"Billy," he said, "you think this punk was messing with the car?"

Billy grinned. "Hey, scum," he called to Ferris. "Get over here. Now."

"No!" Marcia almost screamed the word. "You don't understand. Keep away from him!"

Mikey turned to her. "Are you still here? How'd you like to be stuffed headfirst into one of them garbage cans?"

Billy began to look angry. "Do I have to come and get you?" he shouted to Ferris. The demon began walking slowly in their direction.

Billy slammed his fist into his palm. "I said now!" He strode toward Ferris. "I'm going to drag you by your greasy hair." He stopped in front of him. He was as tall as Ferris, and almost as heavy. "In fact, I might just take you out to the street and drag you around on your fat ass, so everyone can see what a tough guy you are."

He reached for Ferris's hair. The demon casually batted his arm away without taking his eyes from Marcia.

Billy threw himself on Ferris with an enraged snarl. Ferris remained completely immobile. Billy looked like a man trying to attack a telephone pole. Mikey started toward them. Marcia saw Daniel slip from the car.

As Mikey ran up to him, the demon seemed to notice his attacker. With one hand he seized Billy and threw him into Mikey. Their foreheads rapped together sharply and they slumped unconscious to the ground in a heap.

He raised his eyes to Marcia.

"Wicca!" he growled. "Witch! Why do you stand here? Others of your kind would know to avoid me. Do you know what your powers are to mine? As loose ash to wind."

His sneer sat on his face like a scar.

"But it is the man I want. You I will allow to run away." He took two or three quick steps forward, then slowed his advance. "Run, little witch. You are no match for me. Run or I will crush you like a bug."

As Daniel watched, Marcia took a single step toward the demon. He put his hand on her shoulder. She pushed it off without turning. "Stay where you are," she said. "Keep behind me." She took two more steps and stopped.

Ferris continued toward them.

Marcia raised her ring hand to her chest.

The demon stopped. His eyes dropped to her clenched fist.

"What is this?" he said. "Something of power." He bared his teeth. "How surprised you are going to be. How you will squeal when I rip your finger from your hand and throw it away with the ring still on it. Then you will know how profound an error you have made." He stopped. "Still time to run," he said. Marcia did not move. The demon looked at Daniel.

"I am going to open you like a package. Tonight you will find out what you missed before." He returned his yellow eyes to Marcia. When he was four or five paces from her, he stopped.

"Get out of my way," he said in a low growl.

"You may not pass," she said.

The demon loomed over her. He moved one more step forward.

"Tell me, then, whose ring you wear. If it is your own I will not take it from you." He glared down on Marcia like some huge beast on a trapped fawn. "But if you say it is another's I will tear it from your hand." He reached toward her. Daniel braced himself.

Marcia had to tilt her head back to meet the demon's eyes. It seemed to Daniel that she was not able to speak. He expected to see her fall to the ground from sheer terror. He himself had given up any thought of reasoning with the creature that confronted them. It would be like trying to explain something to a polar bear. Marcia moved her other hand to support her arm at her chest. She seemed to waver. Daniel started to help her, then saw her take another step toward the demon.

"This is Elyssa's ring," she said in a low-pitched, quiet voice.

Daniel felt as though he had become permanently attached to the spot of cracked pavement he stood on. He stared fixedly at the demon's reaching hand. In the dim light it looked like a claw. For a moment it was still, as though Daniel's gaze and rooted immobility had trapped it in an endless instant.

When the hand moved, it traveled almost too quickly to be seen. But instead of Marcia's ring, it was her face that it sought, and where it brushed her cheekbone, it left a thin trail of blood.

Daniel watched Marcia sway like a boxer who has just walked into a punch. She remained silent, but Ferris drew his

hand away with a cry of surprise. He looked at his hand, back at
Marcia, and then, suddenly, beyond her, with a fixed stare.

"No!" he shouted. "You have come to cheat me!"

Daniel began to follow the demon's eyes, then jumped, startled. A few feet to his left stood a young woman. He was quite
certain she had not been there a moment before.

"You have touched her," said the woman in a level voice.
Daniel thought it was the most chilling sound he had ever heard.

"I will not be interfered with! I am a king! You have no
right—"

"The passage of these ages has become wearisome to you,
then," she said, interrupting quietly, "and you tire of existence."

Although her eyes were fixed on the demon, Daniel found he
could not look at them, and could not imagine meeting that
deadly gaze, were it to be turned on him. Being careful to make
no movement that might attract attention, he shifted his eyes
back to Ferris and Marcia. Before the arrival of the young
woman, Daniel had had every reason to believe his life was
over, yet it was in her presence that he felt the greatest sense of
danger.

She began to walk slowly toward the others. The demon took
a step backward. The woman raised a hand.

"You will stand where you are."

Marcia faced the demon still; she had not moved. Now she
turned toward the voice.

"Elise," she began.

"No," said the woman, "not Elise. Now you may call me
Elyssa." She reached Marcia and stopped. "You have done what
I asked you to, and you have done it well."

Marcia's eyes dropped. "Your ring," she said, beginning to
remove it from her finger. Elise touched her lightly on the arm.

"Would you keep the ring, for a time, if I offered it?"

For a moment Marcia was silent, then she nodded. "Yes," she
said, in a voice barely above a whisper, "I would."

"Good. You seem"—Elyssa paused, looking at the ring on
Marcia's finger—"suited to it."

Marcia's eyes followed Elyssa's to her hand. "But what . . . ,"
she began.

"No questions," said Elyssa. "We must leave at once—you to go to your home, I with this king to . . . another place."

Daniel heard a soft noise and turned to see the third gangster slipping back into the building. When he looked around again, he saw, or thought he saw, the three figures standing together, their hands joined like children starting some game. Then, at the same instant, he was alone in the alley except for the sleeping thugs.

One of them—in the tangle of suits and haircuts, Daniel couldn't tell which—groaned and began to stir. Daniel looked once more for the women and Ferris, then sprinted to the corner and down the sidewalk. He wanted nothing more to do with Charlie's pals. He flagged a cab. He decided he could take a chance on retrieving his rented car; he was sure the thugs would be busy swearing and lying to each other for a while.

He drove immediately to his hotel. In his room, he forced himself not to pace. When room service brought his scotch, he settled into the old-fashioned comfortable chair next to the phone and cleared his mind of the fears and worries that wanted to clutter it. As was frequently the case, his poker-table discipline was useful with problems that had nothing to do with chips and cards.

He picked up the phone and got an outside line. "One thing at a time," he said.

Charlie answered his phone on the first ring.

"Kid. Is that you? Where are you? Are you okay?"

"What?"

"Willie thought the bikers might have got you."

"The bikers?"

"The gang. How did you get away?"

"I ran. Listen, why are you so worried about my health?"

"Oh. That's right. You don't know. Roxy called. She eloped."

Daniel's instincts told him that laughter would be offensive and rude. He took a very deep breath.

"Where is she?" he asked, trying to sound like an interested cousin.

"California. She just called tonight, all upset. You know what? She didn't realize her credit cards had spending limits.

You tell me, do you believe that?" Daniel could hear very clearly the pride in Charlie's voice. His daughter was a princess.

"That's really something, Charlie," he said. "Tell Roxy I wish her the best, okay."

"Okay. That's nice, kid. Listen, I gotta call some relatives. I'll see you at the game Friday night, okay?"

"Right, Charlie. See you."

"You're a nice kid."

Daniel put down the phone. "This is a crazy world," he said. Five minutes later, he was on his way back downtown.

CHAPTER

· 14 ·

The escort of soldiers crowded the gaming tables at the inn. They were in no hurry to retire to tents or to piles of straw in the stables. Their officers and the diplomats that rode with them had found their beds already, feeling the need to rest for the political ordeals of the morrow. But at the top of the house, in the best room, the candles burned late.

"Iris, please don't look so terribly shocked. You're making me feel like a harlot. How could I fall in love instantaneously?"

"Daniel did."

Modesty felt her cheeks go warm. "You should have heard the things he said."

"And have I not? More than a hundred times?" She smiled softly and lay her hand on her friend's shoulder. "Not that I mind. You tell the most interesting stories since your adventure."

Modesty's eyes filled with tears.

"But where could he be? What has happened to him?"

"More tears? Modesty, you never cry. I cry, then you comfort me. And insult courtiers."

"It's true I did not tell him I loved him, but I told him I liked him. And I showed him. I treated him like a brother. Well, I mean . . ." She began to laugh, tears still streaming down her cheeks. "I mean we were friendly. We talked. We plotted, but we talked, too." She wiped her wet cheeks and smiled. "He was very impressed when I managed to talk to you. He was generous, and he was considerate. . . ."

Iris put her arms around Modesty.

"I don't know what has happened," she said, "but we must hope that he will come to Ambermere. The soldiers said he was released before us. The innkeeper said he had come to pay for . . . your room." The princess blushed. "We don't even know how it is that we came to be released. My odious cousin watched from a window with not so much as a word. Perhaps it was somehow Daniel's doing, and it entailed some further errand before he was free to come to you."

Modesty sat up and made a visible effort to compose herself.

"I am being foolish," she said. "I am only worried about his safety anyway."

"It has only been one day," said the princess.

"A day and a half."

"Tomorrow we will be home. They sent him. Rand will know where he is, and why."

"You're right," said Modesty. "I don't know why I didn't think of that." She hugged Iris.

"Dear Modesty, my formerly sensible friend, I have been pointing that out to you since yesterday afternoon."

"Oh."

By noon the next day, they were on the outskirts of Ambermere. When they reached the little shrine, the princess asked the captain to stop while she and Modesty paid a call.

They looked first in the shrine, then walked through the garden to the back of the house. They found Renzel in the kitchen at the stove.

When she saw her niece, she gave a shriek and ran to her. She caught her in a tight embrace, squeezing her and laughing. She nearly did the same to Iris, but remembered herself in time, and curtseyed instead.

If for a moment the princess looked like a disappointed little girl dressed in very fancy clothing, Renzel did not notice, so delighted was she to see them.

"I couldn't think what had happened to you. And that man at

the castle—a person can't tell if he's telling the truth or lying, because he always sounds like he's lying."

"We have been away, Aunt."

Renzel looked her niece up and down. "Is that a fact?" she said tartly. "That's what the man at the castle has been saying."

She looked at Modesty closely. "Are you sick?" she asked.

Modesty gave a wan smile. "Just tired," she said. "We've come all the way from Ascroval."

Renzel looked shocked. "And not been to the palace yet?"

"We wouldn't pass your shrine without stopping, Mistress," said the princess. Renzel looked pleased.

"But you must go on now, Your Highness. Your poor father, that is, His Majesty, will be waiting."

"No," said Iris, "I don't believe he knows we're coming to-day."

"Well, then, the king is as much in the dark as I was. I must say it seems only right."

From an upstairs window, the priestess happened to look out at the moment Renzel and two fine ladies were walking through the garden. She got up to get a better look. Odd, she thought. One girl looked almost like the royal daughter that was soon to be married. She knew that Renzel had a niece somewhere in the city, but these were persons of rank. It was with considerable surprise that she watched Renzel begin an awkward curtsey. But the young woman came to her and hugged her, planting a kiss on her cheek. When Iris turned from Renzel, she happened to glance toward the window. Catching sight of the priestess, the princess nodded, then turned without witnessing the spectacle of a woman curtseying foolishly to a window.

As it happened, the princess and her escort arrived at the castle at a moment when her father was staring from a window overlooking the main gate. He had been composing, or rather engaged in an ongoing failure to compose, a letter to Finster the Munificent that would succeed in couching a series of transparent falsehoods in language that would somehow make them believable. The fact that Rand, who as a seasoned diplomat had broad experience in saying and writing things that were, as he

liked to put it, "not strictly true," had failed in the same enterprise had not initially dampened the monarch's optimism.

"You know, Rand," he had said only two days before, "I have
something of a gift for language. I'm sure that if I devote an
hour or so to the problem, I shall be able to find an acceptable
excuse for postponing the wedding." The king waved a negli-
gent hand in the air before him, as if to demonstrate how easily
minor problems could be dismissed. "You see," he said, "it's
primarily a problem not of what we say, but how we say it. A
simple matter of . . . Oh . . ."

"Semantics."

"Indeed. Just so. Have the courier ready to go at a moment's
notice."

Since then, the courier had slept two nights in his own bed,
partaken of six meals and numerous snacks, and had been re-
sponsible for the substantial depletion of a freshly broached
cask of ale.

When the first mounted troops came into view, Asbrak
formed the panic-stricken conclusion that their presence her-
alded a surprise visit from King Finster. This idea immediately
became lodged in his mind, so that when he saw his daughter
pass through the gate, his only thought was to wonder what on
earth she could be doing in the company of her future father-in-
law.

"Rand," he shouted, except his shout came out a dry whisper
that could not have been heard ten paces away.

The king turned from the window, and then back to it, twice
in rapid succession. Had anyone at that moment been looking in
from outside, they would have concluded that His Highness had
engaged the services of a dancing master, and was taking instruction.

"Rand!" The king tugged at a bell pull that rang in his adviser's official chambers. He peered anxiously at the scene outside.
Finster the Munificent was not yet in view.

A door opened, and Rand strolled casually into the room. He
made a slight bow to the king's back.

"Your Majesty?"

"Rand, quick! Finster's here. Think of something."

Rand stepped briskly to the window.

"King Finster? Surely not," he said, looking out.

If Rand was rarely surprised, it was even more rarely that he let it show. On this occasion, he did.

"But, Highness . . . the princess, she's . . ."

"Yes, yes. I see her," said Asbrak with an impatient gesture. "Her companion, Mystery, too. But what are we going to say to Finster?"

Rand forced his eyes from the royal hostage and allowed them to roam the yard.

"I see no evidence of King Finster, my liege."

"But he's following." The king looked at his adviser. "Isn't he?"

"As those officers are wearing the colors of Ascroval, I should venture he is not, Your Highness."

"Ascroval?"

"And there, Majesty, is that weasel, Femigris, looking very ill at ease."

The king was lost in confusion.

"Is this diplomacy?"

Rand smiled a thin, mean smile.

"Not yet, Your Highness, but evidently it is about to assume that character."

He left the window. "Come, Majesty. We must welcome the princess. And our guests."

Daniel awoke late the next morning. He had spent a restless night in his own bed, after hours of aimless driving downtown hoping to see the woman with the ring; the witch, as the demon had called her. Even Brenda-Lee had seemed to have disappeared from the face of the earth last night. Her corner had been drab and sexless without her painted face and tight, bright, and shiny working-girl outfit.

By the time he had been up for half an hour, he was fighting the midmorning traffic. He had coffee downtown, half a block from Brenda-Lee's corner. He sat by a window and watched the street as he sipped from the chipped mug. He was no longer able to keep thoughts and images of Modesty from his mind. Nor could he deny or banish the fear that memories of his lover might be all he was ever to have—those few hours, those whispered conversations. His mental images of her were clear and sharp. Her fearless eyes as she confronted him in the tower; her outlandish disguise and hoarse voice as his serving boy; her soft lover's smiles as she lay beside him in the beds they had shared. He wondered if these pictures would become, in time, ambiguous and cloudy. Perhaps he would begin to doubt that any of it had really happened.

He pulled himself away from his memories. If he could not succeed in returning to Modesty, he would have endless time to regret her loss. Meanwhile, he was determined to spend his energies on logic, not regrets.

He could hope that he might, by combing the streets of the city, find the schoolteacher. But he did not want to miss other possibilities. The other woman he would recognize as well, but he doubted, from the things she had done and said, that he would find her on the city streets. The schoolteacher had seemed to have no great powers of her own. She certainly had not been able to control Charlie's thugs. But the younger woman had controlled the demon without noticeable effort, and had then arranged for the three of them to disappear while Daniel had looked away for a second.

The only other connection to the other world that Daniel could even hope to find in this one was the mage, as Remeger had called him, who had brought him back. Daniel ordered another cup of the surprisingly good coffee, and began to make a concentrated effort to recall everything about his magical journey.

The journey itself: They had covered the landscape between Ascroval and Ambermere in a matter of hours—a trip that had taken him four days of efficient walking. Daniel was sure it would be pointless for him to waste time with speculations about the nature of the trip. It had been magical; whether by expanding time or compressing distance was unimportant. What was important, he realized, was that there had been any need to make it at all. Clearly the purpose had been to return him to his own world.

"No," he said aloud, drawing a glance from a ragged old man in the next booth.

He had been returned to exactly where he had come from.

His city. His apartment. His bedroom. To accomplish this, the mage had first had to bring him to Ambermere. The transfer could not be accomplished from Ascroval.

A feeling of optimism, even euphoria, began to rise in Daniel. He suppressed it with a practiced ease that anyone capable of making a living at poker could have duplicated. He was concentrating on a problem, not daydreaming about a result.

When Rogan's spell had called him, he had traveled through a featureless mist, and he had arrived in Rogan's tower. With the mage, on the other hand, he had traveled through a recognizable landscape, and at the end of the journey they had even opened and closed doors while passing through the tavern.

Daniel turned his memory back. He needed only to recall the day before yesterday. He plumbed his mind for pictures of the tavern at Ambermere. It had been on a narrow street only one block in length. They had passed through the common room and opened a door at the back. From there they had passed through a storeroom, climbed a few stairs, and opened a door at the top.

They were in a bar. Daniel strained to see the wood of the countertop, the arrangement of the tables. The floor was bare and dark, old-fashioned wide planks of odd lengths. There were a few people seated by a window. Daniel had a clear image of only one, a young man straddling a chair and watching them as they approached. He couldn't remember, but he thought he had spoken to someone there. His next memory was of awakening the next morning in his bed.

He opened his eyes and checked Brenda-Lee's corner. It was empty, as he expected it to be at that time of day. He ordered a third cup of coffee to stare at as he pondered his recollections.

He reviewed his passage from the tavern to the bar. Why, he wondered, did he always think of the place in Ambermere as a tavern and the other one as a bar? He pictured the man straddling the chair, the vague forms seated by the window.

By the window.

Neon. The window said BAR. Backward. In neon. An old, dead neon sign.

That there were no signs made of neon in Ambermere was not a matter of controversy. Given the unknowable workings of magic, the bar with the neon sign could be anywhere, he supposed, but the only hypothesis of use to him put it somewhere in this city. He and the mage had walked from Ambermere to his world in well under one hundred steps. And, of much more practical interest, they had arrived at a place he could hope to recognize from the street.

Daniel bought a city map at a newsstand. He knew if he didn't approach this in a methodical way, he would end up searching some streets three times and others never. He marked off a small area near the block of strip joints. He intended to begin in downtown neighborhoods where he was most likely to find low-rent bars with broken neon signs. As he started down the first street, he pondered the fact that by some legitimate, if unknown, schemes of measurement, Rogan the Obscure lived closer to his apartment building than his brother and sister-in-law did. That suited Daniel. He sort of liked Rogan.

Ten minutes later, he found he had a problem. He had been prepared to spend hours cruising up and down every street and alley in the city. He had been prepared to face the disappointment of not finding the place at all. He had not, however, been prepared to find a candidate on the second street he drove down.

He was parked almost directly across from the place. He stared at the BAR sign in the window. He tried to picture it from the other side. It looked like the sign he remembered. He wondered how many thousands of them had been put up over the last forty or fifty years.

"Now what?" he said. To go into the bar would be to declare himself, to remove any possible advantage that secrecy might confer. By habit, by experience, and he supposed by nature, Daniel was disinclined to lightly give up an advantage. It was true, he was not prepared to specify what advantage he was protecting. He did not think for a minute that he could break into the place in the middle of the night, go through the door in the back, and then break out of the tavern. The magicians, mages, whatever, would scarcely leave their retreat unguarded.

That, of course, assumed that it was the place, and not just a dingy little bar that resembled it. Daniel got out of the car, crossed the street, and walked past the window. He could see nothing. The glass was dirty, for one thing, and seemed to be

tinted. In any event, it showed him nothing more than a dull reflection of his own face. He thought that if he pressed his nose
against the glass and stared, he might see something of the inside, but that would be worse than simply going in to have a
quick look.

He got back in his car and drove around the block. When he
got back to the street, he parked farther away from the bar, in a
spot where he could watch the door without being seen from the
window.

In a few minutes, Daniel knew, logic was going to force him
to go into the bar to see if it was the right place. There seemed to
be no other answer. He could continue to look for neon signs,
marking any he found on the map. But how stupid that would be
if this was the place.

Which, evidently, it was. He sat up behind the wheel. Coming down the street from the far corner was the young man he
had seen straddling the chair. Had he walked past the bar and
continued up the street, Daniel would have been left in doubt.
But he did not. The door to the bar closed behind him. Daniel
felt his heart pounding.

He looked at the small slice of the city he could see from
where he sat. The buildings, the cars, the stripe of cloudy sky
above. He listened to the traffic noise from the avenue, and
from the downtown spur of the interstate highway a few blocks
away. Yet somehow, a hundred steps from where he sat, people
were walking on the quiet streets of Ambermere, far from any
thought of engines more complicated than the winch at a deep
well or the gears that drove the miller's wheels.

Now that he knew he was in the right place, Daniel was willing to wait and let things develop. At the least, he would be so
cautious as to watch the place for a while before going in.

Ten minutes later a person emerged from the bar who was of
great interest to Daniel. It was a woman, old and with the posture if not the height of a drum major, who was dressed in the
long dark skirt he had seen worn by so many matrons on the
streets of Ambermere. In addition, she sported a hat that could
only have been homemade. Daniel was pretty sure that no matter how many worlds, or Regions, or places of any kind existed,
this hat was in style in none of them. The woman walked at a

brisk pace. She was nearly around the corner before he decided
to follow her.

Five or six blocks later she entered a small park. Daniel
stayed across the street, watching her make her way down the
winding walk. Only when it appeared she was going to be lost
from view did he dart across the street and begin to stroll along
in her wake. He needn't have bothered. She took a seat on a
bench. Daniel leaned against a tree. The woman sat with her
hands folded on her lap and looked straight ahead. She did not
move. Her posture as she sat was a reproach to anyone who had
ever slouched in a chair. Daniel thought she looked rather like a
turn-of-the-century photograph that had been enlarged to life
size and taped to the bench. Surely, he thought, she hasn't come
from Ambermere to sit in a park, listen to traffic noise, and in-
hale exhaust fumes. A noisy truck rumbled past, emitting a
powerful diesel stench.

"To wit," said Daniel.

Besides the truck, the air smelled of rain. Daniel looked up to
check the sky. When he sent what he hoped was a casual glance
at the bench, he saw another woman seating herself next to the
matron. He stared with no attempt at subtlety. It was the
schoolteacher-witch. She was not looking in his direction. He
forced his eyes back to the clouds above, then studied his cuffs
and shoes. He gradually allowed his gaze to drift back to the
bench. Both women were looking directly at him. The lady in
the hat raised her hand slowly and beckoned.

"I would think you would be just a bit tired of adventures,
young man. Not to mention spells and demons," she said as he
walked up. "In the wizards' bar I hear of you rescuing maidens
from towers. Now Marcia tells me you stood with her before the
demon. Apparently you are resourceful and courageous, but
surely you can't be enjoying all these trials. Your aura shows no
great love of risk. I don't know why you were spying at the bar,
but I must tell you, the people there are more dangerous than
they may appear to your innocent eye."

Daniel took a seat on the bench next to Marcia:

"I believe you, but I am desperate. I have to get back to
Ambermere."

"Why? This is your world. I can imagine you might like the

peace and quiet of Ambermere. I certainly do. But there are places here that you can go to. Things in your world are not yet so bad that you need magic to find a place of repose. One or another of these vehicles you people are so fond of can take you anywhere, given a little luck."

"But not to Ambermere," said Daniel. "Even though it seems to be just out the back door of the bar."

Marcia gave an impatient gesture. "Wait a minute," she said. "What are you two talking about?"

Hannah looked surprised. "Oh, that's right. You don't know. That's what I was going to explain to you today." She looked at the younger woman affectionately.

"In the weeks you've known me, you have never asked me where I live. That's just as well, because I don't live in this world at all."

"Are you saying you live on an another planet?"

"Gracious, no. At least, not in the way you mean." The witch looked perplexed. "You know, I don't believe I can explain it at all. You must ask the wizards; they love to explain things. I'm just an old witch; we're much better at doing things than talking about them."

Marcia dropped her hands to her sides in a gesture of resignation. "The wizards?"

Hannah sent a look of displeasure at Daniel. "Young man, I must say, I wish you had picked another day to follow me." She put a wrinkled hand on Marcia's shoulder. "It will all be clear soon enough, child. Don't worry about it."

"But what about Elise? Elyssa? Last night, I don't know what happened. One minute we were standing in the alley, then I was alone in front of my apartment building. Is she a wizard?"

Hannah laughed quietly. "No. Not a wizard," she said, continuing to laugh. "Forgive me, my dear, but when you meet the wizards, you will see how funny that is. Anyway, wizards are always men. Always." The witch turned her attention back to Daniel.

"You say you want to go back? Do you mean you want to stay there?"

"Yes, I do. I found . . . I made a friend there. We were separated. I want to return to . . ."

Hannah interrupted him. "When you say 'a friend,' you are not talking about a pal or a chum, I suppose?"

"A woman. A lover," said Daniel. "I don't want to lose her."

"Young man, you're very handsome. Isn't he, Marcia?"

Marcia stuttered inconclusively.

"Oh, never mind," said Hannah. "Anyway, I must say I still don't see how you managed to acquire a lover in the short time you were there."

Daniel started to say something, but was interrupted by the witch.

"Please do not explain. I wasn't asking for details, believe me." Hannah noticed Marcia glancing at her wristwatch.

"Are you still wearing that thing? I thought we took care of all that weeks ago." She shook her head disapprovingly.

"Well, Daniel," she went on, "have you thought that if you were able to return, you would be leaving everything that is familiar to you? Have you really thought of what you would be leaving behind?"

"Yes, I have," said Daniel without hesitation.

"You are sure you have weighed your choices carefully?"

Daniel smiled. "I'm a gambler by trade," he said.

"Of course," said the witch, nodding. "That should have been obvious; I'm being careless. And tell me, are you certain your lover would welcome your return?"

"Certain? No. Of course not."

Hannah shifted her position on the bench, moving closer to Daniel, as though to see him better.

"You gamble for a living. Have you ever lost everything you owned on the turn of a card?"

"No."

"Why not?"

"Because I have never bet everything I owned on the turn of a card."

"Then why are you willing to do it now?"

"Pot odds."

"What?"

"The prize is worth more than the risk."

Hannah sat back with a smile. "Take this opportunity to study his aura, dear," she said to Marcia.

To Daniel she said, "And what is the name of this lover? This prize?"

"Modesty."

The witch looked at him sharply. "The companion to the princess?"

Daniel sat up with excitement. "You know her? Have you seen her? Are they back in Ambermere? Is she all right?"

"Yes, yes, yes, and yes," said Hannah. "I know her only slightly, but I have seen her. I admit, I had thought she would never suffer a man. . . . Well"—she turned to Marcia—"so much for telling detailed fortunes from auras. Waste of time, usually." She frowned at Daniel.

"I can save you the trouble of going to the wizards for help. They will never let you pass by their doorway. As far as they are concerned, you are already where you belong. In fact, for once I agree with them. You should never have gone to Ambermere in the first place. Imagine that trifler, Rogan, trying to summon a demon," she said indignantly. "Magicians are idiots."

Daniel said nothing.

"You seem calm in the face of my discouraging talk."

"I am waiting to hear all you have to say," said Daniel quietly.

Hannah gave an almost imperceptible nod. "I believe you when you say you earn your living at the gaming table, but I would guess that you gamble very little."

A trio of huge motorcycles thundered past. Hannah glared at them as though she were thinking of turning the bikers into toads. She waited for relative quiet to return.

"I am willing to do this much for you. I will ask an authority beyond the wizards, and if permission is granted, I will take you to Ambermere. I use the wizard's doorway because it is convenient. But I can travel by my own paths if I choose. You think carefully about what you are doing, and then if you still want to, come to this place tonight at precisely midnight, prepared to leave, and I will have an answer for you."

Daniel began to speak, but was interrupted.

"See that you are sure, because this will be your only chance. I am not coming to this place again. . . ."

Marcia started. "You are not coming back?" she said. "But

you are to teach me, I mean, you told me. . . . You told me I am your adept."

"No more," said Hannah. "Now you wear that ring. Have you looked at your aura, my dear? You are no longer an adept of mine."

"But what am I to do? Did I do something wrong?"

"No, no, my girl. Don't worry. You are not being abandoned. Someone will come to you. Probably soon. Do not remove the ring, and do not despair. And you will see me again, if that matters. But it will not be here." She patted Marcia's hand maternally. "Now let me finish with Daniel, then we can talk."

Her eyes locked on Daniel's. "At midnight, then. But be sure. And be prepared to leave if permission is granted."

"I am sure, and I will be ready."

"Then I will see you here tonight. Remember, precisely at midnight. No later. I will not wait. Now go settle your affairs, and leave me to settle mine."

CHAPTER

✦ 15 ✦

Daniel spent the afternoon in his apartment. It was clear that he had to proceed as though sure of leaving tonight. If Hannah brought disappointing news, that would be soon enough to worry about it. Until then he tried to banish thoughts of failure from his mind.

It didn't seem to him that there was much to be done. No suits to pack, no socks to fold. He wrote a letter to his brother in which he spoke vaguely about a last-minute chance to take a lengthy trip, and expressed regret that he might not be back in time for the holidays. He paid his rent for the next month, which seemed only fair, somehow. If all went well, in a few hours the currency of the United States would have no value for him anyway. He went to his bank and made a large withdrawal of cash that he planned to use before he left.

His only other chore was to make an alternative arrangement in case his first plan for the cash went awry. A quick phone call to Charlie was all that was required. The underworld, at least, was still working smoothly.

He had kept the rental car, paying for it, and bribing an employee to retrieve it in the morning. He didn't want to be at the mercy of taxicabs on a day when his schedule meant everything. By late afternoon he had nothing left to do but worry.

It surprised him, but he felt uneasy. As the witch had said, he was abandoning everything familiar. He found that he was vulnerable to doubts about his prospects and his life in Ambermere. The woman he was so desperately in love with had admitted to no more than affection for him, though her manner and her actions had been much more than merely affectionate. Of the world, he did not know enough to judge accurately. He suspected that he was being too glib, but he told himself that it could not be any worse than this one.

His doubts didn't really matter, though. He was going, not for the peace and quiet, not for the quaint tile roofs, not for the appealing simplicity of the life. He was going for Modesty, and it was unthinkable not to.

He tried to read and found it impossible. Finally he drove downtown and went to a movie. He watched the tedious succession of car chases, fistfights, and gunplay with a sense of gratitude. This, after all, was the culture he was preparing to abandon. He wondered if Hannah had ever seen a movie.

He forced himself to stay to the end. He occupied his mind with the question of how it had come to pass that movies were accompanied by music. It was such a strange idea that lovers, for instance, could not manage to get themselves into bed, or even participate in a soulful exchange of meaningful glances, without the accompaniment of masses of violins and other musical gadgets.

When the final cathartic hullabaloo had subsided, and all the sidearms had been fired, and all the cars wrecked, and the handsome hero had displayed his profile one last time, Daniel left the theater feeling quite contented, for he had seen his last high-budget, low-brow movie.

He went to the best restaurant downtown and lingered over a light but elegant and very expensive meal. He sampled, with careful moderation, two of the best wines on the list. After dessert and coffee, he moved his party of one to a paneled room, where he smoked a seven-dollar cigar and sipped fifty-year-old brandy.

It was almost eleven o'clock when he got back to the strip. When he was over a block away, he could see Brenda-Lee on her corner, dressed in clothes that looked like they would glow in the dark. When he drove up, she wobbled toward the car.

"Hop in," he said.

"I don't know. What for? My boyfriend got mad before. He said we were gone too long."

"This time I just want to talk to you for ten minutes. Would you just get in the car, please?"

She opened the door. "Okay, but you have to pay me. I might miss a . . . an appointment while I'm with you."

"Fine. Get in." He watched her bend her way into the front seat. He wondered what her clothes were made of.

"Seat belt?" he said. They had gone through this routine yesterday.

"Seat belt!" She glared at him like a rebellious eighth-grader. "Don't worry about me; I'm not your grandmother. Anyway, my boyfriend says seat belts aren't safe. He says if you're in a wreck, the best thing is to be thrown clear of the car."

"Your boyfriend is a moron. Put the seat belt on."

"Are you paying for this?"

Daniel sighed and put the car in park.

"Brenda-Lee, I want to give you some money."

"Sure."

"No. I mean a lot of money."

She looked apprehensive. "What do you want me to do for it?"

"I want you to go out of business. I'm going to give you enough that you can go somewhere else, get a place to live, and go to school or get a job or something."

"What are you trying to do? What kind of trick is this?" Her voice had a panicky sound, as though he had threatened her. She put her hand on the door. "Pay me or I'm getting out."

Daniel fished a hundred-dollar bill out of his wallet.

"Here." He handed her the money with a flourish. "Now will you sit still, preferably with your seat belt on?"

A roughly dressed man who had been standing near the curb walked around the car to the driver's side. He thrust a badge at Daniel. "Turn the car off, pal; fun's over for the night."

Daniel looked at the clock on the dashboard. It was five past eleven. A police car pulled up beside them.

Daniel tried to explain, with predictable results. By eleven-twenty-five he was at the station house. He made a desperate phone call to Charlie who, despite the highly suspicious fact that Daniel had nearly fifteen thousand dollars in cash on his person, was able to get him out by quarter of one.

The park was empty.

Renzel had finished moving her few belongings back to the cottage. The priestess had completely changed her attitude on the subject, insisting that she had never meant to displace Renzel, except for the temporary accommodation of her guests. She had now decided that they would have to make do with the space she could offer them in the house. Renzel, it turned out, was being "too generous" and the priestess had decided she couldn't permit it.

If Renzel had been of a speculative turn of mind, she would have been completely mystified. But her life had taught her that doing the work and solving the problems that each day supplied was complicated enough already. Making guesses about the motives of her priestess held no interest for her.

In a way, she regretted leaving the house. It was ancient, and had housed the priestesses of the shrine for years past the reach of memory. Despite its new tenant, Renzel associated the place with the old priestess, who had lived her simple quiet life there for over sixty years, moving from room to room like a living ghost. Renzel often imagined her still inhabiting the house and grounds that she had presided over for so much of her life.

The figure silhouetted in her open doorway startled her, but it was her entirely corporeal niece who stood there.

"What's the matter with Eldyna?" she said, entering the cottage. "She practically bowed when I passed her in the garden."

"Modesty, please; you mustn't refer to the priestess with such informality."

"Sorry," said Modesty, without detectable contrition.

"My dear, you don't look well. Are you all right?"

"I'm fine," said Modesty, as her eyes filled with tears.

When Modesty got to the part of her story that required a description of her lover, her aunt listened, then interrupted her.

"But, my dear, I have seen him. Twice, in the shrine."

The girl leapt to her feet. "When?" she cried.

Renzel stood up, shaking her head sadly. "A fortnight ago, I'm afraid. I'm sorry, Modesty. But why . . . ?"

Modesty smiled gently at her aunt.

"The story doesn't end with the rescue, Aunt Renzel."

"I see," said the older woman, sitting down again.

Later, they walked in the garden. Renzel sent worried glances in the direction of niece. She had often known Modesty to be quiet; the girl had always shared her aunt's dislike of speech for its own sake. But this silence was troubling to her.

Modesty stopped at the end of a gravel path.

"I must leave. Iris has to be protected from the dressmaker and from every merchant in the city."

Renzel smiled at her niece. It was as though she could see the resilience in her. She thought of Modesty's parents and wondered where it could have come from.

"Work is better than worry, my dear."

Modesty kissed her aunt on the cheek and gave her a lingering hug.

"I wish I were ten years old," she said, and left.

The king twisted in his chair to follow the movements of his pacing adviser.

"Rand, what can you possibly find to frown about? The princess is upstairs with the dressmaker, the merchants are lined up in the hallways, the wedding is but ten days away, Hilbert has not been stolen by pirates or eaten by trolls; everything is exactly as it should be. My despicable cousin has been undone. Femigris has been groveling to you since his ignominious arrival."

"Forgive me, Your Highness. My only concern is that we have no idea how all of this has been accomplished."

Asbrak looked surprised. "But you told Femigris . . . ," he began, then trailed off. "Of course, that wasn't true," he continued, as though reminding himself of a forgotten bit of information.

"Not strictly according to the actual facts," amended Rand, through force of habit. "Your Majesty is quite correct."

"Still, Rogan has accomplished a marvel," said the king.

"Of which, if I may remind Your Highness, he is unable to give a coherent account."

"But he sent the young man, who carried Modesty—by the way, Rand, I do wish you would stop referring to her as Mystery. I find it confusing. Yesterday I actually called her by the wrong name. Most embarrassing."

"My humble apologies, Your Highness. I will try to remember."

"Anyway, he carried her from the tower, and then they were caught trying to rescue the princess." The king stopped as though struck by a sudden thought. "What a remarkable girl she must be. Of course, I've always recognized her qualities." He tugged at his beard judiciously.

"And now the young man is missing," Asbrak continued. "We must reward him, Rand."

"As Your Majesty has just said, he is missing."

"But he will turn up, surely. What does Rogan say?"

"The royal magician seems to know nothing of his whereabouts, Your Highness. The maiden, Modesty, questioned him most tenaciously in my presence. Ran him quite out of wine, she did." The adviser smiled to himself. "I believe I will ask her to interview Femigris."

In the morning, Daniel had returned his rental car, and then walked to the bar, which was locked and dark. He paced up and down the street for a while, then walked back to the strip to see if Brenda-Lee was around. He drank coffee, watching her corner, then took a long walk by the waterfront.

Next, he took care of Brenda-Lee's money. He had arranged for Charlie to hold the cash for a few days, then get it to the girl if Daniel hadn't reclaimed it. The address Charlie had given him turned out to be the strip joint that the thugs had brought him to the night before last. The bartender took the envelope without comment and tossed it in a drawer next to the cash register. On the stage behind the bar a spectacularly built girl was performing a dance that was meant to be erotic but was merely anatomical. Daniel was not tempted to linger.

It was late in the morning by the time he got back to the bar. From what Hannah had said, it was clear that the place was a gathering place for wizards. Having seen a wizard in action at Ascroval, Daniel no longer cherished any illusions about his ability to gain some advantage over the caretakers of the door-way. He simply opened the street door and walked in.

A few men sat around a table by the window. Daniel looked at the neon sign. The sensations of three days ago returned to him. He could almost see himself coming through the door at the back of the room, his mind cloudy with whatever sorcery his companion had worked.

He looked at the doorway now and saw that it matched the one at the back of the tavern in Ambermere. The door looked heavy. It was of dark wood, and rather wide.

Daniel recognized no one in the room. Neither the wizard from the trial at Ascroval nor the young man he had seen on the street yesterday were in the room. The bartender was a young man, short and somewhat stout.

"Yes, sir," he said when Daniel approached.

"Who is in charge here?" said Daniel.

"Me," said the bartender. "Name's Jackie. What can I do for you?"

"I have to get to Ambermere."

Jackie thought for a moment. "Nope," he said. "You got me beat." He called to the men at the table.

"Any of you gents know where Ambermere Street is?"

No one did.

Daniel sat down and put his elbows on the bar.

"I know what this place is," he said calmly. "I was brought here from Ambermere."

The bartender looked him in the eye.

"What do you want?"

"I want to walk through that doorway," said Daniel, pointing to the back of the room.

"That's not an exit, it's a storeroom."

"Oh. All right," said Daniel in a light tone. "I must have this confused with another bar. Just let me have a draft beer."

As soon as Jackie turned, Daniel slid quietly from the stool and hurried to the doorway. It was not locked. He was through before anyone noticed.

The storeroom seemed smaller than he had remembered it,

and not so dark, but the door on the other wall looked right. He
ran across the room. With any luck he would make it. Incred-
ibly, the door was unlocked. As he opened it he resolved to get
through the tavern at a dead run. Once he was on the street in
Ambermere, they would have to catch him. He opened the door
and burst through.

He was in an alley. The first thing he saw was an abandoned
car from which everything useful had been stripped. He turned
to go back into the storeroom. The door had closed behind him
and was locked.

He walked the length of the alley and around the block to the
bar. He shook his head in disgust. For a few moments, he had
dared to think that audacity and fleetness of foot were going to
be all that he needed to outsmart the wizards.

He reached the bar just behind three businessmen full of office talk and cheerful banter. To his astonishment, they entered.
Daniel was not confused, but he was perplexed. He would have
bet a very great deal indeed against the proposition that these
men were anything other than what they appeared to be. He decided to return later.

"It's very simple, Mistress. Yesterday I was able to give you
an answer; today the cards say nothing." The boy gathered the
array of cards into a neat stack with a few economical motions
of fingers and wrists. Through long black eyelashes he gazed
across the cluttered little room to where the witch sat in a
straight-backed wooden chair.

"All right," said Hannah, "I'm satisfied. You tried." She
popped up briskly from her seat. "Tea?" she asked as she passed
through a doorway almost too low for even one of her stature.

The boy curled his lip and turned his head till his chin rested
on his shoulder. He sent a look after her as though she had offered to shave his head.

"Not just now, thanks," he said. He brought his slippered feet
up to the cushion he sat on and tucked his heels against his
thighs. For a few moments he stared through the window at the
afternoon light in the garden. From the kitchen came the muffled clatter of kettle and teapot. He crossed his hands on his lap
and closed his eyes.

When Hannah had finished her tea and tidied up, she came back to her living room.

"I know you'll do as you please," she said to the boy, ignoring the fact that he appeared to be asleep, "so I'll just tell you that after I go to the potter's with something for the little girl's cough, I'm going on to the shrine." She draped a light shawl over her shoulders. "No telling when I'll be back." When she put her hand on the latch of the front door, the boy opened his eyes.

"I would think you had had quite enough of that sort of thing for a while." He stretched, then rolled to his feet in an easy, fluid motion that looked as though it cost him no effort whatever. He was a little more than Hannah's height, and stood as straight as she, but with no hint of rigidity or discipline in the easy grace of his posture. He stretched again, a quiet wave that seemed to flow from the balls of his feet to the black hair that curled over his ears.

"I am looking for no one at the shrine but Renzel, little Egri. No one else at all. But if I cannot get an answer to my question from divination at home, then I must seek help abroad. And besides, this question affects Renzel. If all else fails, I will simply ask her opinion."

"Which you could have done yesterday as well, leaving me to my own pursuits."

"Pursuits, indeed. Naps in the sun."

Egri smiled and paced to the window. He lowered himself onto the deep wooden sill.

"Anyway," he said, "these matters come under Renzel's authority as much as anyone's."

"Of course; when she gets the authority. But the high priestesses have not yet arrived. Until then foolish and annoying Eldyna is still the priestess, and Renzel is merely the woman who looks after the shrine."

"And she has no inkling?"

The witch adjusted her shawl. "Oh, she knows; I'm sure of it. She just does not know that she knows. But she sensed something—found the encounters troubling. She will work it out. If not before, then when those from the Outer Kingdoms—

the High Servants of the Ladies—come to her and install her as priestess."

In her garden, Hannah spent a few minutes freshening the flowers, leaves, and tiny berries that sprouted all over her unusual hat. Before passing through the gate to the lane, she turned and waved. Peering through the window from where it was perched comfortably on the sill was a small black cat.

Daniel watched the bar from across the street. Two hours before, in the late afternoon, he had come back, determined to at least discuss his situation with someone. But when he strode up to the bar and reached for the door, he found himself groping at the brick wall a few yards down the street. On his next try he ended up at a window of the building next door. Daniel tested the spell, for he had no doubt of the origin of his difficulty, several times more, ending up at trees, parked cars, a telephone pole; everywhere but the door. At one point he had begun to laugh at the thought of what he would look like to anyone watching. A man striding purposefully up to lampposts and other unlikely objects and trying to shake hands with them.

In the two hours since, no one had entered or left the bar. He waited, not knowing what else to do. His only other connection, however tenuous, with Ambermere was the woman, Marcia. He was determined to find her, whatever it took. He had pretty well figured out the wording of a newspaper ad that would catch her attention. How handy, he thought, that in a time of disbelief like the one he lived in, he could openly mention demons and witches with no fear that anyone would imagine that he was actually speaking of demons and witches. In fact, his only problem was how to avoid a flood of calls from cultists and other fringies.

He had learned the word from Brenda-Lee two days before when she had used it to refer to a rather normal-looking man who had been standing on a curb shouting to passing cars that "the end" was at hand.

"Don't run over the fringie," she had said.

"The what?" he had shouted, looking around wildly to see if something was in his way.

"The fringie. You know, like fringe element, or like the lunatic fringe."

When Daniel, annoyed, had suggested that most people considered prostitutes to be on the fringes, Brenda-Lee had sulked for half an hour.

A pair of white-bearded men were strolling up the opposite sidewalk in the direction of the bar. Daniel did not recognize them from earlier that afternoon, but he was not surprised when they went into the bar.

He immediately went across the street. He kept his eye on the entrance to the bar without so much as blinking. As he approached, he saw no hint of funhouse-mirror trickery. Nonetheless, when he came to the door, it was a parking meter.

Daniel realized he was hungry. If he hurried, he could beat the Friday-night crowds to the pizza place, and be in and out in no time.

Brenda-Lee was still not at her corner. Tomorrow, he decided, he could check to see if she could possibly be in jail, though he doubted she was. He comforted himself with the thought that wherever she was, Charlie could find her.

He looked for her again after dinner, swinging by in a cab. Her corner was empty. Up the street he saw the man with the bandaged hand. He thought of Marcia and wondered how she had managed to deal with him and what, precisely, she had done. She had certainly not been particularly resourceful with Charlie's goons.

Back at the bar, one try for the door confirmed that the spell was still in effect. Daniel concluded that his only hope was to try talking to the next person to come out of the place. Unfortunately, no one did. A little after eleven o'clock the window went dark. Daniel waited for another half hour, then left, planning to be back in the morning.

He was looking for a cab when he realized that in ten minutes it would be exactly twenty-four hours since he was to have met Hannah at the park. A cab slowed on the empty street. He waved it on and set out for the park. It was not impossible, he suddenly realized, that Marcia might come there. He quickened his pace. Why, he wondered, had it not occurred to him to check there from time to time during the day?

He entered the park nearly at a run, then slowed abruptly when he saw that the bench was not empty. His breath caught in his throat. He drew closer, trying to prepare himself for the sight of a bag lady or a wino slumped and snoring.

The bench was near a streetlight, but in the shadow of a tree. The outline was indistinct. Daniel stared ahead anxiously. He dared not let himself believe that what he saw was Hannah's hat. Without consciously willing it, he walked more and more slowly, delaying the moment of disappointment as he lengthened the interval of hope.

When he saw it was really the witch seated on the bench, he approached very slowly and quietly, as though he feared she would vanish if he made a sudden movement. She watched him come up the path. When he reached her she stood up.

"About time," she said. "Are you ready to go?"

There were a dozen questions in Daniel's mind.

"Yes," he said, and silently fell into step beside her as she started down the dark, tree-lined path.

They left the park and walked one block before Hannah stopped at a corner.

"If you have anything to say, say it now. We have a long walk ahead of us and I'm going to be too busy finding my way to chat."

Daniel looked down at the little woman in the bizarre hat. His sense of relief and of gratitude was so intense that he wasn't sure he could rely on his voice. He cleared his throat.

"Thank you for coming back for me."

Forty-five minutes later they were still walking the streets of the city. They would go for a block, or a few blocks, then Hannah would stop, look around, sometimes with her eyes closed, before setting off again, more than once turning around and going back over ground they had just covered.

It did not take much of this before it occurred to Daniel that he did not, of his own knowledge, know that Hannah had anything to do with the other world. He might be trudging around the city with an old lunatic who had been wandering these streets for forty years. He comforted himself with the knowledge that Marcia had treated the witch as legitimate. On the other hand, Marcia had been completely unaware of the existence of the other world. But she had known about the demon, and had some connection with the woman who had spoken confidently of returning the demon to the Lower Regions. Besides, he remembered, feeling stupid, he himself had seen Hannah come out of the wizard's bar.

The witch had said nothing since they had set out, and Daniel had not dared to trouble her. She had led them, most circuitously, to a particularly seedy part of the waterfront. Not an area that the Chamber of Commerce would have recommended for a midnight stroll. Daniel had nothing else to occupy his attention, so he kept a careful watch for unfriendly natives.

In the distance, the sound of a bell could be heard. It struck one time. Daniel tried to place it as he stepped around a discarded truck tire that was blocking the sidewalk. They passed into the shadow of an abandoned warehouse. The last echo of the low-pitched bell faded to inaudibility.

Hannah stopped, then turned down a narrow alley between two buildings. In a moment, they came to a blank wall. Daniel started to turn around. The witch prevented him with a hand at his elbow. They stood facing the blank wall for what seemed like a long time. Then Hannah turned and led them back toward the street.

Daniel's heart rate increased. They were going to emerge from the alley onto a street in Ambermere, he was sure of it. Images of Modesty tumbled into his head, only to be displaced by the uncompromising reality of a passing car. Two blocks later they went around the same block twice. Daniel wondered how long this little old lady could continue to walk. As they approached the waterfront again, he watched her for signs of fatigue. At that moment she stopped.

"You see why I use the wizard's doorway," she said in a matter-of-fact voice. "Of course, it's much easier when I'm by myself."

Daniel supposed it was all right for him to talk.

"When will we get there?" he asked, attempting to sound unconcerned.

The little witch stared up at him without answering and with an unreadable expression on her face.

Daniel kept his eyes on her. He was afraid to let them move.

He listened for the noises of the city. The night was silent. He closed his eyes. He heard no siren, no traffic, no mechanical hum from a chorus of compressors and air conditioners.

"I wish you'd get on with it," said the witch.

Daniel opened his eyes. They were on the waterfront. Farther down the street he could see a few flickering lights from buildings that faced high-masted sailing ships moored not far from their doorsteps. A misty rain began to fall. Somewhere, out of sight but not far away, a man was singing in a clumsy baritone.

"You look awful," said Hannah without a trace of sympathy in her voice. She rummaged in the folds of her skirts and handed him some coins. "Get yourself a room at one of these inns. You can make your own way to the castle in the morning." She looked sharply at Daniel. "You're not going to get lost again, are you?"

"We're here," he said.

"So we are."

Daniel looked behind him apprehensively.

The witch shook her head. "The other world isn't there. Don't worry; you won't walk around the wrong block and cross over again." She did not bother to explain that in fact it was possible, and actually happened once every thirty or forty years.

"Which way is the castle?"

Hannah pointed. "Listen to me," she said. "Do not go stand outside the castle all night. Get into a comfortable bed. In the morning get something to eat." She looked at Daniel to make sure he was following what she said.

"When you get to the castle, do not present yourself to Modesty, not to mention the princess, in your strange clothing. Go to Rogan and have him make you presentable. Then will be time enough to go to your lady. You are going to surprise her. See that you make the surprise a pleasant one."

The witch took off her hat. Daniel, having come to regard it as part of her anatomy, was shocked at the action. From a tired-looking stalk that seemed almost to grow from the band, Hannah pinched off a tiny leaf, holding it carefully by the slender green filament that served as its stem.

"Take a glass of sweet red wine to your room," she said. "Bruise this leaf lightly between your fingers and float it on the surface of the wine. Then make yourself ready for bed before you drink." She placed the leaf in his hand. She caught his eye. "Remove the leaf before you drink, unless you want to sleep for two or three days. If you do as I have told you, you will have a peaceful night untroubled by dreams and you will awaken in a much better state than you are in now."

Hannah guided Daniel to a place that offered respectable lodging and saw him through the door. For a moment she stood in the empty street, enjoying the cool rain and listening to the creak of heavy ropes on wood. Then she set off down a cobbled lane and was soon out of sight.

CHAPTER

· 16 ·

When Daniel awoke the sun was already well above the horizon. As Hannah had promised, he was rested and refreshed. He had taken her advice about the sleeping potion, but not about breakfast. He couldn't even think of food, let alone eat any. He hurried through the lanes and streets, asking directions occasionally to make sure he wasn't wandering from his course. His clothing attracted a few glances, but in a city used to visitors from exotic ports, unusual fashions in clothing were almost commonplace. Before long he could see the towers and spires of the castle rising above the tile roofs of the town.

He stopped outside the main gate of the castle. It was open for anyone who wished to enter; Daniel merely wanted to see if his pulse would stop racing if he took a few deep breaths. He had the feeling that if he were at that moment to speak, his words would come out in a rapid soprano.

He had expected to be challenged at the entrance to the castle itself, but the guard was satisfied when he told him he was visiting the royal magician. Daniel made his way through the hallways and staircases until he stood at the foot of Rogan's stairs, in front of the room he had occupied only a week and a half ago, though it seemed much longer. Daniel felt very much disconnected from reality of time and distance. For one panicky moment, the thought that he might at that moment be dreaming stabbed at him, draining his euphoric sense of homecoming. He smiled and touched the cold stone of the wall.

"I refute it thus," he said quietly.

The door to "his" room was partly open. Daniel knocked and then entered. Laid out on the bed was an outfit much like the one he had worn before. Feeling very much an old hand at accepting the unexpected, Daniel changed quickly, trading everything he wore for the local replacements that had been provided.

Once outfitted, his impulse was to rush to find Modesty. Again the realization that she was so near gave him the pulse rate of a chipmunk. He sat on the edge of the bed, reasoning with himself. He did not know how to find Modesty. He could very well wander the halls of the castle all day and never find her.

He took the stairs to Rogan's rooms two at a time. As he raised his hand to knock, the magician's voice came through the door.

"Come in. I know you're here."

Daniel stepped into the room. Rogan was seated in his chair by the window. He raised his glass in salute.

"I know," he said. "You're probably looking for a meal."

Daniel flopped into a chair. He felt as though he had never left. He half expected the magician to begin outlining some insane project. He reached for a goblet.

"Actually," he said, "I believe I'll have a little wine." He poured a third of a glass, hoping that it would help to calm him down. He had been less excited the first morning he had sat here, when he had had much more cause to be in a state of agitation.

"You seem to have been expecting me."

"I was. Your friend the witch saw to that. She was here at dawn. Don't those people sleep?"

"I couldn't say. You're the magician."

"Please," said Rogan. "I don't want to talk about magic. I'm thinking of becoming a cobbler." He put down his glass.

"I must say, you did very well, despite rescuing the wrong maiden. The witch told me the rest this morning. My explanations to the king are going to sound much more plausible now that I have some idea of what happened." Rogan stood up and looked out the window.

"You will be with me of course. I want to give you great credit, my boy, and yet somehow leave the impression that I was the mastermind behind this success. In control every step of the way. That sort of thing." At the sight of Daniel's good-natured grin, Rogan looked relieved.

"Any suggestions?" he asked.

"Don't tell the truth."

Rogan looked shocked.

"Of course not! Do you think I'm an idiot? What I meant was, do you have any *useful* suggestions? The problem is, the king will believe anything and his adviser will believe nothing."

Daniel stood up.

"To tell you the truth, Rogan, I'm not going to be any help at all until I can see Modesty."

"Fine. Just don't bring her here, please. I thought she was never going to stop asking me questions."

"Modesty? Questions about what?"

"Questions about you, of course. What else? And every time I'd give her what I thought sounded like a pretty plausible an-swer, considering that I didn't know anything at the time, she would ask ten more questions. She's worse than Rand, and she gets a look in her eye that could fry an egg."

Daniel felt like a high-school boy talking about a girl he had a crush on.

"What did she ask? What did she say about me?"

Rogan looked at him unenthusiastically.

"She said she was concerned about your safety." He picked his glass up and raised it to his lips. "No, wait. She said she was *only* concerned about your safety."

"Nothing else?"

"Not that I recall."

Daniel reached for the wine, then put his glass down instead.

"How do I find her?"

Rogan gave him directions.

"But then come back, my boy. And before too long. I must make you known to the king. I just need a little time to prepare a palatable story. One that does not mention demons."

In five minutes Daniel was lost. He wondered how Rogan ever managed to make his way around the castle. His sense of direction seemed to be limited to an infallible knowledge of up and down, that is, an ability to detect the urgings of gravity, unaugmented by any real feeling for the horizontal. Daniel quickly discovered that no one lacking the ability to pass through stone walls could hope to follow the magician's instructions.

He wandered into a long hallway that must have run the length of the building, disappearing into a cloud of distant shadows. It was an inner corridor. No windows illuminated its reaches—only lamps spaced far apart and high on the walls of gray stone. The first branching hallway led to a descending stair of hewn stone that, like the long corridor he had just left, could not be seen to its end, but faded into heavy shadow.

Daniel had not seen a soul since leaving Rogan. Hoping to find some signs of life, he started down the stairs. The sound of his boots echoed in the empty spaces. By the time he had passed the second lamp, he was beginning to have doubts. The bare stone of the stairs had become damp, suggesting that he was entering a region of cellars. Thoughts of dungeons came to him. He knew nothing, really, of this kingdom, of this world. Perhaps he would begin hearing cries and moans from those whom this kingdom chose to imprison, to torture.

He had almost decided turn back when he saw the archway at the bottom of the stairs. Certainly there would be no harm in having a look, he thought. And it was still possible that this led to some main hallway, or at least an inhabited part of the castle.

He passed through the arch into a cavernous room. The ceiling was hidden in darkness. The only light came form a distant doorway, where the glow of a lamp spilled a few feet into the gloom. There was an odd mixture of smells, mostly sour, in the damp air that seemed familiar, yet unidentifiable.

Daniel walked toward the light, picking his way among a maze of indistinct obstacles, some of which towered over him. He was not far from the doorway when it was filled with first the shadow, then the form of a huge man, great in both height and girth, who was bent forward and carried one shoulder higher than the other. Daniel could see that his arms hung in front of his body as he lumbered through the doorway and into the room.

He could not help thinking of trolls and giants and other fairy-tale horrors as the shadowy figure approached him. If Daniel had been a schoolboy he would have turned and sprinted for the arch without hesitation. A few more ponderous steps and the giant would reach him. Daniel stepped forward.

"Uh, pardon me," he said, attempting to sound like a rational adult.

"*Ooooooooooahhhhhhhh!!!!*" replied the giant in a deafening bellow that threatened to echo perpetually from the invisible ceiling. The huge form scrambled halfway back to the lighted doorway, then froze in a tense crouch.

"Who . . . who . . . who's there?" said the impossibly deep voice.

"I'm looking for the princess," said Daniel from the darkness.

The man straightened up to his full height, something over seven feet to Daniel's eye.

"The princess? Fairest flower? Shames something or other? Envy of whatever it is?"

"Yes."

"And what dull-witted jackass was it sent you to look for her in the wine cellar?"

"Well, Rogan was . . ."

"Say no more. By the gods!" The man turned and started back to the doorway.

"Come in here," he called. "I want to sit down until I know if my heart is going to start beating again. Be a shame to fall and get all bruised up for my funeral."

Daniel followed the hulking troll-form into a room well lit with candles and a large lamp. In the light the man was still extremely big, but not so big as he had seemed to be in the gloomy cellar. He was perhaps something under seven feet, and more broad than fat. He slumped into an oversize chair and gestured for Daniel to take a seat.

"Wines and cheeses," he boomed. "That's all I have down here. Well, hams and meat pies and that," he added. "But no princesses. No women at all, in fact." He looked around the room as though checking for women. "Nope," he said. "See?"

Daniel agreed there were no women.

"Breksin, that's me. Breksin the cellar master."

"Daniel," said Daniel. Breksin seemed to be waiting for him to say more.

"The gambler," Daniel added.

The giant sat up in his chair.

"Cards?" he said. He had raised his voice to a shout that would have carried across a small lake. Daniel supposed he must be hard of hearing.

Daniel nodded.

"We must have a game," he boomed eagerly. He was half out of his chair before Daniel could protest.

"No. Not now. I must find the princess," he said in a loud voice.

Breksin dropped back into his chair.

"You don't have to shout," he said. "I can hear you."

"I have to find the princess, and her companion."

"Modesty?" The big man broke into a smile.

"Yes."

"She plays cards with me sometimes. I haven't seen her for a while."

"She and the princess were away."

"What?"

Daniel leaned forward in his chair.

"I said, she was away with the princess. They were visiting in Ascroval."

"Well, tell her Breksin—say her friend, Breksin—has saved a pretty little pork pie for her to take to her aunt at the shrine." He rose like a derrick from his chair. Daniel felt like a leprechaun.

"Come," said the cellar master. "I will tell you the way. The right way. But you must come back and play cards one day."

The Princess Iris was distraught.

"But, Modesty, how can you talk of leaving?"

"How can I not?" was the reply.

"But we can send someone to look for him. Someone we trust. A knight."

"I trust me," said Modesty quietly. "Let us leave the cavaliers to their intrigues and their dice."

"But he may arrive here."

"That is why I am waiting for one day more. But if he does not come today, I am going to disguise myself as a page or a squire, borrow your fastest pony, and set off for Ascroval in the morning."

Iris went and sat beside her friend on the chaise.

"I think I almost preferred it when you were weeping." She put her arm around Modesty. "Modesty," she said in a gentle voice, "have you thought that he—"

"I have thought of everything," said Modesty with a sad smile. "But I'm not going in search of my lover, Iris; I am going to try to find the brave man who took such risks to help us."

The princess looked into her friend's dark eyes.

"Modesty," she whispered, "I don't believe you."

Modesty lowered her eyes shyly.

"Iris, I don't blame you; I don't, either. But it is true that he might be lost or hurt or ill. And anyway, I cannot rest until I know something." She got up and began to pace the sitting room. "I wish I had left already. I wish I were in the saddle with my breasts bound under my squire's jacket and my hair hidden under my turban."

"But squires don't wear turbans."

The smile that Modesty flashed at the princess was almost cheerful.

"Well the squire I impersonate is going to, because I know that if I chop off my hair ten days before your wedding you will have me beheaded, so I must hide it instead."

"Very well, I know you will do as you wish. I suppose I should be grateful that you do not intend to strap on armor and depart on a warhorse." The princess got up. "But meanwhile, please stop pacing, my dearest friend. You promised you would try to rest." She took Modesty by the elbow and guided her to the chaise. She pushed her gently onto it.

"I want you to have peace today," said Iris. "I am going to go to the dressmaker before she comes here with her six assistants.

When I return I expect to see you lying there, exactly where I have left you."

The princess closed the outer door behind her quietly. As she passed the main corridor something caught her attention. At the far end, she could see a man walking in her direction. She crossed and went a dozen paces, then stopped. She returned to the intersection and gazed down the corridor. The man passed under a lamp. He was walking quickly, not lounging along like a functionary on an errand.

Iris felt a thrill of hope, followed instantly by an anticipatory twinge of the anguished disappointment she expected to feel in a moment when the man striding in her direction turned out to be a courtier.

He drew closer. When he passed under the next lamp, Iris could tell he was a stranger. She began to fell warm, her skin tingling just as it frequently did during exciting scenes at the theater.

He passed the next lamp. Iris recalled the moment that Daniel had come through the window at Ascroval. She strained her eyes to penetrate the distance that still separated them. She began to walk in his direction. She saw him break stride at the sight of her, then continue forward. Now only three lamps burned between them.

She stopped, raising her hands to her mouth. The suspense, the threat of ruined hopes, seemed intolerable. The less impossible the hope, the more wrenching became the wait. The man slowed his pace. The princess sighed miserably.

Finally he stood before her.

"Your Highness?" he said, bowing uncertainly.

Iris nodded. Her eyes were filled with tears, but she could see him well enough to know him.

"Daniel," she said. She straightened her back; blinked away her tears.

"Every time you see me I am weeping," she said. She looked at him closely. There was no doubt.

"I am so . . . ," she began, then stopped. She thought of Modesty in the room nearby. "Where have you been?" she said. "Why did you not come here before?"

"A magician prevented me. Your Highness."

Iris found that her emotions had deserted her. Her thoughts were all focused on Modesty.

"And now that you are here, what do you mean to do?"

"I want to find Modesty."

"Yes, but why?"

"Well, I mean, I'm . . ."

Iris cut off his stammering preface. She was not prepared to listen to any long-winded circumlocutions.

"Are you in love with Modesty?"

Daniel's answer was prompt.

"Yes, I am."

"Truly?"

"Truly."

The eyes of the princess were once again filled with tears. She threw her arms around the astonished Daniel.

"Then you are my brother," she whispered, and kissed him on the cheek.

The princess entered the sitting room quietly. Modesty still sat on the chaise.

"You see, Your Highness," she said, "I am an obedient subject." She looked at Iris. "What's wrong? Have you been crying?" She got up and went to the princess. "What is it, Iris?"

Iris embraced her. "Modesty. Sister." She stepped back from Modesty. Her eyes filled.

"I have just kissed a man," she said.

Modesty said nothing.

"An extremely handsome man," added the princess.

Modesty stared at her friend. She raised one hand to her heart.

"He says he loves my sister."

A cry broke from Modesty's lips. Iris opened the door and went into the hall. Modesty did not move. When Iris returned, Daniel was with her. She walked with him to Modesty and stood between the lovers. She silenced Daniel with a gesture.

"I am leaving for the dressmaker, Modesty," she said, "as soon as I hear you say it."

Modesty smiled at Iris. She looked into Daniel's eyes.

"I feared I was never to see you again." She paused. "Never to be happy again. Never to tell you that I love you."

Iris left, closing the door softly behind her. Daniel and Modesty did not notice her departure.

The wedding of Iris and Hilbert was a stunning public spectacle, surrounded by days of celebration that threatened the extinction of all known supplies of ales, wines, smoked meats, and sausages. Even Finster the Munificent was impressed by the radiant beauty of his new daughter-in-law as she knelt in public to be joined to his blood and to his kingdom. The royalty of all the known world had come to witness the event. King Razenor, so recently out of his subjects' sight with a mysterious illness, led the delegation from Ascroval, professing himself overwhelmed with emotion at the joyful event.

Not only merchants, but players, musicians, jugglers, magicians, and the like prospered at every square and marketplace. Dibrick the Roaster of Meats was kept so busy that for a period of almost a fortnight he scarcely saw the inside of his ale mug. An out-of-town magician, Remeger by name, played tirelessly at shells and peas for pennies on the street and made a season's income in eight days.

Modesty and Daniel carried the last pork pie in the city to the new priestess of the shrine of Elyssana, the Reverend Mother Renzel, and she in turn did them the favor of marrying them three days later in a quiet ceremony attended only by Prince Hilbert and his royal bride, Iris; Rogan and Obscure, magician to his majesty; and the royal cellar master Breksin, who arrived with a small barrel of His Majesty's rarest wine cradled lightly in one massive arm. Mistress Hannah was on a journey and could not attend, but sent a parcel to Modesty with a note instructing her to open it in private.

Asbrak the Fat settled on Daniel and his bride, with no public ceremony whatever, substantial gifts of land and income in payment to them both for services unnamed.

Modesty made it plain to Daniel, though for form's sake she asked him, that they must move with Iris to Felshalfen. Daniel made it plain to Modesty that where he lived was a matter of complete indifference to him as long as she lived there too.

On the last night of the official celebrations, Rogan the Obscure mounted a display of fireworks that all agreed would be remembered for a hundred years.

A stinging sleet fell, invisible in the darkness. Marcia walked carefully on the slippery pavement, staying as close as possible to the buildings. She pulled her arms close to her body and flipped her wet collar up against the biting wind. She had lost track of what block she was in. There seemed to be no restaurant or even drugstore where she could take refuge. The storm had been sudden and unexpected, and rush-hour traffic was in a hopeless snarl. Getting a cab or a bus, even had it been possible, would have offered only a continuation of the frustration she felt already with the additional possibility of being in a wreck. Her decision to walk home from work had been sound, except for being impossible. The wind began to blow harder. Marcia took shelter in the doorway of a bank that had been closed for hours.

The nearly motionless traffic seemed tired and dispirited. Hardly a horn sounded. Those that did were choked off and muffled by the furious weather. Marcia decided that if she ever did get home tonight, she would stay in bed all day tomorrow. Mr. Figge's pet schedule for the current project would suffer, but it seemed unimportant at the moment. Too bad, she thought, that Colette had resigned back in the summer. She would have considered Mr. Figge's schedule as important as he did. Mr. Figge needed a Colette to stand by him in time of need.

A woman stepped into the doorway. Marcia nodded. The woman smiled as though they were old friends and looked her in the eye. Marcia blinked and glanced away uncomfortably.

"Marcia." The woman's voice was barely audible in the wind.

Marcia looked back at her. Her eye was drawn to the thin golden ring on the woman's hand.

"You are exactly as you were described to me," the woman continued, as though the two had just met at an office party. "I'm sure the clothes I got for you will fit perfectly."

"Clothes?"

"Yes, it's summertime where we're going, and I knew we

wouldn't have time later to collect a wardrobe. The task we have been assigned must be seen to without delay."

Marcia felt that her brain must have quit working. She wished she could get in out of the cold. "I'm, I mean, what . . .?" she stammered.

The woman laughed. "I don't blame you," she said. She gestured at the street. "This is just awful. You'll feel better when we get home. I have your things all ready."

Marcia stared, shivering in the wind. "Get home?" she said.

"Marcia. Sister. It is time for you to join us. The ring you wear is one of ours—from Elyssana."

"Elyssana?"

"That's a formal name. You may know her as Elise, or some other name. But you must call her Elyssa now. It is an intimate name from far back, and it's the one the Sisterhood uses." The woman looked at the street again. "I'd really rather explain this when we're both warm and dry." She extended her hand. "If you are ready, we can leave this place."

Marcia remembered, months before, taking Elyssa's hand and traveling miles in the blink of an eye. She looked at the traffic and the sleet, felt the wind and the cold. She looked at the stranger who had called her sister. The woman smiled, waiting patiently, arm extended. Marcia reached out and took her hand.